GRANTA

GRANTA 92, WINTER 2005
www.granta.com

EDITOR *Ian Jack*
DEPUTY EDITOR *Matt Weiland*
MANAGING EDITOR *Fatema Ahmed*
ASSOCIATE EDITOR *Liz Jobey*
EDITORIAL ASSISTANT *Helen Gordon*

CONTRIBUTING EDITORS *Diana Athill, Sophie Harrison, Gail Lynch, Blake Morrison, John Ryle, Sukhdev Sandhu, Lucretia Stewart*

FINANCE *Margarette Devlin*
ASSOCIATE PUBLISHER *Sally Lewis*
MARKETING/PLANNING DIRECTOR *Janice Fellegara*
SALES DIRECTOR *Linda Hollick*
TO ADVERTISE CONTACT *Lara Frohlich* (212 293 1646)
PRODUCTION ASSOCIATE *Sarah Wasley*
PUBLICITY *Jenie Hederman*
SUBSCRIPTIONS *Dwayne Jones*
LIST MANAGER *Diane Seltzer*

PUBLISHER *Rea S. Hederman*

GRANTA PUBLICATIONS, 2-3 Hanover Yard, Noel Road, London N1 8BE
Tel 020 7704 9776 Fax 020 7704 0474
e-mail for editorial: editorial@granta.com
Granta is published in the United Kingdom by Granta Publications.
This selection copyright © 2005 Granta Publications.
All editorial queries should be addressed to the London office. We accept no responsibility for unsolicited manuscripts
GRANTA USA LLC, 1755 Broadway, 5th Floor, New York, NY 10019-3780
Tel (212) 246 1313 Fax (212) 333 5374
Granta is published in the United States by Granta USA LLC and distributed in the United States by PGW and Granta Direct Sales, 1755 Broadway, 5th Floor, New York, NY 10019-3780.
Granta is indexed in The American Humanities Index
TO SUBSCRIBE call toll-free in the US (800) 829 5093 or 601 354 3850 or e-mail: grantasub@nybooks.com or fax 601 353 0176
A one-year subscription (four issues) costs $39.95 (US), $51.95 (Canada, includes GST), $48.70 (Mexico and South America), and $60.45 (rest of the world).
Granta, USPS 000-508, ISSN 0017-3231, is published quarterly in the US by Granta USA LLC, a Delaware limited liability company. Periodical Rate postage paid at New York, NY, and additional mailing offices. POSTMASTER: send address changes to Granta, PO Box 23152, Jackson, MS 39225-3152. US Canada Post Corp. Sales Agreement #40031906.
Printed and bound in Italy by Legoprint on acid-free paper.
Design: Slab Media.
Frontcover photograph: Chris de Bode/Panos Pictures
Back cover photograph: Geert van Kesteren/Magnum Photos

ISBN 1-929001-22-3

DISCOVER THE WRITER'S LIFE IN NEW YORK CITY.

Over more than six decades of steady innovation, The New School has sustained a vital center for creative writing. The tradition continues with our MFA in Creative Writing, offering concentrations in fiction, poetry, nonfiction, and writing for children. Study writing and literature with The New School's renowned faculty of writers, critics, editors, and publishing professionals. Fellowships and financial aid are available.

FACULTY 2005-2006
Jeffery Renard Allen, Jonathan Ames, Susan Bell, Mark Bibbins, Sven Birkerts, Susan Cheever, Jonathan Dee, Elaine Equi, David Gates, Vivian Gornick, Cathi Hanover, Shelley Jackson, Zia Jaffrey, Joyce Johnson, Hettie Jones, James Lasdun, David Lehman, Suzannah Lessard, David Levithan, Philip Lopate, Pablo Medina, Honor Moore, Maggie Nelson, Sigrid Nuñez, Dale Peck, Robert Polito, Francine Prose, Liam Rector, Helen Schulman, Tor Seidler, Dani Shapiro, Prageeta Sharma, Laurie Sheck, Darcey Steinke, Benjamin Taylor, Jackson Taylor, Abigail Thomas, Paul Violi, Sarah Weeks, Susan Wheeler, Stephen Wright, and Matthew Zapruder.

VISITING FACULTY
Joshua Beckman, Frank Bidart, Max Blaqq, Micheal Hoffman, Deborah Brodie, Patricia Carlin, Glen Hartley, Dave Johnson, Rika Lesser, Harry Matthews, Sharon Mesmer, Marie Ponsot, David Prete, Matthew Rohrer, Lloyd Schwartz, Jon Scieszka, Susan Shapiro, Jason Shinder, Ira Silverberg, Frederic Tuten, and Susan Van Metre.

Director: Robert Polito
Application Deadline: January 15, 2006

CREATIVE WRITING

For more information:
nsadmissions@newschool.edu
66 West 12th Street, NYC
212.229.5630

www.writing.newschool.edu

THE VIEW FROM AFRICA

GRANTA

GRANTA

INTRODUCTION

THE MANY VOICES OF AFRICA

John Ryle

It has been the year of Africa, the year, according to *Our Common Interest*, the report of Tony Blair's Commission for Africa, when a combination of indigenous resolve and cash from Western governments was to launch a new assault on the roots of poverty in the continent, stimulating trade, increasing aid, tackling corruption, cancelling debt. In the months since the appearance of the Commission's report, events in African countries have had higher than usual media visibility—but not because of progress in combating poverty. It's been the familiar cavalcade of war, famine and mass killing—in Sudan, then Uganda and Côte d'Ivoire, then Sudan again. In the West, in the world's lucky countries, it may have been the year of Africa; but for many Africans, in much of Africa, it was another year of living on the edge.

Still, the Commission could be right to see change on the way. In a number of African countries things do seem to be getting better. Across the continent civil wars are fewer and gross national product is on the up. The mistake is to generalize. The very word Africa— that sonorous trisyllable—seems to invite grandiloquence. Because the continent has a clear geographical unity it is tempting to hold forth about it. Cecil Rhodes wanted to colour everything imperial red from the Cape to Cairo; since then the tendency has been for Westerners— and often Africans too—to seek to impose a single reality, a general explanation, on the whole place. So one newspaper report can say that 'Africa has never been more dangerous, nor more ready to join the rest of the world'; another that 'Africa is coming together, taking its fate into its own hands.' Which Africa is being discussed in each case? Can Botswana, that haven of stability, be more dangerous than ever? Is Equatorial Guinea ready to join the rest of the world? Is the African Union 'taking its fate into its own hands'?

The idea that the diverse polities of Africa—even of sub-Saharan Africa—form a single entity is, as the philosopher Kwame Anthony Appiah has argued, the product of European colonialism, of romantic imperialism. It is a notion since embraced by other epic dreamers: Rastafarians, pan-Africanists and now, it seems, Tony Blair and Gordon Brown. In truth Africa is far less homogenous—geographically, culturally, religiously and politically—than Europe or the Americas. South Africa and Burkina Faso have as much in common as Spain and Uzbekistan. To say that Africa has 'never been more dangerous'

9

because of wars in Congo or Sudan, is like saying Eurasia has never been more dangerous because of Chechnya. It is generalizing that is dangerous. A century of colonization by Europe, which failed to bring Cecil Rhodes' vision to pass, is the principal source of any historical affinities that exist between one African country and another. And this is the ultimate source of the combination of strategic interest and moral concern that finds expression today in the Commission for Africa, a body that brings together the great and the good of both continents.

Our Common Interest duly warns against generalization, then goes on to generalize. Africa, it says:

> has suffered from governments that have looted the resources of the state; that could not or would not deliver services to their people; that in many cases were predatory, corruptly extracting their countries' resources; that maintained control through violence and bribery, and that squandered or stole aid.

All of this is true. But why the past tense? Has the violence and corruption ceased? And why are there no specifics of this looting and embezzlement? Should those responsible not be named and the exceptions be applauded? The recommendations of the Commission include, after all, an unprecedented level of debt forgiveness and financial aid to African governments. There is, to put it mildly, some risk of throwing good money after bad. A look at the list of Commissioners provides a clue to this reticence in the report. They include two African heads of state, former President Benjamin Mpaka of Tanzania and Prime Minister Meles Zenawi of Ethiopia. On the whole African big men don't pull their neighbours down, whatever their crimes against their own people. That's why South African President Thabo Mbeki refuses to condemn Robert Mugabe. And why Mugabe gives refuge in Zimbabwe to Mengistu Haile Mariam, Meles Zenawi's murderous predecessor. Perhaps it is surprising that those who drafted the report of the Commission, a well-researched and frequently forceful document, got as much plain talk into it as they did.

The optimism of the Commission should not be dismissed, either. The capacity for hope in the face of catastrophe is a characteristically African gift. How else could people who suffer so much survive? In

Sudan, where I work part of the year, the conflict in Darfur has claimed the lives of hundreds of thousands of civilians, victims of a government counter-insurgency campaign that uses tribal militias as proxy fighters. In January 2005, members of this government concluded a peace agreement with rebels in the south of the country, the Sudan People's Liberation Movement, ending the twenty-year civil war there. The government calculated, no doubt, that international pressure over the massacres in Darfur would be constrained by unwillingness on the part of the West to put in jeopardy the deal with the SPLM. And they were right. Despite huffing and puffing by various parties, the government of Sudan got away with mass murder. The North–South peace deal in Sudan is called, optimistically, a Comprehensive Peace Agreement, but comprehensive peace in large parts of the country is absent. Peace there, as a Sudanese saying has it, is the milk of birds.

The language of peace-making is everywhere, though. Sometimes it is curiously belligerent. ANGELIC PEACE LOCOMOTIVE CRUSHES LIFE OUT OF WAR DEVIL MONGERS was the headline in one Khartoum newspaper reporting the agreement. The less peace there is, the more people want to hear the magic word. A South Sudanese hip-hop artist, Emmanuel Jal, and a veteran northern Sudanese musician, Abdel Gadir Salim, recently recorded an album called *Ceasefire*. The two singers have never met: their album was made by sending recorded tracks back and forth between London, Khartoum and Nairobi, in Kenya, where Jal has been living. The result of this collaboration-at-a-distance is a wondrous fusion of the 6/8 *merdoum* rhythm of western Sudan with rap techniques honed in the dance halls of Nairobi. The songs are in a mix of English, Arabic, Nuer (Jal's native language) and Sheng, a street language that is Kenya's equivalent of the Spanglish spoken by Latinos in North America. In July, Jal performed in Cornwall at one of Bob Geldof's Live 8 concerts. In August, he sang at the memorial event in London for John Garang, leader of the SPLM, who was killed in a helicopter accident shortly after the formation of the new government in Khartoum.

To meet him, Jal is the model of a modern hip-hop artist, all torn T-shirt, fatigues, neck chains, and back-to-front baseball cap. His lyrics, though, are a long way from the febrile swagger of gangsta rap. Jal was a child soldier in Sudan, where guns are easier to get hold of than iPods, so he has seen enough of the real thing. As anti-

John Ryle

war poetry, his songs, 'Gua' ('Good' in Nuer) and 'Ya Salaam' ('Yo! Peace' in Arabic), may not be quite in the Wilfred Owen league. But Wilfred Owen never had this array of tablas and saxophones and ululating backing vocalists supporting him:

> Just think for a minute
> It will be so good when there'll be peace in my homeland
> Not one sister will be forced into marriage
> Not one cow will be taken by force
> And not one person will starve from hunger again
> Children will go to school, I hope we can do this
> I can't wait for that day

Our Common Interest puts a stress on culture as a driving force in the fate of nations. By 'culture' the report means mainly political culture, the energy of local communal organizations and, contentiously, religious networks. There's a tip of the hat to language and the arts, but this could have been taken further. Take Jal's multilingualism—striking on the world stage, but not so remarkable in sub-Saharan Africa, where everyone speaks two languages at least. The continent is home to more than 2,000 of them—2,058 according to the website www.ethnologue.com (and they're not counting Sheng). That's a third of the global total. Most of these languages were born to blush unseen, known beyond their spoken range only by proverbs, part of the great treasury that the Commission on Africa refers to as 'intangible cultural heritage'. No one has counted the number of proverbs in Africa. A recently-published collection of sayings of the Akan of Ghana catalogues 7,015 from this single ethnic group. As Francis Bacon wrote, 'the genius, wit and spirit of a Nation are discovered by their proverbs'. If every African language boasted as many proverbs as the Akan do there would be fourteen million altogether, enough to tie several government commissions in knots.

Language is an area where Africans have an edge over Europeans or Americans. And in this respect many outsiders such as myself, who claim some understanding of African countries, practise a double standard. No respectable British or American news organization would dream of sending a representative to France who was not fluent in French, or to Russia without Russian, but it is rare to find a Western journalist—or a foreign aid worker—who speaks any African language properly. This is true even in places that have been the subject of quite intense, long-term, sophisticated news coverage, such as South Africa. How many of the Western correspondents who have made their reputations there speak Sotho, Xhosa, Sindebele or Afrikaans?

Some months back I called in on an acquaintance in Nairobi, Dr Bellario Ahoy, a medical doctor who served for many years in the Sudan People's Liberation Army and has recently been appointed to a post in the new government in South Sudan. In the interstices of war service, Dr Bellario managed to make a collection of proverbial lore in his native language, Dinka. Like all such collections these Dinka sayings combine universal received wisdom with cultural specificities, clichés with odd and striking images, admonitions with their opposites. Some are oracular and hard to understand. When I saw him, Dr Bellario, contemplating the destruction of his homeland, quoted the words of the early twentieth-century Dinka prophet Ariathdit. On returning home after long imprisonment by the British, Ariathdit spoke these words, which have become a Dinka catchphrase: *Piny nhom abi riak mac*, 'the land may be spoiled yet it will remain intact'. Dr Bellario glosses the phrase as Ariathdit's realization that although he had lost his battle against the British, this did not mean that the whole Dinka world would be destroyed. War and peace, good and bad fortune, all offer the chance of renewal. This dignity in the face of catastrophe is a kind of optimism. It combines fatalism, opportunism, and a sense of the limitations of human understanding. As the Mongo, in neighbouring Central Africa, put it, the root does not know what the leaf has in mind.

Dr Bellario has a personal project that he would like to organize: a cultural exchange scheme where young people from one area of Sudan will go and live in the territory of another tribe and learn their language (and presumably their proverbial wisdom too). In other parts of Africa, not held back by war, this has happened already. Though most African countries are still predominantly rural, they will, on average, become fifty per cent urban in a couple of decades. And, as elsewhere in the world, the city is the site of hybrid vigour. Sheng, the language of East African hip-hop, is an example: a third-generation hybrid, mixing Swahili (an East African lingua franca, with a Bantu

13

backbone and Arabic extremities) with English, our familiar Anglo-Saxon creole, it has spread by hip-hop artists like Jal, and by the drivers and turnboys who operate *matatus*, the devil-may-care minibuses that are the core of the public transport system in East Africa.

Kwani? is a literary and political magazine published in Nairobi. (The name means 'So What?' in Sheng.) Although most of the contents of *Kwani?* are in English, the magazine includes pieces where Sheng gets one of its earliest outings as a literary language. In the same spirit, the editor of *Kwani?*, Binyavanga Wainaina, has celebrated the visual art of *matatus*, intricately customized vehicles whose paintwork is startling enough to cause a traffic accident. 'Brash, garish public transport vehicles,' he calls them, 'so irritating to every Kenyan except those who own one, or work for one'. On the streets of Nairobi the turnboys hang from the doors of *matatus*, half-cut on *miraa* (the stimulant leaf favoured by Somalis, grown in central Kenya), calling out destinations at the stopping points and cramming passengers into the vehicle until the wheels splay outward and the transmission hangs a few inches from the ground. Herds of these *matatus* career around Nairobi with cool disregard for other road users. It is hard not to be struck by them, or be struck down while trying to make out the intricate typography of the slogans that bedeck them: HARD TARGET, SWEET BABY, HAPPINESS, SLANDER, DOWN WITH HOMEBOYS, TOLERANCE OF LADIES, DESTINATION. And, seeming to confirm the upbeat conclusion of the Commission for Africa, NO CONDITION PERMANENT. Another Kenyan commentator, Joyce Nyairo, compares the traffic in Nairobi to music. *Matatus*, she says, are jazz.

African music, like language, has been the site of endless mutation, within Africa and beyond. It is Africa's most triumphant export. Jal's Nilotic hip-hop and his duets with Abdel Gadir Salim are just one expression of an inexhaustible hybridity that has had the peoples of northern countries dancing to an African beat since the late nineteenth century. Music is where the traditions of Europe and African meet on equal terms. As the musicologist Stephen Brown puts it:

> One of the most important events of the twentieth century was the marriage of African and European musical languages. It wasn't just one marriage, but a series of marriages—in the American South, in

Cuba, in Jamaica, in Brazil, and, of course, Africa. There is
something about each of the two music cultures that seems to need
the other... European music provided harmonic progressions
organized round a tonal centre—an idea which, once you've heard
it, is irresistible. African music offered its polyrhythms, rhythms
that occur in layers—a kind of beat which, once heard, is hard to
live without.

Hard to live without. Africa is part of everyone's life, whether they
know it or not. Along with ivory, slaves, diamonds, gold and oil, it
has given us the soundtrack of modernity. And—here is one
generalization it is safe to make—Africa is where we come from. Our
ancestral home is in the Rift Valley, somewhere between Nairobi and
the Red Sea. This is worth remembering: if it were not for Africa we
would not be here at all. □

GRANTA

THE MASTER
Chimamanda Ngozi Adichie

Nigeria

The Master was a little crazy; he had spent too many years reading books overseas, talked to himself in his office, did not always return greetings and had too much hair. Ugwu's auntie said this in a low voice as they walked along the path to the Master's house. 'But he is a good man,' she added. 'And as long as you work well, you will eat well. You will even eat meat every day.' She stopped to spit; the saliva left her mouth with a sucking sound and landed on the grass.

Ugwu did not believe that anybody, not even this master he was going to live with, ate meat every day. He did not disagree with his auntie, though, because he was too choked with expectation, too busy imagining his new life away from the village. They had been walking for a while now, since they got off the lorry in Nsukka, and the afternoon sun burned the back of his neck. But he did not mind. He was prepared to walk hours more in even hotter sun. He had never seen anything like the streets that appeared after they went past the university gates, streets so smooth and tarred that he itched to lay his cheek down on them. He would never be able to describe to his sister Anulika how the bungalows here were painted the colour of the sky and sat side by side like polite, well-dressed men, how the hedges separating them were trimmed so flat on top that they looked like tables wrapped with leaves.

His auntie walked faster, her slippers making slap-slap sounds that echoed in the silent street. Ugwu wondered if she, too, could feel the coal tar getting hotter underneath, through her thin rubber soles. They went past a sign, ODIM STREET, and Ugwu mouthed *street*, as he did whenever he saw an English word that was not too long. He smelled something sweet, heady, when they walked into a compound, and was sure it came from the white flowers clustered on the bushes at the entrance. The bushes were shaped like slender hills. The lawn glistened. Butterflies hovered above.

'I told him you will learn everything fast, *osiso-osiso*,' his auntie said. Ugwu nodded attentively although she had already told him this many times, as often as she told him the story of how his good fortune came about: while she was sweeping the corridor in the faculty of sciences a week ago, she had heard the Master say that he needed a houseboy to do his cleaning, and she had immediately said that she could help, speaking before his typist or office messenger could offer to bring someone.

'I will learn fast, Auntie,' Ugwu said. He was staring at the car in the garage; a strip of metal ran around its blue body like a necklace.

'Remember, what you will answer whenever he calls you is, "Yes Sah!"'

'Yes Sah!' Ugwu repeated.

They were standing before the glass door. Ugwu held back from reaching out to touch the cement wall, to see how different it would feel from the mud walls in his mother's hut that still bore the faint patterns of the fingers that had moulded it. For a brief moment, he wished he were back there now, in his mother's hut, under the dim coolness of the thatch roof, or in his auntie's hut, the only one in the village with a corrugated iron roof.

His auntie tapped on the glass. Ugwu could see the white curtains behind the door. A voice said, in English, 'Yes? Come in.'

They took off their slippers before walking in. Ugwu had never seen a room so wide. Despite the brown sofas arranged in a semicircle, the side tables between them, the shelves crammed with books and the centre table with the vase of red and white plastic flowers, the room still seemed to have too much space. The Master sat on an armchair, wearing a singlet and a pair of shorts. He was not sitting upright, but slanted, a book covering his face, as though oblivious that he had just asked people in.

'Good afternoon, Sah! This is the boy,' Ugwe's auntie said.

The Master looked up. His complexion was the colour of old bark, and the hair that covered his chest and legs was a lustrous, darker shade. He pulled off his glasses. 'The boy?'

'The houseboy, Sah.'

'Oh, yes, you have brought the houseboy. *I kpotago ya.*' The Master's Igbo felt feathery in Ugwu's ears. It was Igbo coloured by the sliding sounds of English, the Igbo of one who spoke English often.

'He will work hard,' his auntie said. 'He is a very good boy. Just tell him what you want done. Thank Sah!'

The Master grunted in response, watching Ugwu and his auntie with a faintly distracted expression, as if their presence made it difficult for him to remember something important. Ugwu's auntie patted Ugwu's shoulder, whispered that he should do well and then turned to the door. After she left, the Master put his glasses back on and faced his book, relaxing further into a slanting position, legs stretched out. Even when he turned the pages he did so with his eyes on the book. Ugwu stood by the door, waiting. Sunlight streamed in through the windows and from time to time, a gentle breeze lifted the curtains. The room was silent except for the rustle of the Master's page-turning. Ugwu stood for a while before he began to edge closer and closer to the bookshelf, as though to hide in it, and then, after a while, he sank down to the floor cradling his raffia bag between his knees. He looked up at the ceiling, so high up, so piercingly white. He closed his eyes and tried to re-imagine this spacious room with the alien furniture, but he couldn't. He opened his eyes, overcome by a new wonder, and looked around to make sure it was all real. To think that he would sit on these sofas, polish this slippery-smooth floor, wash these gauzy curtains.

'What's your name?' the Master asked, startling him.

Ugwu stood up.

'What's your name?' the Master asked again and sat up straight. He filled the armchair with his thick hair that stood high on his head, his muscled arms, his broad shoulders; Ugwu had imagined an older man, somebody frail, and now he felt a sudden fear that he might not please this Master who looked so youthful and capable, who looked as if he needed nothing.

'Ugwu, Sah.'

'Ugwu. And you've come from Obukpa, *okwia*?'

'Opi, Sah.'

'You could be anything from twelve to thirty.' The Master narrowed his eyes. 'Probably thirteen.' He said *thirteen* in English.

'Yes Sah.'

The Master turned back to his book. Ugwu stood there. The Master flipped past some pages and looked up. '*Ngwa*, go to the kitchen, there should be something you can eat in the fridge.'

'Yes Sah.'

Ugwu entered the kitchen cautiously, placing one foot slowly after the other. When he saw the white thing, almost as tall as he was, he knew it was the fridge. His auntie had told him about it. A cold barn, she had said, that kept food from going bad. He opened it and gasped as the cool air rushed into his face. Oranges, bread, beer, soft drinks, many things in packets and cans were arranged on different levels and, on the very top, a roasted, shimmering chicken, whole but for a leg. Ugwu reached out and touched the chicken. The fridge breathed heavily in his ears. He touched the chicken again and licked his finger before he yanked off the other leg, eating it until he had only the cracked, sucked pieces of bones left in his hand. Next, he broke off some bread, a chunk that he would have been excited to share with his siblings if a relative had visited them and brought it as a gift. He ate quickly, in case the Master came in and changed his mind. He had finished eating and was standing by the sink, trying to remember what his auntie had told him about opening it to have water gush out like a spring, when the Master walked in. He had put on a print shirt and a pair of trousers. His toes, which peeked through leather slippers, seemed feminine, perhaps because they were so clean; they belonged to feet that always wore shoes.

'What is it?' the Master asked.

'Sah...' Ugwu gestured to the sink.

The Master came over and turned the metal tap handle. 'You should look around the house and put your bag in the first room on the corridor. I'm going for a walk, to clear my head, *inugo?*'

'Yes Sah.' Ugwu watched him leave through the back door. His walk was brisk, energetic; he looked like Ezeagu, the man who held the wrestling record in Ugwu's village.

Ugwu turned off the tap, turned it on again, then off. On and off and on and off until he was laughing at the magic of the running water and the chicken and bread that lay balmy in his stomach. He went past the living room and into the corridor. There were books piled on the shelves and tables in the three bedrooms, on the sink and cabinets in the bathroom, stacked from floor to ceiling in the study and, in the pantry, old journals were stacked next to crates of Coke and cartons of Premier beer. Some of the books were placed face down, open, as though the Master had not yet finished reading them but had hastily gone on to another one. Ugwu tried to read the titles, but most were too long, too difficult. *Non-Parametric Methods. An African Survey. The Great Chain of Being. The Norman Impact Upon England.* He walked on tiptoe from room to room, because his feet felt dirty, and as he did so he grew increasingly determined to please the Master, to stay in this house of meat and cool floors. He was examining the toilet, running his hand over the black plastic seat, when he heard the Master's voice.

'Where are you, my good man?' He said *my good man* in English. Ugwu dashed out to the living room, still on tiptoe. 'Yes Sah!'

'What's your name again?'

'Ugwu, Sah.'

'Yes, Ugwu. Look here, *nee anya*, do you know what that is?' The Master pointed and Ugwu looked at the metal box studded with dangerous-looking knobs.

'No Sah,' Ugwu said.

'It's a radiogram. It's new and very good. It's not like those old gramophones that you have to wind and wind. You have to be very careful around it, very careful. You must never let water touch it.'

'Yes Sah.'

'I'm off to play tennis, and then I'll go on to the staff club.' The Master picked up a few books from the table. 'I may be back late. So get settled and have a rest.'

'Yes Sah.'

After Ugwu watched the Master drive out of the compound, he went and stood beside the radiogram and looked at it carefully, without touching it. Then he walked around the house, up and down, touching books and curtains and furniture and plates. When it got dark, he turned the light on and marvelled at how bright the bulb that dangled from the ceiling was, how it did not cast long shadows on the wall like the palm oil lamps back home did. His mother would be preparing the evening meal now, pounding *akpu* in the mortar, the pestle grasped tight with both hands. Chioke, the junior wife, would be tending the pot of watery soup balanced on three stones over the fire. The children would have come back from the stream and would be taunting and chasing one another under the breadfruit tree. Perhaps Anulika would be watching them. She was the oldest child in the household now and as they all sat around the fire to eat she would break up the fights when the younger ones struggled over the strips of dried fish in the soup. She would wait until all the *akpu* was eaten and then divide the fish, so that each child had a piece, and she would keep the biggest for herself, like he had always done.

Ugwu opened the fridge and ate some more bread and chicken, quickly stuffing the food in his mouth while his heart beat as if he were running, then he dug out extra chunks of meat from the breast and pulled out the wings. He slipped the pieces into the pockets of his shorts before going to the bedroom. He would keep them until his auntie visited and he would ask her to give them to Anulika. Perhaps he could ask her to give some to Nnesinachi, too. That might make Nnesinachi finally notice him. He had never been sure exactly how he and Nnesinachi were related, but he knew that they were from the same *umunna* and therefore could never marry. Yet he wished that his mother would not keep referring to Nnesinachi as his sister, saying things like 'please take this palm oil down to Mama Nnesinachi and if she is not in, leave it with your sister.'

Nnesinachi always spoke to him in a vague voice, her eyes unfocused, as if his presence made no difference to her either way. Sometimes she called him Chiejina, the name of his cousin who looked nothing at all like him and when he said, 'It's me,' she would say, 'Forgive me, Ugwu my brother,' with a distant formality that meant she had no wish to make further conversation. But he liked going on errands to her house. They were opportunities to walk into their yard and find her bent over and fanning the firewood until the tiny specks of light flared, or chopping *ugu* leaves for her mother's soup pot, or just sitting outside looking after her younger siblings, her wrapper hanging low enough for him to see the tops of her breasts. Ever since they started to push out, those pointy breasts, he had wondered if they would feel mushy-soft or hard like the unripe fruit from the umbrella tree. He often wished that Anulika wasn't so flat-chested—he wondered what was taking her so long, anyway, since she and Nnesinachi were about the same age—so that he could feel her breasts. Anulika would slap his hand away, of course, and perhaps even slap his face as well, but he would do it quickly, squeeze and run, and that way he would at least have an *idea*, know what to expect when he finally touched Nnesinachi's.

But he worried that he would never get to touch them, now that her uncle had offered to have her live with him and learn a trade in Kano. She would be leaving for the North soon. Ugwu wanted to be as pleased and as grateful as the rest of the family; there was, after all, a fortune to be made in the North and he knew of people who had gone up there to trade and came home to tear down their huts and build houses with corrugated iron roofs. He feared, though, that one of those pot-bellied traders in the North would take one look at her, and the next thing he knew somebody would bring palm wine to her father and he would never get to touch those breasts. They, her breasts, were the images saved for last on the many nights when he touched himself, slowly at first and then vigorously until a muffled moan escaped him. He always started with her face, the fullness of her cheeks and the ivory tone of her teeth, and then he imagined her arms around him, her body moulded to his. Finally, he let her breasts form, sometimes they felt hard, tempting him to bite into them, and other times they were so soft he was afraid his imaginary squeezing caused her pain.

For a moment, he considered thinking of her tonight. He decided not to. Not on his first night in the Master's house, on this strange bed that was nothing like his hand-woven raffia mat. First, he pressed his hands into the springy softness of the mattress. Then he examined the layers of cloth on top of it, unsure whether to sleep on them, or whether to remove them and put them away before sleeping. Finally he climbed into bed and lay on top of the layers of cloth, his body curled into a tight knot.

He dreamed that the Master was calling him—*Ugwu, my good man!*—and when he woke up, the Master was standing at the door, watching him. Perhaps it had not been a dream. He scrambled out of bed and glanced at the windows with the drawn curtains, in confusion. Was it late? Had that soft bed deceived him and made him oversleep? He usually woke with the first cock crows.

'Good morning Sah!'

'There is a strong roasted chicken smell here.'

'Sorry Sah.'

'Where is the chicken?'

Ugwu fumbled in his shorts pockets and brought out the chicken pieces.

'Do your people eat while they sleep?' the Master asked. He was wearing something that looked like a woman's coat, and was absently twirling the rope tied round his waist.

'Sah?'

'Did you want to eat the chicken while in bed?'

'No Sah.'

'Food will be restricted to the dining room and the kitchen.'

'Yes Sah.'

'The kitchen and bathroom will have to be cleaned today.'

'Yes Sah.'

The Master turned and left. Ugwu stood trembling in the middle of the room, still holding the chicken pieces with his hand outstretched. He wished he did not have to walk past the dining room to get to the kitchen. Finally, he put the chicken back in his pockets, took a deep breath and left the room. The Master was at the dining table, the teacup in front of him placed on a pile of books.

'This has just come out,' the Master said, looking up from a magazine. 'Not that I ever doubted it, of course. You know who really killed Lumumba? It was the Americans and the Belgians. It had nothing to do with Katanga.'

'Yes Sah,' Ugwu said. He wanted the Master to keep talking, so he could listen to the sonorous voice, the musical blend of English words in his Igbo sentences.

'You are my houseboy,' the Master said. 'If I order you to go outside and beat a woman walking on the street with a stick, and you then give her a bloody wound on her leg, who is responsible for the wound, you or me?'

Ugwu stared at the Master, shaking his head, wondering if the Master was referring to the chicken pieces in some roundabout way.

'Lumumba was Prime Minister of Congo. Do you know where Congo is?' the Master asked.

'No Sah.'

The Master got up quickly and went into the study. Ugwu's confused fear made his eyelids start to quiver: would the Master send him home because he did not speak English well, kept chicken in his pocket overnight, did not know the strange places the Master named? The Master came back with a wide piece of paper that he unfolded and laid out on the dining table, pushing aside books and magazines. He pointed with his pen. 'This is our world, although the people who drew this map decided to put their own land on top of ours. There is no top or bottom, you see.' The Master picked up the paper and folded it, so that one edge touched the other, leaving a hollow between. 'Our world is round, it never ends. *Nee anya*, this is all water, the seas and oceans, and here's Europe and here's our own, Africa, and the Congo is around here. Further up here is Nigeria, and Nsukka is here, in the south-east. This is where we are.' He tapped with his pen.

'Yes Sah.'

'Did you go to school?'

'Standard two, Sah. But I learn everything fast.'

'Standard two? How long ago?'

'Many years now, Sah. But I learn everything very fast!'

'Why did you stop school?'

'My father's crops failed, Sah.'

The Master nodded slowly. 'Why didn't your father find somebody to lend him money?'

'Sah?'

'Your father should have borrowed!' the Master snapped, and then in English: 'Education is a priority! How can we resist exploitation if we don't have the tools to understand exploitation?'

'Yes Sah!' Ugwu nodded vigorously. He was determined to appear as alert as he could, because of the wild shine that had appeared in the Master's eyes.

'I will enroll you in the staff primary school,' the Master said, still tapping on the piece of paper with his pen.

Ugwu's auntie had told him that if he served well for a few years, the Master would send him to commercial school where he would learn typing and shorthand. She had mentioned the staff primary school, but only to tell him that it was for the children of the lecturers, who wore blue uniforms and white socks and held handkerchiefs so intricately trimmed with wisps of lace that you wondered why anybody had wasted so much time on mere handkerchiefs.

'Yes Sah,' he said. 'Thank Sah.'

'I suppose you will be the oldest in class, starting in standard three at your age,' the Master said. 'And the only way you can get their respect is to be the best. Do you understand?'

'Yes Sah!'

'Sit down, my good man.'

Ugwu chose the chair farthest from the Master, awkwardly placing his feet close together. He preferred to stand.

'There are two answers to the things they will teach you about our land: the real answer and the answer you give in school to pass. You must read books and learn both answers. I will give you books, excellent books.' the Master stopped to sip his tea. 'They will teach you that a white man called Mungo Park discovered River Niger.

That is rubbish. Our people fished in the Niger long before Mungo Park's grandfather was born. But in your exam, write that it was Mungo Park. Soon, very soon, we will change things so that the real truths will be told. Do you understand?"

'Yes Sah.' Ugwu wished that this person called Mungo Park had not offended the Master so much.

'Can't you say anything else?'

'Sah?'

'Sing me a song.'

'Sah?'

'Sing me a song. What songs do you know? Sing!' The Master pulled his glasses off. His eyebrows were furrowed, serious. Ugwu began to sing an old song he had learned in his father's farm. His heart hit his chest painfully. *'Nzogbo nzogbu enyimba, enyi...'*

He sang in a low voice at first but the Master tapped his pen on the table and said, 'Louder!' so he raised his voice and the Master kept saying 'Louder!' until he was screaming. After he had sung it a few times, the Master asked him to stop. 'Good, good,' he said. 'Can you make tea?'

'No Sah. But I learn fast,' Ugwu said. The singing had loosened the knots inside him, he was breathing easily and his heart no longer pounded. And he was convinced that the Master was mad.

'I eat mostly at the staff club. I suppose I shall have to bring more food home now that you are here.'

'Sah, I can cook.'

'You cook?'

Ugwu nodded. He had spent many evenings in his mother's hut, watching her cook. He had started the fire for her often, or fanned the embers when it started to die out. He had peeled and pounded yams and cassava, blown out the husks in rice, picked out the weevils and stones from beans, peeled onions and ground peppers. Often, when his mother was sick with the coughing, he wished that he, and not Anulika, would cook. He had never told anyone this, not even Anulika; she had already told him that he spent too much time in the kitchen, and that he would never grow a beard if he kept doing that.

'Well, you can cook your own food then,' the Master said. 'Write a list of what you'll need.'

'Yes Sah.'

'You wouldn't know how to get to the market, would you? I'll ask Jomo to show you.'

'Jomo, Sah?'

'Jomo takes care of the compound. He comes in three times a week. Funny man; I've seen him talking to the sunflower bush.' The Master paused. 'Anyway, he'll be in tomorrow.'

Later, Ugwu wrote a list of food items and gave it to the Master.

The Master stared at the list for a while. 'Remarkable blend,' he said in English. 'I suppose they'll teach you to use more vowels in school.'

Ugwu disliked the amusement in the Master's face. 'We need wood, Sah,' he said.

'Wood?'

'For your books, Sah. So that I can arrange them.'

'Oh yes, *shelves*. I suppose we could fit more shelves somewhere, perhaps on the corridor. I will speak to somebody at the works department.'

'Yes Sah.'

'Odenigbo. Call me Odenigbo.'

Ugwu stared at him doubtfully. 'Sah?'

'My name is not Sah. Call me Odenigbo.'

'Yes Sah.'

'Odenigbo will always be my name. *Sir* is arbitrary. You could be the *sir* tomorrow.'

'Yes Sah...Odenigbo.'

Ugwu really preferred *Sah*, the crisp power behind the word, and when two men from the works department came a few days later to install shelves in the corridor, he told them that they would have to wait for Sah to come home, that he could not sign the white paper with typewritten words. He said *Sah* proudly.

'He's one of these village houseboys,' one of the men said dismissively, and Ugwu looked at the man's face, and murmured a curse about acute diarrhoea following him and all of his offspring for life. As he arranged the Master's books he silently promised himself that he would learn how to sign forms one day.

In the following weeks, the weeks when he examined every corner of the bungalow, when he discovered that a beehive was lodged in the cashew tree and that the butterflies converged in the front yard when the sun was brightest, he was just as careful in learning the rhythms of the Master's life. Every morning, he picked up the *Daily Times* and *Renaissance* that the vendor dropped off at the door and folded them on the table next to the Master's tea and bread. He had the Opel washed before the Master finished breakfast, and when the Master came back from work and was taking a siesta, he dusted the car over again, before the Master left for the tennis courts. He moved around silently on the days that the Master retired to the study for hours. When the Master paced the corridor talking in a loud voice, he made sure that there was hot water ready for tea. He scrubbed the floors daily. He wiped the louvres until they sparkled in the afternoon sunlight, paid attention to the tiny cracks in the bathtub, polished the saucers that he used to serve kola nut to the Master's friends. There were at least two visitors in the living room each day, the radiogram turned on low to strange flute-like music, low enough for the talking and laughing and glass-clinking to come clearly to Ugwu in the kitchen or in the corridor as he ironed the Master's clothes.

He wanted to do more, wanted to give the Master every reason to keep him and so, one morning, he ironed the Master's socks. They didn't look rumpled, the black ribbed socks, but he thought they would look even better straightened. The hot iron hissed and when he raised it, he saw that half of the sock was stuck to it. He froze. The Master was at the dining table, finishing up breakfast and would come in any minute now to pull on his socks and shoes and take the files on the shelf and leave for work. Ugwu wanted to hide the sock under the chair and dash to the drawer for a new pair but his legs would not move. He stood there with the burnt sock, knowing the Master would find him that way.

'You've ironed my socks, haven't you?' the Master asked. 'You stupid ignoramus.' *Stupid ignoramus* slid out of his mouth like music.

'Sorry Sah! Sorry Sah!'

'I told you not to call me sir.' The Master picked up a file from the shelf. 'I'm late.'

'Sah? Should I bring another pair?' Ugwu asked. But the Master had already slipped on his shoes, without socks, and hurried out. Ugwu heard him bang his car door and drive away. His chest felt weighty; he did not know why he had ironed the socks, why he had not simply done the safari suit. Evil spirits, that was it. The evil spirits had made him do it. They lurked everywhere, after all, and whenever he was ill with the fever, or once when he fell from an umbrella tree at the village entrance, his parents had tended to his aching body, all the while muttering, 'We shall defeat them, they will not win.'

He went out to the backyard and sat under the mango tree near the garage, resting his head against the trunk. The evil spirits would not win. He would not let them defeat him. He got up and walked to the front yard, past stones which were placed side by side around the manicured lawn. There was a round grassless patch in the middle of the lawn, like an island in a green sea, where a thin palm tree stood. Ugwu had never seen any palm tree that short, or with leaves that flared out so perfectly. It did not look strong enough ever to bear fruit and, like most of the plants here, did not look useful at all.

He picked up a stone and threw it into the distance. So much wasted space. In his village, people farmed the tiniest plots outside their homes and planted useful vegetables and herbs. His grandmother had not needed to grow her favourite herb *arigbe* though, because it grew wild everywhere. She used to say that *arigbe* softened a man's heart. She was the second of three wives and did not have the special position that came with being the first or the last so before she asked her husband for anything, she told Ugwu, she cooked him spicy yam porridge with *arigbe*. It had worked, always. Perhaps it would work with the Master.

Ugwu walked around the compound in search of *arigbe*, past the line of pink African lilies just below the study window. He looked under the cashew tree with the spongy beehive lodged on a branch, the lemon trees that had black soldier ants crawling up and down the trunks, and the pawpaw trees whose ripening fruit were dotted with fat bird-burrowed holes. But the ground was clean: no herbs. Jomo's weeding was thorough and careful; nothing that was not wanted was allowed to be.

The first time they met, Ugwu had greeted Jomo and Jomo nodded and continued to work without saying anything. He was a small man with a tough, shrivelled body that Ugwu felt needed a watering more than the plants that he targeted with his metal can. Finally, Jomo looked up and stared at Ugwu. '*Afa m bu* Jomo,' he announced as if Ugwu did not know his name. 'Some people call me Kenyatta, after the great man in Kenya. I am a hunter.'

Ugwu did not know what to say in return because Jomo was staring right into his eyes, as if expecting to hear something remarkable from him in return.

'What kind of animals do you kill?' Ugwu finally asked. Jomo beamed, as if this was exactly the question he had wanted and began to talk about his hunting and Ugwu sat on the stairs that led to the backyard and listened. From the first day, he did not believe Jomo's stories—of fighting off a leopard barehanded, of killing a baboon with a single shot—but he liked listening to them and he put off washing the Master's clothes for the days Jomo came so that he could sit outside while Jomo worked. Jomo moved with a slow deliberateness. His raking, watering, planting all seemed filled with wisdom. He would look up in the middle of trimming a hedge and say, 'That is good meat' and then walk to the raffia bag tied behind his bicycle to rummage for his catapult. Once, he shot a bush pigeon down from the cashew tree with a small stone and then wrapped it in banana leaves and put it into his bag. 'Don't go to that bag unless I am around,' he told Ugwu, 'Or you might find a human head there.' Ugwu laughed, but had not entirely doubted Jomo.

He wished so much that Jomo had come to work today. Jomo would have been the best person to ask about *arigbe*, indeed to ask for advice on how best to placate the Master.

He walked out of the compound, to the street, and looked through the plants on the roadside until he saw the rumpled leaves close to the root of a whistling pine. He had never smelled anything like the spicy sharpness of *arigbe* in the bland food the Master brought back from the staff club; he would cook a stew with it and offer it to the Master with rice and, afterwards, plead with him: *Please don't send me back home, Sah. I will work extra for the burnt sock. I will earn the money to pay for it.* He did not know exactly what he could do to earn money for the sock, but he planned to tell the Master that anyway.

If the *arigbe* softened the Master's heart, perhaps he could grow it and some other herbs in the backyard. He would tell the Master that the garden was something to do until he started school, since the headmistress at the staff school had told the Master that he could not start mid-term. He might be hoping for too much, though. What was the point of thinking about a herb garden if the Master would ask him to leave, if the Master would not forgive the burnt sock?

He walked quickly into the kitchen, laid the *arigbe* down on the counter, and measured out some rice.

Hours later, he felt a tautness in his stomach when he heard the Master's car: the crunch of gravel and the hum of the engine before it stopped in the garage. He stood by the pot of stew, stirring, holding the ladle tightly. Would the Master ask him to leave before he had a chance to offer him the food? What would he tell his people?

'Good afternoon, Sah! Odenigbo,' he said, even before the Master had come into the kitchen.

'Yes, yes,' the Master said. He was holding books to his chest with one hand and his briefcase with the other. Ugwu rushed over to help with the books. 'Sah? You will eat?' he asked in English.

'Eat what?'

Ugwu's stomach got tighter. He feared it might snap as he bent to place the books on the dining table. 'Stew, Sah.'

'Stew?'

'Yes Sah. Very good stew, Sah.'

'I'll try some, then.'

'Yes Sah!'

'Call me Odenigbo!' the Master snapped before going in to take an afternoon bath.

After Ugwu served the food, he stood by the kitchen door, watching as the Master took a first forkful of rice and stew, took another and then called out, 'Excellent, my good man.'

Ugwu appeared from behind the door. 'Sah? I can plant the herbs in a small garden. To cook more stews like this.'

'A garden?' The Master stopped to sip some water and turn a journal page. 'No, no, no. Outside is Jomo's territory, and inside is yours. Division of labour, my good man. If we need herbs, we'll ask Jomo to take care of it.' Ugwu loved the sound of *division of labour, my good man* spoken in English.

'Yes Sah,' he said, although he was already thinking of where would be the best spot for the herb garden: near the back hedge where the Master never went. He could not trust Jomo with the herb garden and would tend it himself when the Master was out and this way, his *arigbe*, his herb of forgiveness, would never run out. It was only later in the evening that he realized the Master must have forgotten about the burnt sock long before coming home.

Ugwu came to realize other things. He was not a normal houseboy; Doctor Okeke's houseboy next door did not sleep on a bed in a room, he slept on the kitchen floor. The houseboy at the end of the street who Ugwu went to the market with did not decide what would be cooked; he cooked whatever he was ordered to. And they did not have masters or madams who gave them books to read, saying, 'This one is excellent, just excellent.'

Ugwu did not understand most of the sentences in the books that the Master gave him, but he made a show of reading them. Nor did he understand the conversations of the Master and his friends but listened anyway and learned that the world had to do more about the black people killed in Sharpeville, that the spy plane shot down in Russia served the Americans right, that de Gaulle was being clumsy in Algeria, that the United Nations would never get rid of Tshombe in Katanga. Once in a while, the Master would stand up and raise his glass and his voice—'To that brave black American led into the University of Mississippi!' 'To Ceylon and to the world's first woman prime minister!' 'To Cuba for beating the Americans at their own game!'—and Ugwu would enjoy the clink of beer bottles against glasses, glasses against glasses, bottles against bottles.

More friends visited on weekends, and when he came out to serve their drinks, the Master would sometimes introduce him, in English of course. 'Ugwu here helps me around the house. Clever boy and a fantastic cook.' Ugwu would continue to uncork bottles of beer and Coke silently, while feeling the warm glow of pride spread up from the tips of his toes. He especially liked it when the Master introduced him to foreigners, like Mister Johnson who was from the Caribbean and stammered when he spoke, or Professor Lehman, the nasal white man from America who had eyes that were the piercing green of a fresh leaf. Ugwu was vaguely frightened the first time he saw him because he had always imagined that only evil spirits had grass-coloured eyes.

He soon noted the regular guests and brought out their drinks before the Master asked him to. There was Doctor Patel, the little Indian man with thick black hair that fell over his ears, who drank Golden Guinea beer mixed with Coke. The Master called him 'Doc'. Whenever Ugwu brought out the kola nut, the Master would say, 'Doc, you know the kola nut does not understand English,' before going on to bless the kola nut in Igbo. Doctor Patel laughed each time, with great pleasure, leaning back on the sofa and throwing his short legs up as if it was a joke he had never heard before. After the Master broke the kola nut and passed the saucer around, Doctor Patel always took a lobe and put it into his shirt pocket; Ugwu had never seen him eat one. There was tall, skinny Professor Ezeka with a voice so hoarse he sounded as if he spoke in whispers. He always picked up his glass and held it up against the light, to make sure Ugwu had washed it well. Sometimes he brought his own metal bottle of gin. Other times, he asked for tea and then went on to examine the sugar bowl and the tin of milk, muttering, 'The capabilities of bacteria are quite extraordinary.' There was Okeoma, who looked younger than all the other guests, who always wore a pair of shorts, and whose hair had a parting at the side and stood higher than the Master's. It looked rough and tangled, unlike the Master's, as if Okeoma did not like to comb it. Okeoma drank Fanta. On some evenings, he read his poetry aloud, holding a sheaf of papers, and Ugwu would look through the kitchen door to see all the guests watching Okeoma, their faces half-frozen, as if they did not dare breathe. Afterwards, the Master would clap and say, in his loud voice, 'The voice of our generation!' and the clapping would go on until Okeoma said, sharply, 'That's enough!'

And there was Miss Adebayo, who drank brandy like the Master and was nothing like Ugwu had expected a university woman to be. His auntie had told him a little about university women. She would know; she worked as a cleaner at the faculty of sciences during the day and as a waitress at the staff club in the evenings. Sometimes the lecturers paid her to come in and clean their homes. She said that they kept framed photos of their student days in Ibadan and Britain and America on their shelves. For breakfast, they had eggs that were not cooked well so that the yolk danced around, and they wore maxi dresses that grazed their ankles and bouncy, straight-hair wigs. She told a story once about a couple at a cocktail party in the staff club, who climbed out of a nice Peugeot, the man in an elegant cream suit, the woman in a green dress. Everybody turned to watch them, walking hand in hand and, then, the wind blew the woman's wig off her head. She was bald. From the hot combs they used to straighten their hair, his auntie had said; they wanted to look like white people, although all they ended up doing was burning their hair off. Ugwu had imagined the bald woman: beautiful with a straight nose that stood up, not the sitting-down flattened noses that he was used to. He imagined quietness, delicacy, the kind of woman whose sneeze, whose laugh and talk, would be as soft as the under-feathers closest to a chicken's skin. But the women who visited the Master, the ones he saw at the supermarket, at church, or on the streets, were different. Most of them did wear wigs (others had their hair woven or plaited with thread) but they were not delicate stalks of grass as he had imagined from his auntie's stories.

These women were loud. The loudest was Miss Adebayo. She was not an Igbo woman; Ugwu could tell from her name, even if he had not once run into her and her housegirl at the market and heard them both speaking rapid, incomprehensible Yoruba. She had asked him to wait so that she could give him a ride back to the campus; he thanked her and said he would take a taxi because he still had many things left to buy, although, really, he had finished shopping. He did not want to ride in her car. He did not like how her voice rose above the Master's in the living room, challenging and arguing. He often fought the urge to raise his own voice from behind the kitchen door and tell her to shut up, especially when she called the Master a 'sophist'. He did not know what 'sophist' meant, but he did not like that she called the Master that. Nor did he like the way she looked at him. Even when somebody else was speaking and she was supposed to be focused on that person, her eyes would be on the Master.

One Saturday night, Doctor Patel dropped a glass and Ugwu came in to clean up the shards that lay on the floor. He took his time cleaning. The conversation was clearer from so close by and it was easier to make out what Professor Ezeka said. It was almost impossible to hear him from the kitchen.

'We should have a bigger pan-African response to what is happening in the American South really,' Professor Ezeka said.

The Master cut him short. 'You know, pan-Africanism is fundamentally a European notion.'

'You are digressing,' Professor Ezeka said and shook his head in his usual superior manner.

'Maybe it *is* a European notion,' Miss Adebayo said. 'But in the bigger picture, we are all one race.'

'What bigger picture?' the Master asked. 'The bigger picture of the white man! Can't you see that we are not all alike except to white eyes?' The Master's voice rose easily, Ugwu had noticed, and by his third snifter of brandy he would start to wave his glass around, leaning forward until he was seated at the very tip of the chair. Late at night, after the Master was in bed, Ugwu would sit on the same chair and imagine himself speaking swift English, using words like *decolonize* and *pan-African*, shaping his voice like the Master's, and he would shift and shift until he was on the tip of the chair, talking to rapt imaginary guests.

'Of course we are all alike, we all have white oppression in common,' Miss Adebayo said dryly. 'Pan-Africanism is simply the most sensible response to this.'

'Of course, of course, but my point is that the only authentic identity for the African is the tribe,' the Master said; he was on the tip of his seat now. 'I am Nigerian because a white man created Nigeria and gave me that identity. I am Black because the white man constructed Black to be as different as possible from his White. But I was Igbo before the white man came.'

Professor Ezeka snorted and shook his head, his thin legs crossed. 'But you became aware that you were Igbo because of the white man. The pan-Igbo idea itself came only in the face of White domination. You must see that tribe as it is today is as colonial a product as nation and race.' Professor Ezeka recrossed his legs.

'The pan-Igbo idea existed long before the white man!' the Master shouted. 'Go and ask the elders in your village about your history.'

'The problem is that Odenigbo is a hopeless tribalist; we need to keep him quiet,' Miss Adebayo said.

Then she did what startled Ugwu: she got up laughing and went over to the Master and pressed his lips close together. She stood there for what seemed a long time, her hand to his mouth. Ugwu imagined the Master's brandy-diluted saliva touching her fingers. He stiffened as he picked up the shattered glass. He wished that the Master would not sit there, shaking his head and gesturing with his glass, as if the whole thing was very funny.

Miss Adebayo became a threat after that. She began to look more and more like a fruit bat, with her pinched face and cloudy complexion and print dresses that billowed around her body like wings. Ugwu served her drink last and wasted long minutes drying his hands on a dish towel before he opened the door to let her in. He worried that she would marry the Master and bring her Yoruba-speaking housegirl into the house and destroy his herb garden and tell him what he could and could not cook. Until he heard the Master talking to Doctor Patel: 'What a woman! You're lucky, Odenigbo.'

The Master shook his head. 'I've never respected a colleague more. But she's not for me.'

And Ugwu was relieved. He did not want Miss Adebayo, or any woman, coming in to intrude and disrupt their lives. Some evenings, when the visitors left early, he would sit on the floor of the living room and listen to the Master talk. The Master mostly talked about things Ugwu did not understand, as if the brandy made him forget that Ugwu was not one of his visitors. But it didn't matter. All Ugwu needed was the deep voice, the melody of the English-inflected Igbo, the glint of the thick eyeglasses.

He had been with the Master for four months when the Master told him, 'A special woman is coming for the weekend. Very special. You make sure the house is clean. I'll order the food from the staff club.'

'But Sah, I can cook,' Ugwu said, with a sad premonition.

'She likes fried rice, my good man. I'm not sure you could make something suitable.' The Master turned to walk away.

'I can make that, Sah, very well,' Ugwu said, quickly, although he had no idea what fried rice was. 'Let me make the rice, and you get the chicken from the staff club.'

'Artful negotiation,' the Master replied in English. 'All right then. You make the rice.'

'Yes Sah,' Ugwu said. Later, he cleaned the furniture and scrubbed the toilet and bathroom carefully, as he always did, but the Master looked at them and said they were not clean enough and went out and bought another jar of Vim powder and asked, sharply, why Ugwu didn't clean the spaces between the tiles. Ugwu cleaned them again. He scrubbed until sweat crawled down the sides of his face, until his arm ached. And on Saturday, he bristled as he cooked. The Master had never complained about his work before. It was this woman's fault, this woman that the Master considered too special for him to cook for. He could not bear to think of her and when the doorbell rang, he muttered a curse under his breath, about her stomach swelling from eating faeces. He heard the Master's raised voice, excited and childlike, followed by a long silence and Ugwu imagined their hug, and her ugly body pressed to the Master's. Then he heard her voice. He stood still. He had always thought that the Master's English could not be compared to anybody's, not Professor Ezeka whose English one could hardly hear, or Okeoma who spoke English as if he was speaking Igbo, with the same cadences and pauses, or Patel whose English was a faded lilt. Not even the white man Mister Lehman, with his words forced out through his nose, sounded as dignified as the Master. The Master's English was music, but what Ugwu was hearing now, from this woman, was magic. Here was a superior tongue, a luminous language, the kind of English Ugwu heard on the Master's radio, rolling out with clipped precision. It reminded him of slicing a yam with a newly sharpened knife, the easy perfection in every slice.

'Ugwu!' the Master called. 'Bring Coke!'

Ugwu walked out to the living room. She smelled of coconuts. He greeted her, his 'good afternoon' a mumble, his eyes on the floor.

'*Kedu?*' she asked.

'I'm well, Mah.' He still did not look at her. As he uncorked the bottle, she laughed at something the Master said. Ugwu was about to pour the cold Coke into her glass when she touched his hand and said, '*Rapuba*, don't worry about that.'

Her hand was lightly moist. 'Yes Mah.'

'Your master has told me how well you take care of him, Ugwu,' she said. Her Igbo words were softer than her English, and he was disappointed at how easily they came out of her. He wished she would stumble in her Igbo; he had not expected English that perfect to sit beside equally perfect Igbo.

'Yes Mah,' he mumbled. His eyes were still focused on the floor.

'What have you cooked us, my good man?' the Master asked, as if he did not know. He sounded annoyingly jaunty.

'I serve now, Sah,' Ugwu said, in English, and then wished he had said, 'I am serving now,' because it sounded better, because it would impress her more. As he set the table, he kept from glancing at the living room, although he could hear her laughter and the Master's voice with its irritating new timbre.

He finally looked at her as she and the Master sat down at the table. Her face was smooth like an egg, the lush colour of rain-

39

drenched earth, and her eyes were large and slanted and she looked like she was not supposed to be walking and talking like everyone else; she should be in a glass case like the one in the Master's study, where people could admire her curvy, fleshy body, where she would be preserved untainted. Her hair was long; each of the braids that hung down to her neck ended in a soft fuzz. She smiled easily; her teeth were the same bright-white as her eyes. He did not know how long he stood staring at her until the Master said, 'Ugwu usually does a lot better than this. He makes a fantastic stew.'

'It's quite tasteless, which is better than bad-tasting, of course,' she said and smiled at the Master before turning to Ugwu. 'I'll show you how to cook rice properly, Ugwu, and you shouldn't use so much oil.'

'Yes Mah,' Ugwu said. He had invented what he imagined was fried rice, frying the rice in groundnut oil, and had half hoped that it would send them both to the toilet in a hurry. Now, though, he wanted to cook a perfect meal, a savoury jollof rice or his special stew with *arigbe*, to show her how well he could cook. He delayed washing up so that the running water would not drown out her voice. When he served them tea, he took his time rearranging the biscuits on the saucer so that he could linger and listen to her, until the Master said, 'That's quite all right, my good man.' Her name was Olanna. But the Master said it only once; he mostly called her *nkem*, my own. They talked about the quarrel between the Sardauna and the Premier of the Western region, and then the Master said something about waiting until she moved in and how it was only a few weeks away after all. Ugwu held his breath to make sure he had heard clearly. The Master was laughing now, saying, 'But we will live here together, *nkem*, and you can keep the flat as well.'

She would move to Nsukka. She would live in this house. Ugwu walked away from the door and stared at the pot on the stove. His life would change. He would learn to cook fried rice and he would have to use less oil and he would take orders from her. He felt sad, and yet his sadness was incomplete; he felt expectant, too, an excitement that he did not entirely understand.

That evening, he was washing the Master's linen in the backyard, near the lemon trees, when he looked up from the basin of soapy water and saw her standing by the back door, watching him. At first, he was sure it was his imagination, because the people he thought the most about often appeared to him in visions. He had imaginary conversations with Anulika all the time and right after he touched himself at nights Nnesinachi would appear briefly with a mysterious smile on her face. But Olanna was really at the door. She was walking across the yard towards him. She had only a wrapper tied around her chest and, as she walked, he imagined that she was a yellow cashew, shapely and ripe.

'Mah? You want anything?' he asked. He knew that if he reached out and touched her face, it would feel like butter, the kind the Master unwrapped from a paper packet and spread on his bread.

'Let me help you with that.' She pointed at the bed sheet he was rinsing and slowly he took the dripping sheet out. She held one end and moved back. 'Turn yours that way,' she said.

He twisted the sheet to the right while she twisted to the left and they watched as the water was squeezed out. The sheet was slippery.

'Thank Mah,' he said.

She smiled. Her smile made him feel taller. 'Oh, look, those pawpaws are almost ripe. *Lotekwa*, don't forget to pluck them.'

There was something polished about her voice, about her; she was like the stone that lay right below a gushing spring, rubbed smooth by years and years of sparkling water, and looking at her was similar to finding that stone, knowing that there were so few like it. He watched her walk back indoors.

He did not want to share the job of caring for the Master with anyone, did not want to disrupt the balance of his life with the Master, and yet it was suddenly unbearable to think of not seeing her again. Later, after dinner, he tiptoed to the Master's bedroom and rested his ear on the door. She was moaning loudly, sounds that seemed so unlike her, so uncontrolled and stirring and throaty. He stood there for a long time, until the moans stopped, then he went back to his room.   □

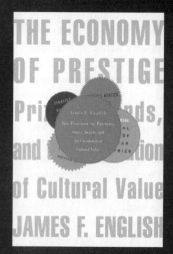
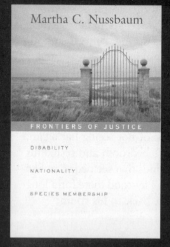

GRANTA

THE WAR OF THE EARS
Moses Isegawa

Uganda

Beeda stood on the school veranda and watched the last pupils disappear down the road. He thought of this as the road swallowing pupils. The day's climax, a question-and-answer session, came back to him and he heard his voice rise to fill the classroom:

'What is twelve times five?'

'Sixty,' the pupils sang cheerfully.

'What is twelve times seven?'

'Eighty-four.'

'What is twelve times twelve?'

'One hundred and forty-four.'

He loved the interaction and the pupils' rapt attention, which placed him at the centre of their world, and made him feel alive. The world outside school was full of questions he could not answer and things he could not control. But when he stood in front of his class, he knew everything and there was nothing he could not do.

Now his class was gone and he was back on the periphery of their lives, and the school, with its abandoned classrooms and silent playground, made him think of an empty shell. When he tried to imagine what would happen if the road did not regurgitate pupils tomorrow a feeling of near panic crept over him.

Night was falling. On the left side of the school the trees in the forest were slowly sinking into darkness. On the right side, the details on the hills were disappearing, the profiles hardening. This was the loneliest time of the day and Beeda hated it.

He listened to the wind rustling the leaves of the mango and the bright red flowers of the flamboyant trees in the compound. It drew his attention to the sharp sound of the typewriter coming from the headmistress's office. He could see his mother's fingers flying over the keyboard, striking the letters with great precision. He liked to watch her type blind, her eyes fixed to the text, her hands a seeming extension of the machine. It was the only surviving typewriter in an area of dozens of square kilometres, and its sound made him feel proud.

Ma Beeda had started Nandere Primary School as a small operation under the mango tree in the middle of the compound twelve years ago. It had become a large school with nine classrooms, creamy, rough-cast walls and a red roof. She had invested her inheritance, as well as her heart and her soul, in the school. She had bought the materials to build it and had chosen the colours to paint it, and she had planted the seashore paspalum which covered the entire compound. Measuring himself against her, Beeda often wondered what kind of mark he would make on the world.

'Beeda, where are you? Come and help me,' he heard her calling from her office. Her voice carried well, it was used to issuing commands and addressing school parades. In church, rising in song, it made the rafters quake.

'I am coming,' he murmured, but made no effort to move.

'Where are you? Do you think we are going to camp here all night?'

He did not reply. He looked at the hills and the darkening sky. He heard the trumpeter hornbill crying *waaa-aaa-aaa*. It was his favourite bird and he loved to watch it fly.

Beeda had detected a note of anxiety in his mother's voice. It made him both uncomfortable and reluctant to find out what had happened. She was so good at camouflaging anxiety and absorbing pressure that whenever it leaked out, he became fearful. And then he would hear the plaintive baby cries of the hornbill.

Ma Beeda looked up and shook her head when he entered. The head-shake was a bad sign; it always meant there was a crisis. It always meant that the big world with its perplexing questions had intruded on their predictable little world.

'We have a problem,' she said, lifting her fingers off the keyboard and looking him in the eye, as if the answers were hidden there. 'I got another letter this morning.'

'What does it say?' Beeda whispered in a voice almost foreign to his ears. He tried to regain his composure by staring at the oil lamp burning on his mother's table. But its sharp smell nullified any calming effect of the yellow flame.

Ma Beeda handed him a piece of paper the writer had torn out of an exercise book. The handwriting was compact and just legible in the mediocre light.

We have warned you many times to close your disgusting school and to stop poisoning God's children with your filthy ideas. But you have refused. We know that you are a government agent and a tool of the Devil. Above all, we know that you are proud of standing in the way of God's work. Who will come to your aid when your hour comes? Remember, nobody spits at our warnings

with impunity. The Most High, who gave us the Ten
Commandments to guide us in all matters, sent us to stamp
corruption out of this country. He sent us to cleanse the entire land
with fire. God's Victorious Brigades are watching you day and
night. Your punishment will be both heavy and harsh. The War of
the Ears has begun. And as the ancient saying goes, *Ears which
don't listen to their master get chopped off.* You are next.
For God and our Revolution.
Colonel Kalo, Chief of Operations.

Colonel Kalo: the mastermind, so most people believed, of the
local branch of the rebels of God's Victorious Brigades. A specimen
of the Colonel's thumbprint made in blood marked the end of the
letter. It was the proof that the letter was authentic.

'He should know that we are going to continue with our work,'
said Ma Beeda. 'We have nowhere else to go. Everything we own is
in this soil. We are teachers, and we are going to teach whoever wants
to learn.'

Her voice was too calm for Beeda's liking. It meant that there was
no room for compromise, a position he did not find wise. Beeda
hoped that, as before, the threats would come to nothing. A war was
going on in the forest and in the hills, where rebels and government
forces occasionally clashed. In the period between engagements, the
rebels attacked civilians, furthering a campaign of terror, while the
government forces, in turn, looked for rebel collaborators.

'Did you speak to the teachers?'

'Yes. The majority wants to stay. Two or three want to run away.'

'Did you hear from the regional commander?'

'He assured me that everything will be all right,' Ma Beeda said,
as if the commander had lied to her.

'When is Uncle Modo coming?' Beeda's voice was still hoarse with
fear. Modo was a former soldier and Beeda wanted him to come and
help them.

'I don't know.'

'I thought he made a promise,' Beeda said, staring at the lamp as
if his uncle was hidden in its belly.

'I am sure he will come, but I cannot say when,' his mother said
firmly. 'Don't worry. We will manage. There are always people

looking out for us. Do you think they will allow the only school in the area to close?'

'No, they won't,' Beeda said without conviction. There was a limit to what unarmed people could do.

Ma Beeda went back to her typing, filling the room with the sound of the keys. When the letter was finished, she pulled it from the machine, read it over, signed and sealed it in an envelope, which she locked in a drawer.

She put a waterproof cover over the typewriter, pulling the edges to make it fit snugly. She cleared her table quickly, putting the files in a big metal cabinet, which she locked, and dropped the key in her bag. She turned down the wick and the lamp went out, the darkness merging the office with the compound outside. She picked up her bag and started humming *Kumbaya, my Lord, kumbaya...* She did that every evening. It was the signal that the day had officially ended.

Beeda walked out of his mother's office and stood on the carpet of grass in the compound. Behind him, he heard his mother closing and locking doors, her voice coming nearer. She insisted on closing the school herself. She liked to hear the sound of the locks.

She stood on the veranda, holding the railing, and swept the compound with her eyes. She felt grateful for the trees, the grass and a well-used day. She walked down the steps into the deepening darkness, which had glued the trees together and turned the forest into a solid mass.

Beeda and his mother took the small, stony road to their house, a half a kilometre from the school. Beeda walked with his eyes half on the ground, half on the sky. The area had no electricity because the rebels had destroyed the transformer, leaving everybody at the mercy of the moon and the stars. He was disappointed that there were so few stars this evening. Here and there lanterns in the houses along the road punctured the darkness, but they only reinforced Beeda's feeling that he was swimming in a lake of black ink. He disliked his mother's humming at that time of the day, for he feared it might invite the rebels to silence her. But she was incorrigible.

'I miss the full moon,' he said, looking straight ahead.

Ma Beeda said nothing. Beeda racked his brain for something to say for the rest of the way, but came up with nothing. They did not meet anybody, as most people went home early and were barricaded inside their houses by nightfall.

'You are thinking about him,' Ma Beeda said suddenly, making Beeda stub his foot on a stone. She had the ability to guess what he was thinking and at times he disliked it intensely.

'Yes, I was thinking about my father,' he replied, stressing the last two words with a touch of annoyance. 'Was he brave?'

'Yes. He knew what to do, and when to do it,' she replied in a low voice. 'I miss him.'

Beeda kept quiet and she started humming again. Beeda knew very little about his father, who had died when he was four. He thought about him at difficult moments, and prayed to him for protection. And whenever he heard the go-away-bird saying *go-away, go-away, go-away*, he thought it was his father shooing troubles out of his path.

When they reached their house, Ma Beeda stopped humming and Beeda stepped aside to let her pass. He stood in the paspalum and looked at the fruit trees, which seemed larger than during the day. Behind the house, the banana trees resembled a high wall. He looked forward to the first flash of the match, and the first flame.

Ma Beeda stopped in front of the main door and searched for the keys in her bag. The huge lock opened with a snap, like a pistol shot. Ma Beeda entered and her son heard her strike a match, and he smiled when the darkness round the flame parted. He followed her inside and locked the door.

It was a victory to arrive home. Ma Beeda always celebrated with a strong cup of tea. While she went to light the stove, Beeda filled a basin in the bathroom with water from a jerrycan, took a sponge, rubbed it with soap and scrubbed his body. He scooped water in his palms and rinsed himself. The feel of the water and the sound it made on the floor relaxed him more than anything he knew. He let the water glide off him until his skin was dry. He put on a pair of shorts and a T-shirt, lay down on his bed and tried not to think about anything. As his mind drifted, he saw the school, his pupils, the other teachers and his uncle. Finally he dozed off.

'Beeda, Beeda. Tea is ready,' he heard his mother calling him.

In the kitchen, the smell of ginger and lemon grass made his mouth water. He drank a big cup of tea while his mother tended to the Irish potatoes cooking on the stove. She was tired and did not want to talk or hum 'Kumbaya', and he was content to listen to the music of the stove and to think about making plans for next day's lessons.

Beeda was not a trained teacher; he was still in secondary school himself. He was just filling in for a teacher who had run away several weeks ago. But with his mother's guidance, he did things like a trained teacher. And the longer he stayed at the school, the more he enjoyed his work.

At home, there was one rule regarding cooking. If it was your turn, you did all the work. Today, it was Ma Beeda's turn; tomorrow, it would be his. They shared all the housework equally, which Beeda liked because it made him self-sufficient: he could cook, wash and iron clothes, tend the garden.

Beeda finished his tea, thanked his mother and put the cups in the sink. A little later, Ma Beeda told him to lay the table, as the food was ready. She served his favourite dish: Irish potatoes with fish cooked in thick groundnut soup. Beeda bent his head over his steaming plate and the aroma went deep into his nose. After a day at school, with the voices of the pupils fresh in their heads, they ate in silence, with only the whistle of a bird intruding.

At the end of the meal, Beeda thanked his mother for cooking and left the kitchen. She did the dishes and then went to her room. She had school finances, teachers' motivation, the security situation to think about before going to bed.

Beeda made the next day's lesson plans and at nine o'clock he said goodnight to his mother. Deep in the night, tucked under the sheets, he woke with a start. A sound like a rock thrown on to the roof had scared him awake. With a thumping heart, he lay still and waited for his mother to call him and tell him what had happened. But there was only a chorus of crickets outside. Eventually, it dawned on him that an avocado had fallen from the tree behind the house. *It is an avocado... an avocado... an avocado*, he whispered until he felt calm enough to fall asleep again.

Two kilometres from Beeda's house three boys squatted in a banana plantation and watched a fourth boy cut up a big jackfruit. The leader was given a slab larger than the rest and he attacked it immediately. It was after nightfall, but this was their first meal of the day and it felt wonderful to be feasting on a jackfruit.

They munched loudly and threw the seeds at their feet. Irritated, the leader raised his sticky hand and slapped one of the boys on the back.

'Lieutenant, you are a pig. The whole village can hear you chew!'

'I am sorry, Major,' the boy whispered. The others took heed and the noise died down.

Major Azizima liked to be addressed by his rank. It made him feel older than his fourteen years. His boss, Colonel Kalo, was only three years older yet his face looked like old leather. Major Azizima envied him his menacing look, for he disliked his own choirboy face, which had endured despite the hardship in the bush.

Today, they had walked thirty kilometres from their base, hiding in the forest and in tall grass. They were on a mission to spread God's glory and that of God's Victorious Brigades. Major Azizima liked to be sent on missions. He dreamed of becoming a general, which would make him a member of the High Command. Fighters who volunteered stood a better chance of advancement, and nobody volunteered as much as he did.

Life at the base was an ordeal. Sex was forbidden, except for the four middle-aged generals who made up the High Command. Colonel Kalo made sure that anybody who broke this rule got one hundred strokes of the hippo-hide whip. He punished rape with amputation of the left hand, and desertion and theft with death. He planted spies everywhere, against whose word there was no appeal. In the mornings, he put the fighters through military drills; in the afternoons, he made them recite the Ten Commandments and chant the Generalissimo's vitriol against the Ugandan government for hours on end. Major Azizima usually came away from such exertions with a headache.

The only time the fighters relaxed was when Colonel Kalo was away, which was rare. The only time everybody was happy was on the Generalissimo's birthday and on Sudan's National Day, when Colonel Kalo allowed them to steal two bulls and hijack a truckload of Coca-Cola for a great feast. All the rules and guidelines came from the Generalissimo, who spoke with God and whose name it was forbidden to pronounce.

Major Azizima's mother had died six years ago, killed by other rebels of God's Victorious Brigades. Every day Major Azizima saw the face of Blue Beast, the man who had killed her and forced him to cut off her ears. She took advantage of the interminable waits between attacks to slip into the cracks in his mind and call his name. 'Azizima, who are you? Who are you?' It was an eerie voice, rising from the bowels of the earth, and it made him shudder.

Now that the War of the Ears had started, he feared his mother's voice even more. It would bother him until he lost his mind. He had started to think about the most dangerous thing a rebel could do: escaping. If caught by his comrades, he would be killed. If caught by government soldiers, he would be tortured or killed or both. The uncertainty made him think of his father, who had been arrested by government soldiers shortly before his mother was killed. Major Azizima believed the soldiers had wrongly accused his father of collaboration with the rebels and killed him. He wanted to avenge his parents, and to find out what had happened to his siblings, who had disappeared. For that reason, he wanted to survive.

After the meal, Major Azizima and his boys left the safety of the plantation and crept past the back of the house. They moved slowly, careful not to alert anybody to their presence. They passed under a window and heard one of the people inside snoring. This would have been the perfect time to storm the house and carry off both food and money. But Colonel Kalo had not given them orders to do so. Instead Major Azizima gave a signal to proceed to Nandere Primary School. They walked on the outer edge of the road, where the grass muffled their footsteps.

When they reached the compound, they spread out. Major Azizima hid behind a tree and looked at the building. He imagined his father standing in front of a class, teaching boys who looked like him. He saw the children doing examinations. He saw his father marking them and announcing that all of them had passed. He felt a yearning to return to school, to study and get a certificate. But he hated having to take orders from teachers. He wanted to be like his father, but it would mean surrendering his power, something he knew he would not do freely. He wanted to cry out. But just then he lost the image of his father and the pupils, which made him angrier.

He walked around the school building. Trying to regain his composure, he drove the butt of his rifle through a window. The sound of the shattering glass soothed him, bringing closer the day Colonel Kalo would order him to burn down the building.

He signalled his boys to leave the compound and head for the nearby trading centre. They made their way silently along the empty road. The bushes were filled with the cries of nocturnal creatures.

They found a spot near shops with Coca-Cola and Nile Beer billboards. The place had the feel of a dead town, with no light anywhere. Shielded by shrubs, they lay in the wet grass and waited. Major Azizima tried to identify the animals shrieking in the forest. After a while, his mother started calling him, her voice rising and falling, fading and swelling. He saw her falling down, her bullet-riddled body covered with widening patches of blood. He saw her asking for mercy, beseeching heaven to intervene. He heard Blue Beast barking at him to take the knife or else he would share her fate. He felt intense pain, which spread from his chest to his stomach and he bit back a crying fit.

It was approaching midnight. Major Azizima heard footsteps. A man appeared from behind the shops, looked left and right, and walked towards the road. The boys waited till he was very near and cocked their rifles. Hearing the sound, the man froze, his hands going up above his head.

'I am a local resident,' he said. 'Please don't shoot!'

'Where are you going at this hour?' Major Azizima asked.

'My wife is very sick. I am getting her some medicine. Please let me go.'

'Are you a government supporter?' Major Azizima asked in a chilly voice.

'Please, let me go. My wife...'

'Are you a rebel sympathizer?'

'Please, have mercy. Every minute counts. Please...'

'Don't think you can fool me, you lout,' Major Azizima said. Here was the chance to do God's will and enhance the reputation of His Victorious Brigades. There was nothing like it, and he could never get enough of it. 'You are a disobedient and impertinent lout. As the ancient proverb says, *Ears which don't listen to their master*—'

'—*get chopped off*,' one of the boys said in a high voice.

'Well said, Lieutenant,' Major Azizima said, emerging from the long grass and approaching the man. Much to his pleasure, he saw the man's legs wobble. When he was barely two metres away from him, he saw the man fall on his knees, his arms held high above his head, the words coming out of his mouth incoherent.

'Don't waste my time, lout,' Major Azizima said, moving nearer. 'You should be happy that you have become a part of God's grand plan.'

He stood over the man and took his knife out of his sheath. He pulled the man's left ear, shouted, 'To God's glory!' and severed it. The man moaned and his bowels screamed as they emptied into his clothes.

'My ear! My ear!'

'Shut up, you lout,' Major Azizima said as he put the ear in his trophy pouch, wiped the dagger on the man's shirt and ordered him to go.

The one-eared man put his palms on the ground and crawled for a number of paces. He then struggled to his feet, swayed, and ran off behind the shops.

To be on the safe side, Major Azizima and his boys moved to another spot, lay down in the shrubs and trained their rifles on the shops. Nobody came outside to confront them.

Major Azizima looked at the stars and decided it was time to find a place to sleep. He signalled his boys to enter the forest and head for the derelict house they occasionally used on missions.

Beeda woke up at six, greeted his mother, washed his face and went outside. Standing in the cold air, he thought that the only thing he hated about teaching was waking up early; he wished he could sleep till ten o'clock. He often spent part of the night awake, praying that their house remained invisible to the rebels.

He raked the leaves which had fallen from different trees overnight, collected them in heaps and threw them in a compost pit near the banana plantation. He found last night's avocado, which had cracked open, and threw it in the pit five metres away. He smiled at his perfect aim.

He emptied yesterday's garbage into the pit. He washed out the garbage can and wiped the floor of the living room and the kitchen with a wet cloth. This was the part he liked least, for he had to get down on his knees, and he was glad when it was over. He fetched a knife from the kitchen and cut some dry banana leaves. He took the leaves to the latrine, put some at the mouth of the hole and struck a match, producing tongues of orange flame and plumes of odoriferous white smoke. He withdrew, the scent sharp in his nose, the smoke making his eyes water. Using a long stick, he pushed more leaves into the fire and smoke filled the entire place. He watched it pushing from under the iron sheets, spreading and chasing away flying insects. When the fire died down, he swept the latrine.

After a bath and a big mug of coffee, which he sipped very hot, he stood on the veranda, arms akimbo, waiting for his mother to appear. Farmers going to their plantations, with hoe in one hand and panga in the other, greeted him. He replied in a cheerful voice, eager to get started with the day's business. The clear weather, the jabbering monkeys and the singing birds all served to lift his spirits higher. He was looking forward to the coming hours, during which he was going to take centre stage in his pupils' lives.

Ma Beeda locked the house, pocketed the key and they left for school. She hummed 'Kumbaya', stopping only if she had to greet somebody. She had slept badly, waking up several times with the feeling that a messenger was at the door, waiting to break the news that her school was no more. It was a daily ordeal, which reached its peak at this time of the morning.

When they were one hundred metres from the compound, they saw the roof peeping through the trees. Ma Beeda stopped humming and made the sign of the cross. 'Thank you Mother Mary, thank you Jesus,' she murmured, her face breaking into a big smile. Beeda watched her in silence, pleased with the transformation that came over her, grateful that they had another day. Ma Beeda walked faster and Beeda had to increase his stride to keep up.

She inspected the premises and saw the broken window. She wondered if the rebels planned to dismantle the school piece by piece; it was only the day before that Colonel Kalo had promised to make an example out of her. She picked up the fragments, remembering what it had cost her to build the school, and tossed the shards in the latrine.

She hurried to the main door and told Beeda to wait by the side of the building. She inserted the key in the lock and held her breath for a number of seconds, for she lived in fear that one day the rebels would booby-trap the door. It was one reason she insisted on opening up herself. If somebody was going to be killed at the entrance to her school, she wanted it to be its founder. This time the door opened safely.

'You can come in now,' she turned and beckoned Beeda. His face was clouded by irritation with this little act, which he thought unnecessary, if not downright degrading. 'I can't take any chances with you,' Ma Beeda replied every time he complained. He no longer bothered.

Beeda inspected the classrooms to make sure they were clean and provided with enough chalk. He examined the charts on the walls to make sure nobody had tampered with them. Finally, he checked the desks and the chairs to make sure none were broken. Satisfied, he went to his mother's office to report and then returned to his class, where he arranged the books he needed for the first lesson neatly on the desk. Now all he needed were his pupils. He picked up a thin bamboo stick and went outside. He stood in the compound, waving the stick absent-mindedly, and waited for the first arrival.

Minutes later, a teacher emerged from the light mist on the side of the hills. She was walking fast, her body rigid, her bag held tight in one hand. Beeda knew something was wrong, for usually she took her time, her movements graceful, her gestures calculated. She did not stop to say hello; she just waved awkwardly and rushed into the headmistress's office before he could ask her what was wrong. He followed her.

'Ma Beeda, Ma Beeda,' she called breathlessly.

'What is the matter, Miss Bengi?' Ma Beeda said lifting her eyes to her.

'They cut off a man's ear last night! We heard him crying as he fled.'

'I am very sorry to hear that,' Ma Beeda said in a soothing voice. 'Do we know the unfortunate fellow?'

'Yes. He is a parent of one of our pupils. He had gone to collect medicine for his wife.'

'It marks the start of the War of the Ears in our area,' Ma Beeda sighed, remembering Colonel Kalo's letter.

'The government must do something.'

'They are going to hunt down those criminals and punish them.'

'They must or else we are lost.'

'The rebels have no chance of victory. They don't have the people's support. It is the reason why they are doing things like that. Breaking our windows won't help them either,' Ma Beeda said.

'What windows are you talking about?'

'Beeda, show her,' Ma Beeda said in a voice which told him that she wanted to get rid of Miss Bengi.

Beeda took Miss Bengi to the broken window. She did not say anything, but he saw that she was frightened. He cautioned her not to tell anybody as it was school policy to avoid alarming the teachers and pupils. She nodded her head in agreement.

Beeda asked her to help him inspect the pupils, who had started arriving. The school compound was filling with noise, which pushed his worries further and further away as his favourite part of the day had begun. They checked to see if the pupils' school uniforms were clean, and issued warnings to those who were untidy.

Other teachers arrived and organized their pupils to pick up leaves in the grass and to get ready for the parade.

At eight o'clock, the bell rang and all the pupils stood in long, straight lines in front of the school. Ma Beeda stood on the veranda behind the railing with the teachers to her left and to her right. She was wearing a dark blue dress with black shoes. She told the pupils to be punctual, to be calm, and to do their work well. When she dismissed them, they walked to their classes in silence.

Beeda taught Mathematics and Science. He derived the greatest pleasure from Mathematics, which he had begun by teaching the multiplication table until every pupil knew it by heart. He made the pupils sing it whenever they were sleepy or distracted. This morning though, he taught division. He took his class outside to collect mangoes and pebbles, which he used as teaching aids.

When the bell rang for the break, the pupils streamed out of the class and he was left alone. He went to the window and looked outside, hoping to see Uncle Modo entering the compound. A man walked towards the school, and he waited expectantly, the noise in the compound seeming to rise higher and higher. But it was a stranger. He sucked his teeth in frustration. It struck him that his uncle might be in trouble. The bell for class rang.

When lunch break came Beeda saw Miss Bengi walk past his classroom. 'How are you feeling now? You seemed quite shaken by last night's events.' His throat felt parched and he swallowed hard. He hoped that, unlike his mother, she could not read his thoughts.

'I am feeling much better, thank you.'

Miss Bengi had the most beautiful voice he had ever heard. He often saw her in his sleep, leading him into the forest, and singing to him as they ran among the trees.

'I am glad to hear that.'

'I cannot live like this any more. I am thinking about going to the city.'

Beeda did not want her to go. It was such a joy to hear her voice when she led the school choir. He now believed Miss Bengi was one of the two teachers Ma Beeda had talked about. 'Are you sure you want to leave? Who will teach the children music? Nobody does it like you.'

'I don't know,' she said softly, as if her resolve had crumbled.

'Stay with us, please. The war will not last forever.'

'Whose propaganda are you listening to?'

Beeda thought the word 'propaganda' was very beautiful, fitting to come out of the mouth of the woman whose voice he adored. He vowed to think of her as Miss Propaganda.

'Your pupils have such respect for you. You can't just leave them,' he said, looking for more convincing reasons to win her over.

'I did not start this war. I won't wait my turn to have my ears cut.'

At that moment Beeda's mother sent a messenger calling him to her office. Beeda suspected she had seen them talking and decided to spoil the moment for him. 'I am a man. I am no longer a kid,' he said to himself in protest.

'What were you saying?' Miss Bengi asked, looking at him closely.

'I have to go,' he said reluctantly. 'But don't forget that we need you.'

'Did your mother send you to tell me that?'

'Of course not. I didn't know you had told her.'

Beeda went to his mother's office and found her listening to the man she called her 'eyes and ears'. Everybody else called him Nightcrawler. He was giving Ma Beeda details of what several people had heard and seen the night before, and she was noting everything down in a black book with waterproof covers. Beeda was not allowed to look in that book. He did not even know where she kept it. On one occasion, however, he had taken a look when his mother was called outside to attend to a playground emergency. It was a record of killings and other atrocities suffered by the people at the hands of both the rebels and government agents. Both the rebels and the government hunted collaborators and spies and treated them roughly, but the former routinely attacked civilians. Beeda pretended he had never looked in the book.

At last Ma Beeda stopped writing, closed the book and handed Nightcrawler last evening's letter, which Beeda saw was addressed to the Regional Army Commander. Nightcrawler put the letter in his inner jacket pocket.

'Have you already had lunch?' Ma Beeda asked when she saw that Beeda was becoming restless.

'No.'

'Why not?'

'I am not hungry.'

'It is still a long way to supper. I would eat something if I were you,' she said and turned her attention back to Nightcrawler.

Feeling redundant, Beeda excused himself and left his mother's office. He went back to the window, but found Miss Bengi gone.

A short while later, he saw Nightcrawler leaving the premises and he wondered what else his mother had confided in him. He felt afraid for Nightcrawler's sake, as he could not imagine what the rebels would do to him if they intercepted that letter. It occurred to him that there might be rebel spies at the school. He spent the day thinking about it and trying to determine whether the spies were teachers or pupils.

On the way home, he wanted to talk about his feelings with his mother, but he could not find the right words. He did not want Ma Beeda to think he was a coward.

'What is bothering you? You have been moody all day,' she said.

Feeling ashamed of his thoughts, he tried to brush her off. 'Nothing really.'

'I hope it is not about Miss Bengi.'

'Not at all. She is too old for me,' he said, forcing a laugh.

'I am all you have. Feel free to tell me your problems.'

'Don't forget Uncle Modo.'

'At the moment he is not here,' she said and, when he kept quiet, she went back to her humming.

They arrived home safely and the door did not explode when Ma Beeda opened it. It was his turn to cook and he immersed himself in his duties. After a while, his mind began to wander and to turn again towards the question of spies in the school. How to identify them? How to trap them? It came as no surprise when the food burned. The pungent odour filled the kitchen and spread throughout the house. Afraid to let in mosquitoes, he did not open the windows, which made the situation worse.

Ma Beeda rushed into the kitchen fanning her nose with a book and found him dumping the food into the garbage can. Biting back the urge to scold him, she asked if she could help. He turned her down. As she turned to go back, he started peeling fresh green bananas. He put them in a pan, added water and put the pan on the stove. He felt ashamed.

When the food was ready, he called his mother. The smell of burning food had given her stomach ache, but she forced herself to eat a little.

There was one radio in the house, which Ma Beeda kept in her room. She lent it to him for the night, hoping the music would soothe him and ease him into sleep.

Beeda spent the next two hours listening to a mixture of current news and music on both local and foreign stations. He luxuriated in this ephemeral connection with other worlds and the resulting suspension of fear. He would have liked to listen all night, but he had to wake up early. At his usual bedtime, he switched off the radio and fell asleep.

Deep in the night, he was awakened by gunfire, though it was difficult to tell where it was coming from. He lay still, the silent radio near his heart, and waited. But nothing happened. He prayed to his father to keep him safe and, after a while, he switched on the radio and pushed the earphones deep in his ears. □

GRANTA

PASSPORT CONTROL
Kwame Dawes

Ghana/Jamaica

2

DESCRIPTION — *SIGNALEMENT*

Bearer—*l'titulaire*

Profession
Profession } PROFESSOR OF ENGLISH

Place and date
of birth
Lieu et date } ACCRA
de naissance 28:7:1962

Residence } U.S.A.
Résidence

Height } 1m 84 cm
Taille

Colour of eyes } BROWN
Couleur des yeux

Colour of hair } BLACK
Couleur des cheveux

Special peculiarities }
Signes particuliers

CHILDREN — ENFANTS

Name *Nom*	Date of birth *Date de naissance*	Sex *Sexe*

3

My father left me no nation. It is hard to blame him for this, but he could have offered more sustained concepts of home and nationalism. I have inherited this absence of home and will now pass it on, somehow, to my children. The facts alone, which I sometimes rehearse to baffle strangers, offer some hints as to why 'home' is a curious concept for me. When my children were born, two in South Carolina, one in Canada, I realized that at one level they would be calling North America, and perhaps the United States, home. Yet I realized, also, that they would be conflicted about home, and the source from whence they would expect to receive their legal and psychic sense of home—their father—would be most unreliable, most unhelpful. This is what my children entered the world with.

I am Ghanaian. This is my legal label. I was born there. It is my inheritance. My mother is Ghanaian—she was born there and her ancestors came from Togoland and from Ghana. Now anyone listening to me or reading my poetry or fiction would recognize that I am culturally largely Jamaican. It is because I grew up in Jamaica. My father was Jamaican and in the early 1970s, when I was eight years old, he decided to take his family from Ghana to go and live in Jamaica. This is all simple enough. I am a product of my parents, and, technically, I should have access to both nationalities. But I don't. I tried to have this arranged when, in 1983, I was going to the Dominican Republic for two weeks to train some fellow students in evangelistic techniques.

I called the Embassy of the Dominican Republic to see if I would need a visa to enter that country. They said I wouldn't. They asked me no questions except if I had a passport. I did. I was to travel through Haiti, spending a couple of hours there in transit. It was late afternoon when I arrived in the congested and hot Port-au-Prince airport. I joined a line that led me to the customs desk where they examined the papers of those taking the connecting flight to Santo Domingo. That is where the trouble began. I was asked to stand aside. I strained to make out what they were saying in this babble of language that jumped from a consonant-free Spanish to a truncated, coded French, to a fluid but utterly incomprehensible patois. I picked up enough to know that my Ghanaian passport was a problem. They asked for my visa. I said I was told I did not need a visa. They asked where I lived. I said Jamaica. But they seemed not to believe me. I tried to show them from my passport my last record of travel and to prove that I lived in Jamaica. It did not seem to work. There was no permanent resident stamp in my passport. As far as they were concerned, I was a Ghanaian trying to get into the Dominican Republic illegally. They would not let me in. They suggested I get a visa from their embassy in Haiti. The Haitians, of course, were happy to have an African. I loved Haiti for that. But not the Dominicans.

Getting a visa was going to be a problem. It was Friday and the following Monday was a public holiday. It was past five in the afternoon. I was stranded. I ended up spending almost a week in Haiti before I could get the visa. I did my work in Santo Domingo, but it was never pleasant. I was annoyed at the inconvenience and disturbed at my abject vulnerability. Over the years, I would come to accept this kind of intense scrutiny and suspicion as part of my journey through customs anywhere in the world. When you have a Ghanaian (or Nigerian or Bangladeshi) passport, you never feel welcomed at any port, even your own country's port. The ritual of customs is one characterized by the assumption of your criminality, of your guilt. You approach the desk with all your papers intact, yet with a sense of being called to prove yourself. You learn to be clear, polite, and efficient, because you recognize that these people have incredible power, unilateral power. You approach the desk aware that the task before the clerk is to find out why not to let you in rather than when to let you in. The impression is that the country you are entering does not want you there. In many ways, it is an unreasonable feeling, a very personal feeling of shame, but I have been through quite enough long interrogations at airports when my papers were in perfect order, to make me declare this ritual of arrival a deeply painful one.

I contemplated, after Haiti and the Dominican Republic, being rid of the Ghanaian passport. At least a Jamaican passport would give me access to the Caribbean *sans problèmes*, and Jamaica was not officially blacklisted at most customs desks. I struggled with this because all through my ten or so years in Jamaica, I took pride in being different, in being someone else, in being from Ghana. It was how I explained my inability to cope with the violence of Jamaican society, for instance. In Ghana, that kind of volatile violence—sudden, efficient, and totally inexplicable—was not the norm. And then there were the

Afrophobes in Jamaica—that group of Jamaicans who liked to tell me that despite all the hand wringing and groaning about slavery and about being torn from 'Mother Africa', they were glad it had happened for they had been rescued from the uncivilized world of that continent by the glorious world of the West. I did not want to give them the pleasure of saying, 'See, you too can't stand your Africanness.' But I needed some stability. Eventually, I decided to go to the passport office in Kingston and apply for a new passport—a Jamaican passport.

The passport office was somewhere on Marcus Garvey Drive, a busy dual carriage-way filled with coughing trucks, ancient vans, road-weary and weighed-down minibuses stuffed to overflowing with passengers, who did not seem to recognize their complete recklessness in boarding such vehicles that swayed and staggered their way between the potholes that littered the boulevard. Marcus Garvey Drive was flanked by some of the toughest areas in Kingston; 'ghetto' is too organized a word for the chaos and squalor of those clotted fields of zinc, cardboard, and timeworn cement where people eked out a living. Riverton City, riverless, a glinting monolith of colour and rust, was on Marcus Garvey Drive, along with an assortment of long-established factories: the Tia Maria factory with its exotically shaped gigantic bottle overlooking the road; the soap factory that spewed a nauseating chemical stench into everything. The trees and bushes that survived this onslaught of exhaust fumes, stinking chemicals, and the relentless sun had an olive green unhealthiness about them; a peculiar dullness of colour that made their very survival appear a mistake.

When you walked along Marcus Garvey Drive, you felt you were quite totally in Jamaica, in a place of violent and complex energy, a place in which hardship was scored to a reggae sound: gritty, unvarnished, and yet miraculous. It was a blazing morning. I caught a bus in Papine, a small square and bus depot tucked into the foothills of the Blue Mountains, and continued downhill, south towards the coast, passing through the bustling Half-Way Tree and all the way down to the Three Mile roundabout. I came off the bus on Marcus Garvey Drive which runs parallel to the shoreline of Kingston Harbour, my body reacting at once to the dust and the stench from the soap factory. I spat. In my head was a strange feeling—a sense that I was going to get this thing done, this thing that would take an hour at the most, this thing that would secure my status as Jamaican. I was aware that I was planning to give up something, to give up my uniqueness, to give up the African in me—but I was being pragmatic. I was a New World man, now. I was a writer, a Jamaican writer and that was the simple fact of it.

It did not occur to me that Jamaica would not want me, would even hesitate to have me. At the time, I had lived in Jamaica for fourteen years. I had no intentions of leaving the country. England was an impossibility—I had no ties there—and America was only for the fickle, the sell-outs, the unpatriotic, the materialistic, the *lickey-lickey*, the bourgeois. America was *Mee-ami*, the haven for those who valued foreign things over local things. I was overbearingly dogmatic about this. Perhaps I could afford to be because I had no prospects of going to America and I had no desire to do so. At the time I was writing my Master's dissertation. After it was done, I planned to go on to do a doctorate, perhaps, and get some teaching work somewhere in the Caribbean. America was not an especially useful option because I found I was revolted by the thought of going to the American embassy to join the long line of desperate people looking for escape, to grovel before rude and smug embassy officials. I was not planning to do this. So I was going to stay in Jamaica and I thought I might as well legalize my status.

I was confident about my Jamaicanness. I spoke patois. I was educated in Jamaica. I had won a national scholarship to university in Jamaica. I did not pay differential fees for school. I had won national awards as a playwright, reviewers were calling me a Jamaican playwright of promise; there were newspaper clippings to prove all this. I was not just Jamaican, I was making Jamaica proud. I was called up to the National Youth Cricket trials to represent Jamaica at cricket. I did not make the team, but I was at the trials. Everyone knew I was Jamaican. My father was the great Jamaican novelist, he was one of the custodians of Jamaican culture in his position as Director of the Institute of Jamaica. People knew him. I could call his name if need be.

During those early years in Jamaica when I was nine, ten and eleven, I spent much of my time battling the ignorance of Jamaicans about Africa and things African. I could tell that my mother was constantly being given a hard time by all ranks of society about her Africanness. They asked daft questions about her comfort with clothes, about how people dressed in Africa, about cars, about the food we ate, and so on. The problems were exacerbated by the fact that my mother was my father's second wife. The first was a brilliant Jamaican theatre director who was quite well known in the country. I have learned over the years that the marriage between my father and his first wife was regarded as a perfectly excellent match among the pseudo elitists and the artistic community in Jamaica. He was, after all, an Oxford man and she was on her way to great things as a UWI graduate who would soon head off to Yale where she would eventually get her PhD as a theatre director. For some reason, the news of the demise of their marriage did not sit well with the Jamaicans.

Africa, in the middle-class Jamaican imagination, was a quagmire of twisted manners and ancient memories, not unlike the peculiar uncertainty existing between humans and monkeys: they look so much like us, but don't tell me we came from them! Please don't. Africans, in other words, were not exactly associated with racial pride and dignity for the colonized Jamaicans. This is a generalization, but a fair one. When Marcus Garvey started to speak of repatriation to Africa in the 1920s, he did muster up a following in Jamaica, but he also managed to secure for himself quite a grand opposition who made it clear in editorials in the newspapers that returning to Africa amounted to a backward step, a step into savagery, from whence Jamaicans had been rescued, albeit through the horrendous system of slavery; but that was a long time ago, and how could we question God's wondrous wisdom in ordering the affairs of humans. Africa, then, became associated with illegal workers of spiritual deviancy—the obeah man, the myal man, the Pocomania adherent—all people who had sustained, through much oppression and censure, a sense of Africa in their communities. Then Africa became associated with Rastafarians who started to take Garvey at his word and speak very forcefully and creatively about going back to Africa. And many did go, including a tragic 'uncle' of mine, Uncle Freddy, who ended his African sojourn in Ghana, no longer a Rastaman, but certainly a thoroughgoing rumhead and an exceptional carpenter. Freddy would come to our home in Ghana each Christmas and drink himself into a strange and tragic stupor after handing us the handcrafted gifts of toy guns and toy dolls, and the like. He would vomit in the house and sleep for long hours. That was Freddy. When in the 1970s he returned to Jamaica, to Spanish Town, to retire, he had long given up the vision of repatriation to Africa, but he was an exception. Africa was Rastafarian and Rastas were the lowest of the low in middle-class eyes. So my mother was African and I was African, and we were teased. My siblings and I were teased. My older brother, Kojo, was given the name Unka—as in *Unka, Unka, kill, kill*—a simulation of the chant of cannibalistic Africans. I was labelled Little Unka or Young Unka.

Invariably, our need for survival, our desire to battle this kind of racial prejudice, helped build in us an instinct for nostalgia. It was one of many ways to cope with the insult. There were other ways, far more amusing and perhaps more satisfying. My sister and I— the one closest in age to me, Adjoa—found ourselves in Shortwood Primary School together for two years. She started in grade five and I in grade four. We exchanged stories of the kind of insults we had undergone. At first it was difficult. Jamaican dialect, or nation language, is *not* English. It is a terribly complex and difficult language to master. I thought I spoke fairly good English—in fact we had spent two years in London before moving to Jamaica and I had acquired a quite credible cockney accent which tempered my Ghanaian one. That should have ensured that they would at least think I spoke 'proper' English. So while I was understood (or accommodated politely) by the teachers and the students, I could not understand them. They did not speak English, despite their claims to the contrary. I struggled for the first six months, trying my best to follow the dance and turn of the Jamaican language. And Jamaican children did not, at that age, have the notion of bilingualism—they simply shouted louder when I said, 'eh?' The teacher felt pity on me and started to attempt translating for me in class. But her St Catherine accent was rather thick and that proved to be an amusing comedy of errors and confusion. But I did well in class. I could read and that helped. Yet my difference posed problems because children decided to try out their knowledge of Africa, well gleaned from authoritative sources like Tarzan movies, Hollywood films like *The African Queen*, Phantom comics, and very reliable information from older brothers and sisters who had seen things in magazines and on television about Africans, about their way of life and about their abject savagery. So I was tested: Did I like shoes? Did I live in a house? Did I know Tarzan? Did I ever see a tiger, an elephant, a cheetah, a lion, a chimpanzee...? Did I like to wear clothes? Did I see women's *titties out a door* all the time? Did I ever meet the Phantom?

At first I was defensive and embarked on a major education campaign, but it soon became clear that this was futile and, anyway, this was not what they wanted to hear. If I denied anything, they would call me a liar. So I lied. I lied first about eating snakes. They enjoyed that and I decided to embellish. I developed such an uncanny system of lying about things that it was soon clear that they believed I had met Tarzan and that I did not like him because he still talked like an Ape and, contrary to the impression given by the comics, he did not wear loincloths but went around grossly naked, his member an awful and ugly looking monstrosity. My stories grew in grandeur and I must have become possessed of the spirit of Elizabethan explorers like Walter Raleigh or tale-weavers like Hakluyt. The other children devoured the stories. So I fed them. I kept feeding them these tales. When, after a few months, there began to be a growing sense of distrust, a questioning of my tales (it may have been when I started to talk about the pet lion I had at home), I consulted with my sister who found my manner of deflecting these fools so ingenious that we conspired together to have our stories properly formalized. From then on, when I was challenged about anything, I would tell them to go ask my sister. She agreed with everything. And when I was approached by her older, but equally gullible friends, I would answer with such flippant boredom and slight impatience, while embellishing some more for effect, that they bought it all. I look on that and still say to myself: Ah, the fools. For they were fools to believe all of this, but they could not be blamed entirely for their stupidity. Still, our action was one of self-protection, of self-preservation for we were being insulted at all times and it was difficult, very difficult. We took secret pleasure in our game.

It was within such a context, then, of some hostility and a strong negativity towards Africa, that we developed our own sense of nostalgia about Ghana. Ghana was a place of great stories, family stories. We preserved stories like most families do, by passing on tales

Kwame Dawes

of the exploits of one child to the rest of the children. There were
five of us, and we had enough stories to go around and around until
they formed the fabric of nostalgia. There was the story of my older
brother who brought a stone, almost twice his size, instead of a
switch when my mother asked him to bring something for her to
beat him with. He was two and understood irony. The story of that
same brother who drove the car at age four, down a hill and into a
ditch—he lived to tell the tale, as he did when he was ten and set
the entire field of corn and shoulder-high wild grass at the back of
our house and along a ridge afire. He was punished by having to
walk out with a bucket, stark naked, to battle the blaze. The story
of our first communal whipping for missing school, the story of my
infant brother, Kojovi, who drained all the glasses of liquor left by
guests after one of my father's parties, and became so drunk that he
assumed the position of a Chief: 'Bring me my *chokota*!' We would
repeat the story and roll with laughter. The story of my accidents,
the poisonous plants I ate, the pills I consumed, the car that ran over
me and left me for dead, and so on. And there were songs, songs of
our childhood in Ghana, songs that reminded us about our
grandparents, our grandmother singing her Gospel songs in Fanti on
the last day that we saw her before leaving Africa. We would sing
those songs with sadness and my mother would weep. We remembered
the house, the school, the university campus, the fresh bread we would
get from the bakery located at the top of the hill in Legon, the games
we played at the Africa Centre with drumming and dancing, trying
to mimic the professional dancers of the theatre company there.

We had strong tales of remembrance and we spoke them as people
trying to ensure that the memory of our origin was not lost. It was
part of who we were and we had no good reason to battle that
nostalgia for that nostalgia sustained us. So the names of our relatives,
our cousins, our friends would have the sound of a litany—a strange
cadence that remained locked in the mind as a song would. Nostalgia
was rich. The food: the *fufu*, the *banku*, the *kenke*, the *kelewele*, the
okra soup, the palm nut soup, the groundnut soup, the *yoyi* tree, the
akra, the *garri* done a million ways, the monumental legend of the day
Aba, my oldest sister, and I ate plates and plates of yam and corned
beef until we were almost sick, but how we relished that meal and
how we remembered it like a legend of incredible proportions.

We could afford the nostalgia of Ghana because Ghana was a place of childhood and the complications of coups, of political intrigue, of the corruption in the government, of the executions and the arrests—while a part of our imagination and while quite acutely remembered—remained muted by the relative safety that we felt as children, protected from the fear of our parents. It was their task to fear. Once we had to leave Accra in a grand hurry to speed to my grandmother's house in Cape Coast and remain there for nearly a week in the middle of a school term. It did not occur to us that my father was actually running for his life and trying to avoid deportation for his political actions. We did not know. All I remember of that trip was the excitement of a sudden departure and my father getting sick on whisky and coconut water—apparently a horrendous combination. It was the first time that I had seen him become sick like Uncle Freddy. There was a sense of foreboding and sadness about that, but it passed and then we were happily running around playing games with our cousins. There were more memories of gunfire at night during coups, the news of Kotoka's dramatic and tragic killing, the flight of President Nkrumah after the coup that ousted him, and so on. I even sang songs about the Biafran war— but we were children, and it is part of the condition of children to be able to alchemize the hardships of life into a litany of nostalgia and adventurous memory.

So in Jamaica, we held Ghana as a place of hope. We wanted to return, and we felt with our mother when she walked through the house singing Ghanaian songs in Fanti, or singing songs that would invoke her mother. We mourned with her when her father died and she was not able to go and see him. We mourned too when her mother died and she had to go home to be there with the family. And even as time began to erode our connection with Ghana through the loss of the languages we used to speak so well—Ga, Fanti, Ewe—we preserved the memory always. It was our way of sustaining ourselves and finding dignity in our Africanness. I embraced my Africanness quite gladly. There was little else I wanted to do. By the time I had reached high school I had abandoned calling myself Neville and started to call myself Kwame. I was linked up nicely with the Rastafarians who liked to talk to me, liked to connect with someone from the Motherland.

To return to that day in 1985 when I tried to get a Jamaican passport: I knew nothing about what I had to do to get one. I arrived at the office—a huge hangar-like structure with a zinc roof—with nothing but my Ghanaian passport tucked into my book bag. I did not expect to receive the blue Jamaican passport that day, but I did expect to fill out the forms and get the process started within the hour.

I was sent upstairs to a darkened floor with a maze of cubicles carved out of this space. Table fans whirred. White-shirted, tie-wearing clerks and uncomfortably dressed women in skirt-suits sipped iced juices while looking lazily involved with their labours. I found the woman I was to talk to. She wore a dark suit. Her coiffure was helmet-steady, the processing not able to undermine the stern roots of her hair. Her forehead gleamed with sweat and lotion; round lips, fist-like nose, plucked brown eyebrows, efficient gold earrings. I remember her well.

I explained quickly that I wanted to get a Jamaican passport.

'You ever have one before?' she asked, not looking at me. Slow, non-committal, very detached.

'No, not a Jamaican,' I said.

'But you have a passport, then?' she asked.

'Yes.'

'What kind?' She looked at me.

'Ghanaian,' I said, taking out the passport.

'Guyanese? So why you want a Jamaican passport, anyway? Don't you have a Guyanese passport already?' She seemed genuinely puzzled by my request.

'Ghanaian. From Ghana,' I said.

'Africa?' Her nose curled. 'Africa?'

'Yes, West Africa. My Ghana passport has expired and I decided to get a Jamaican one instead.' I tried to sound convincingly Jamaican. Her reaction to my Africanness was not a good sign.

'So you are Ghanaian... How do you say it?'

'Ghanaian. Yes,' I said.

'Then you must get a Ghana passport. You were born there, right?' It was now as if she was talking to a child. Perhaps I had hoped she would be puzzled by my strong Jamaican accent. I wanted a point of connection, a sense that we were one, that we were Jamaican together.

'No, but I am Jamaican too,' I said and then quickly added, 'I have lived here for fourteen years. Went to school here and everything. I am at UWI now. My father is Jamaican.'

'Born here?' she asked.

'No. He was born in Nigeria, but he came here when he was two,' I added.

'Your mother?' she asked.

'But I have lived here for fourteen years...' For some reason, this was not going as I had planned. I was feeling the urge to pull out my information about scholarships and the like—all the evidence that everyone saw me as Jamaican. Everyone.

'Your mother is Jamaican?' she asked again.

'No. Ghanaian,' I said.

'So you are Ghanaian.' She said this with a note of triumph, as if she had just won an argument.

'I know...' I stated. She interrupted me.

'And you have not been naturalized?'

'I came for a passport. To get a Jamaican passport...'

Perhaps it was me who caused what happened afterwards. It may have been my sense of being put-upon, it may have been inordinate pride for, all of a sudden, here I was looking like a poor supplicant come to beg something from this country that I had, after much consideration, decided to embrace as my own. I had given up years of feeling almost superior in my Ghanaianness, my difference; I had come to offer my identity to this country and this woman was starting to make me feel as if I was in the American embassy trying to get a visa. I kept wondering how many people came to her in a year asking to be made a Jamaican. Was she relishing this sense of superiority, this sense that at last a poor African was now seeing how valuable it was to be a Jamaican? Was that what was coming out, or was it all in me, in my shock at being treated as a beggar, my shock at the thought that perhaps the racist poison that I had managed to deflect as a child with a sense of superiority, was now back to destroy me?

Whatever it was, I know I became curt and that the edge in my voice and manner was apparent. I am not being juvenile in saying that she started it, though. She actually looked at me and laughed, and then quite haughtily (at least so it seemed to me then), but sternly said: 'You think we just give out Jamaican citizenship like that? You think it so easy? You think we just give it out to any and everybody?' Then she gave that 'humph' which was at once amused and impatient. Beyond that, her tone assumed that saccharine civil servant quality of complete lack of interest. 'I am sorry, sir, but you can't inherit nationality from your father. He is Jamaican, but naturalized. He could get it from his father, but you can't get it from him because he is Nigeria-born. So I can't help you. If you want to be naturalized, you going to have to apply for citizenship, and I don't deal with that.'

She was finished. I was livid. I had been stupid to have come without finding out any of this, but she did not have to assume that air, that manner. At that moment, I began to rehearse all the things I hated about this little island, this tiny colonial dot of insignificance. I was frustrated by my helplessness, by the sheer logic of what she said, and by the absurdity of the notion that fourteen years in the country did not qualify me for status. I told her that I resented her tone, that I did not come begging for nothing, that they could keep their damned passport for all I cared, and I stormed out of the building, my armpits stinging with anger and heat.

My father had left us with a confusing heritage, a complicated inheritance. Of course, that last sentence sounds like blame. It really is not. It is a simple observation. And it is the kind of observation that, at some level, is quite disturbing to me. There is an implication that the choices that my parents made about where we would grow up have significantly complicated our lives. It is in this basic truth that my own disquiet lies. In February 1992, when my wife Lorna and I began to have children in North America, we expected to live in Jamaica. Sena was born in Canada, but I expected to complete my doctorate and return to Jamaica to work. Lorna had already successfully applied for a library position at the University of the West Indies, while my application for a position at the Creative Arts Centre was looking promising. Jamaica it would be. True, Sena would be a Canadian child, but this would simply be a safeguard, an option for her in later life. We did not plan it that way, but it was something that made sense.

The job in Jamaica fell through. Not long after that, in the summer of 1992, an opportunity came up in America. This meant a complete realignment of what we were doing. The decision to take the position in South Carolina was a tough one. There was the obvious pressure of finances: we wanted more children and so had to start planning for more stability. I needed a job. Our lives during my student years were hard, very difficult, and when the scholarship money had dried up, I had to work in all kinds of unusual areas to supplement the money Lorna was making as a telemarketer. We were hurting. The band—the reggae band—I played with, Ujamaa, was constantly on the verge of a great deal but it did not happen, over and over again. South Carolina was offered; America was offered and I was surprised at how easily I became drawn into the idea of moving to America.

It may have been another reaction to Jamaica, to my sense of having been rejected by Jamaica. It may have been exactly the same feeling of anger at the troubling way Jamaica had dealt with me, that made the decision to think about America so easy. My father had detested America but ironically it was his experience in Jamaica— the dark years of unemployment, of being avoided by people who had once claimed to be his friends, the job he took teaching high school because he could get nothing else—that came back to me and suddenly made taking the job in America seem like fitting revenge, a kind of lashing out against the affront of his rejection.

I too had been rejected and from what I could tell I had fallen victim to one of those insidious Jamaican problems of 'connections'. The position I had applied for at the Creative Arts Centre in Jamaica seemed perfectly suited to my experience and abilities. I was actually assured that I was favoured for the position. But soon I stopped getting calls from Jamaica asking about my plans to arrive to take up the position. I called some friends at the Centre and was told that someone else, a friend of my family in fact, had been hired. No one thought to tell me. I was later told that it was because of a deal with this family friend that I had been pushed aside. I did not want to believe this, but it was enough that I had been shafted in a rather rude and unprofessional manner. That was Jamaica for you, I thought. I would go to America, go anywhere. □

GRANTA

GIFTED
Segun Afolabi

Nigeria

The mother woke to the sound of screaming. One of the sons was trying to take something from the other, and the youngest had found his lungs. She moved swiftly, past fatigue, throwing the robe over the places where she had been beaten, past the bedroom door, into the chill of the corridor, into the room where the screaming was. She shut the door behind her and cupped her mouth as if she were about to vomit. The boys looked round at her and fell silent. She did not have to speak or scold or raise her hand. They understood.

'What *is* it?' she asked. 'Why are you misbehaving this early in the morning? Don't you know your papa is sleeping?'

The boys' eyes grazed the carpet and then each other guiltily. The youngest tried not to smile with shame.

'He stole my toy!' the other one started. 'He won't give it back.'

His brother held the bright red plastic machine behind him, and inched away.

'And so what!' the mother said. 'He is your brother. Don't you know you must share your things? Ah, ah! You must show a good example. How many times do I have to tell you?'

He shuffled his feet and glanced at his brother. He did not feel generous towards him at all. He felt everything would be taken from him eventually and given to the younger one.

'And you too, Dayo—did you ask your brother if you could play with his toy?'

'Yes!' The boy looked wildly about and clutched the machine to his chest. He could not meet his mother's eyes.

'Hmm—always ask before you take something. Otherwise you've done a wrong thing. You understand?' She held the flat of her palm against her hip. She had been ignoring the pain; now the danger had passed and she winced as she remembered the kick.

'What's wrong?' the older boy asked.

'Nothing's wrong. *Oyo* now, time to get ready for school.'

The mother left the room and checked on her husband who was still sleeping, and went to the bathroom and locked the door. She removed the robe and inspected the nightgown which had been torn beyond repair. She squeezed her shoulders, trying to ease the ache, and moved her head from side to side. She could hear her own breathing in the silence and it disturbed her so much she turned on the taps for the bath. She returned to the mirror and removed the

79

gown and stared at the places that were spoiled like old fruit. She touched herself: her shoulders, her breasts, her thighs. She examined the new areas—the ladder of her ribs, the imprint of his shoe against her hip—kneading the flesh gently. She did not know whether anything was broken. The bath filled and she lowered herself into the water and felt the heat leaching away the pain. Foam drifted to the floor. She craned her neck and listened, but there was only silence now. She did not have to worry about the boys. She lay back and thought of nothing except how tired she was and how her head felt like wet, twisted cloth.

'I don't like it,' the youngest boy complained, stirring the porridge back and forth, not eating.

'You *will* eat it,' the father said.

The boy looked up and moved the spoon towards his face, turning his mouth down, feeling the slimy pulp against his tongue.

'Who was making so much noise this morning?' the father asked.

The boys looked at each other and then to their mother and back to their breakfasts again. No one said anything.

'Eh?' His voice was a calm river, but it was the calm before the waterfall. They knew this.

The youngest one began to whimper.

'They were excited because of the snow,' the mother said.

'Snow?' The older boy pushed away from the table and ran to the window. His brother followed.

'Everything's white!' the older boy said.

'I can't see!' the younger one cried.

His brother dragged a dining chair to the window and together they gazed out at the city from the apartment window.

'Is that your school?' The youngest one pointed to a high-rise towards the centre of the city.

'No, silly—my school isn't high like that. It's over there—see where the park is?'

'Who told you to stand on the chair?' The father came from behind and brought his hand down, hard, on the backs of their legs. The youngest one buckled and lost his grip on the chair, but his brother caught him before he fell. 'Who told you to carry the chair to the window?'

The youngest one began to cry while his brother clenched his teeth, his head shaking a little. The mother looked at them, the china cup of tea against her lips, but she did not drink. She knew what was coming.

'Why do you let them behave like this?' he began. 'Every day they deteriorate. They are becoming wild, these children, and you sit there looking at them. Why don't you do anything, eh?'

The boys were quiet. They looked at their mother and then stared down at their bowls. They could not eat. They could hear the father's breathing, and in the distance, the rumble of the Odakyu express train. The doorbell rang and the mother flinched. Her husband noticed this and smiled. '*Oya, oya*—time to go!' he said to the older boy. 'Go and carry your satchel.'

As they waited in the hallway for the elevator, Mrs Nakamura arrived with her little girl. The mother and father greeted them in English and then the younger boy used the Japanese words. They rode the elevator with only the giggles of the younger boy and the girl to break the silence.

The embassy bus shuddered outside the lobby doors while the other children and staff talked among themselves as they waited. Beyond the entrance the snow still fell. Mrs Nakamura and her daughter waved to the family and walked in the snow towards the bus stop at the bottom of the hill. The father and the older boy entered the embassy bus, and the mother and the other son waved as it departed. She exhaled as if for the first time.

'I want to go to school too.' The boy looked up at his mother. 'I want to go in the bus.'

'When you are older,' she said. 'Don't you want to see your friends in the nursery? You don't want to stay at home with me?'

'I do, I do!' the boy cried. He had already forgotten about his brother's school and the crowded embassy bus. He skipped across the marble lobby as his mother collected the letters and they rode the elevator back to the seventh floor. This was a ritual: sometimes when she was tired she would carry her son and tiptoe the length of the corridor so no one would hear them. Today she could not lift him. She touched a finger against her lips so that the boy would play the game, and they moved quietly across the tiles. But the door opened.

'*Gooden morgen*,' Mr Mihashi said. 'Mrs Odesola, small Dayo.

Enter. You must enter.' The old man stood at the door wearing a navy wool kimono and grey obi, waving them in. The boy looked up at his mother and grinned. They had lost the game again. She touched his head and smiled and they moved into their neighbour's apartment as he shuffled behind them in worn Western slippers.

'Mr Mihashi, you are cooking something—something sweet,' the mother said. She stood in the centre of the living room and closed her eyes and inhaled. She counted: 'Nutmeg, cloves, cinnamon,' bouncing the palm of her hand on her son's soft curls. 'What is Mr Mihashi cooking today?'

'Ah, sit, sit. *Assey-vous*,' he said. 'Beginning, you must take some tea. And then I must illustrate to you.' He clapped his hands in excitement. 'Am I correct, Mrs Odesola—I must illustrate? I have been learning.'

The mother thought for a moment and said, 'Show, Mr Mihashi. You are going to show us something?'

'Yes, yes. I must show to you what it is, and then you will eat it.' He clapped his hands again and looked from the boy to the mother, and fled to the kitchen, the kimono creating a breeze as he moved.

The boy left the dining table and switched on the television set in the corner of the living room. He located the remote control and began to search for the cartoons about the machines that talked and fought and changed their shapes, like his brother's toy. The mother looked out of the window, at the snow which was falling faster now. She shifted in the seat to ease the gnawing in her hip, her shoulders. She turned away, towards her son and the aroma-filled room. There was a painting on the wall between the television and kitchen, of the sea, showing exaggerated waves and a ship's crew, terrified.

'Snow, so much snow,' Mr Mihashi said as he carried in the tray of tea. 'In your country you do not have so much snow? Am I correct, Mrs Odesola?'

'You are correct, Mr Mihashi. In my country there is no snow at all. Only hot, hot sun and sometimes plenty of rain. How it can rain, Mr Mihashi. You cannot imagine.' She thought of the time she had played with her sisters in the road outside their house during a downpour. How quickly their dresses had been soaked. How they had carried on regardless, their faces upturned, drinking in the rainwater as it fell.

'Come and have some biscuits,' she said to her son who was now engrossed in a documentary about bowhead whales.

'Biscuit and what?' he asked.

'Biscuits—biscuits and tea,' she said. 'And Mr Mihashi has made you some cocoa.'

He came to the table and sat between them and tasted the hard biscuits the old man had baked.

'It is good?' Mr Mihashi grimaced, the lines of his face moving, wavering, the eyes darting like flies.

The boy nodded and continued to eat, staring at the television screen.

'Mrs Mihashi, she could make it very nice, no problem,' he said. 'So many things she could do; I can make only this.'

'It's very good,' the mother said. 'Isn't it, Dayo?'

The boy nodded again as he sipped his cocoa, both hands wrapped around the cup. 'You must eat more,' the old man insisted, and he pushed the plate of biscuits towards him. The boy took a handful of biscuits and carried his drink to sit on the floor in front of the television set.

'She could make many delicious things,' Mr Mihashi continued. 'She was very beautiful woman, Mrs Odesola. She was speaking French; it was her work—French teacher. My children, now they can all of them speak French. She had many, many skills, Mrs Odesola. How do you say it, when someone can do many things?'

'Well, you were right the first time—your wife had many skills, you could say, or talents. She was talented, or you could say that she was gifted. There are different ways to describe your wife, all of them correct.'

Mr Mihashi closed his eyes for a moment. 'Gifted—I must write it on a paper. She will like it.'

This time the mother did not correct him.

When it was time, the boy and his mother went downstairs to walk to the nursery. The snow had stopped falling then. It was so fresh it hurt their eyes to look at it. She inhaled and it felt like crystals were forming in her lungs. The mothers huddled in the entrance to the nursery. When Mrs Odesola arrived, one or two turned to smile at her. The other mothers had formed groups according to where they came from. She did not have her own group and she did not stay. She left the boy, happy enough with the other children, pulled her coat tight around herself and hurried down the hill.

The stallholder asked, 'You want two, three? How many do you want?'

The mother shook her head and squinted and held up four fingers. He threw the mangoes into a plastic bag and wrote the figures on a pad of paper. She counted the money quickly and hastened away from the stall, her heart pounding against her will. But she was warm now and she could take her time as she waited for her son to finish at the nursery. She stared in the windows, at the shops with their impossible prices: the clothes, the gadgets, the parade of glazed food. She looked at the rows of televisions on display and saw the machines again: changing, moving, fighting. She did not know why they were always there. She began to shiver and it intensified the ache in her body.

The mother had grown used to so much in such a short time: the language, the cold, her husband's violence. She did not know why he hated her now. He was so strange in this country, away from their home. She could not understand it. Every day she waited like this— she lived her life, but she was waiting—for him to return from the office, for the anger to surface again. She began to anticipate it, to long for it almost, so that it would be finished for a time. She looked around her—everything was a shade of white: the snow, the people, the sky above. She felt utterly alone. She thought of her sisters, how they had danced in the rain. She wanted to dance in the snow this minute. A van hooted and screeched and she moved away as it came skidding beside her. Her heartbeat quickened again.

The mother collected the boy from the nursery and they made their way back up the hill. He ran ahead of her, kicking furiously at the snow until he grew tired of this and settled beside her.

'What should we do?' he asked.

She was quiet now, and he noticed this. She looked at him, her head tilted slightly. 'Can we play a game?' he tried again.

She continued to stare as if she could not recognize him, and he began to be afraid. 'I don't think so,' she said, finally. She smiled and held his hand. 'We will play later. It's too cold now. Wait until we get inside.'

Later, the older boy arrived and she let them play in the garden at the back of the building while she watched from the warmth of the lobby. They became tired quickly and felt the winter in their hands and it wasn't long before they returned to the apartment.

The mother began to prepare the evening meal. She made small movements and did not speak. At the same time the boys grew raucous. At one point she missed the onion she was slicing and cut her finger, but the knife was not sharp. She wiped away the blood and sealed the wound with a plaster.

'He keeps coming into my room and I don't want him there!' the older boy shouted.

The younger boy ran into the kitchen and beamed at them. And then the chasing began and the screaming, and she could not concentrate. She stood with the knife in her hand listening to the racket of her children in the apartment, and to the thoughts swirling in her head. Her limbs dragged and she could not continue with the meal. She did not know whom to phone, whom to talk to. The trouble would soon begin again and the days seemed never-ending.

The boys ran into the kitchen, breathless. They stood at the door and wondered why their mother was so quiet, why she did not scold them.

'Did you cut yourself?' The older boy walked towards her and touched the injured finger.

The other boy followed. 'I want to feel it too.'

'It's nothing.' She turned back to the chopping board. She looked outside at the snow which was falling again in the late afternoon, the lights of the city beyond. She could see the reflection of the boys in the window as they waited quietly for her. She saw her own face, how her cheeks were sunken, the ghostly eyes. She put down the knife. 'Are you going to help me?' she said at last.

'Help? How?' the older boy asked.

'How?' the younger one mimicked.

'Well, you could bring me the silver pot. And Dayo, you carry the lid. And you could take the juice to the table, and draw the curtains. Could you do that for me?'

They carried out their tasks slowly, conferring all the time. Soon she heard the sound of the television set in the living room, but the boys were no longer fighting.

She allowed them to turn on the television in the kitchen as they ate their meal. She only picked at her food, but they did not notice this. She watched them, the curve of their necks as they twisted to look at the screen, their glistening eyes, the way their hair grew—the youngest would have a widow's peak like his father—how one would always be darker than the other. She noticed everything about them. She tried to imagine them grown, living independent lives, but it was too strange for her. She glanced at the oven as it hummed, keeping her husband's meal warm.

'Bath time!' she clapped. 'We have to hurry.' She got up to clear the table.

'Now?' the older boy asked.

'Yes, now,' she replied. 'I don't have time to do it later.'

She filled the tub while they undressed, and after a moment she went to help the younger one with his shirt buttons and shoes.

'Are you cold?' the older boy asked her.

'No. Why?'

'Look, your hands are shaking.'

The younger one reached out to touch her fingers.

'Well…maybe I'm a little cold,' she said. She rubbed her hands vigorously along her arms, but the trembling did not stop.

The boys bounded to the bathroom, shrieking, chasing one another. The mother switched off the televisions in the kitchen and the living room. She drew the curtains they had only partially managed to draw.

'Can we get in now?' the older boy asked.

She nodded and closed the door behind her and rested on the stool next to the bath.

'Will it snow again tomorrow?' the younger one asked.

'I think so,' the mother replied. 'Maybe for a long time to come. Did you like it?'

The boy scrunched up his face and looked away. 'Mmm, maybe. But it was too cold. It hurt my fingers.'

'Yes…it's cold,' she said, but she did not say anything else and she moved back into her thoughts.

The boy plunged his face into the water in front of him and blew bubbles. When he surfaced, he laughed, then tipped his head backwards. When he was beneath the water he opened his eyes for a moment, then floated up again.

'Very good,' the mother said. 'You might become a diver one day. You like being underwater, don't you?'

'I can't stay long,' the boy complained. 'Can you hold me?' He rolled back so that he was submerged again. The mother reached out and held his chest for a moment, then released him. When he emerged he began to shriek with delight. 'Again! I want to go again!'

'Me too!' his brother cried.

They both dipped their heads back and then there was no more noise.

She held them there, quietly, beneath the surface, as they looked up at her. They were smiling, but the mother could no longer smile. There was a thin film of scum around the edge of the bath. The extractor fan laboured to remove steam from the windowless room. She sighed and closed her eyes. If she screamed no one would hear. She knew this; she had screamed before. She looked down at their smiling faces, their wide eyes, the brown skin against white enamel. She wondered how a person could live, yet not be alive. The only sound was the whirr of the ventilation. 'Quickly!' she said. She pulled the boys up and spoke urgently to them. 'It's time to move quickly, you hear me?'

'I want to play under the water again,' the younger one cried.

'I promise we'll play again next time.' She pulled him out of the water and wrapped him in a towel. She helped his brother climb out of the bath and rubbed his wet hair. The youngest one opened the door, threw his towel to the floor and ran across the apartment, yelling.

She knew where everything was, what she would take, what she would leave behind. She had rehearsed this many times, but it had only been fantasy: the money, the passports, the essential clothes, the diary containing her sisters' phone numbers. She worked hard and fast and in no time she was ready. She told the boys what was going to happen, and they were quiet and afraid.

'Should I put my clothes on again?' the older boy asked. They were both wearing pyjamas.

'It's all right,' she said. 'Just wear your socks and sweaters. There are clothes in the suitcase. You can wear them later.'

She fetched their jumpsuits and gloves and helped them to dress over their nightwear. She pulled on their fur-lined boots. They watched obediently while she tied the strings of their hoods. Their little faces peered out from within their enclosures and she began to cry. They were her boys and she loved them more than her own life. She could not go on without them, but she could not go on. This was the only solution she could think of. She touched the front-door handle and then withdrew her hand. She looked at the boys and closed her eyes and said some words in her head to whomever was listening.

'Where are we going?' the older boy asked when they were in the hallway.

'Sshh,' the mother said. 'We must be quiet now.' But it was already too late. The door was opening, and he stood peering at them, Mr Mihashi. The mother stopped, paralyzed.

'You...you are going out?' Mr Mihashi asked.

'Yes, yes. We are going... We are going to...' She could not find the words, the excuses, the lies she needed.

'You go on holidays?' Mr Mihashi suggested, noticing the suitcase.

'Yes, yes. We go on holidays,' she nodded quickly. 'We are going on a holiday.'

But he could see the face, tear-stained, and the way the hands shook, and he had an inkling he might never see her again. 'You...you must wait. One moment. You must wait, Mrs Odesola,' he said. He shuffled into his apartment.

The mother glanced at the elevator doors at the end of the hallway. If the doors opened and her husband appeared she did not know how she would survive. She thought she would leave now, before it was too late. But then she heard his voice. 'I can find not so many things.' Mr Mihashi came towards them stuffing fruit and biscuits and rice crackers into a shoulder bag. He gave it to the older boy to carry.

'When, when you are on holidays my English will decline.'

'Your English is very good, Mr Mihashi,' the mother said. 'You have nothing to worry about.'

'Our talking, Mrs Odesola, it brings me many, many pleasures. You must have a good holidays, a good rest,' he said.

'Gifted, Mrs Odesola. You also are gifted. You see, I use it already.' He gave a broad smile.

'Thank you, Mr Mihashi. You are very kind. You have always been kind to us. But we must go now or we will be late.'

They walked to the elevator and waited. As the doors opened and the mother picked up the suitcase, Mr Mihashi called, 'Mrs Odesola,' from his open door, but then he was quiet. He waved to the boys.

'Look, it's still snowing,' the older boy said. The ground was thick with it as they trudged down the hill towards the bus stop. The mother struggled with the suitcase as the pavement was too soft with snow to wheel it.

'Is anyone inside?' Dayo asked as they walked past the nursery.

'No, stupid,' his brother said. 'Everyone's at home.'

The boy thought about this for a moment. 'I'm not at home,' he said.

They walked in silence until they arrived at the bottom of the hill. It was busier here; cars came and went, and passers-by stared at them. When they turned to cross the road, the mother slipped. She came down hard and lost her grip on the suitcase. She felt it all in her thin body: her thighs, her ribs, her neck, the bruised places. But the snow cushioned the impact. The boys came running to her, making noises of concern. She looked at them. She looked up at the sky, at the snow falling in her face, and she began to laugh. When they saw her laughing, the boys smiled uncertainly. They helped her up and the older boy dragged the suitcase for a while, but he was not strong enough to take it across the road.

When they were in the hotel room, the mother began to remember things she had forgotten: their slippers, her nightgown, all their toothbrushes, her underwear. She would have to buy these things the next day. She thought of everything she would have to do: the phone calls, the travel arrangements, the decisions she would make back home. The chaos.

'I left the oven on!' she gasped.

The boys turned away from the television to look at her. They were sitting on the carpet, eating the biscuits Mr Mihashi had packed for them.

The older boy asked, 'What should we do?'

The mother shrugged and said, 'It doesn't matter now.'

She began to notice a side of herself that wanted to return to switch off the oven, to be back in the apartment, and she would always have to fight this side.

The boys still looked at her because they were anxious.

'It's all right,' she said. 'You watch your programme. You shouldn't worry.'

She sat on the edge of the bed, gazing beyond their heads at the glowing television screen, at the machines that changed and moved and fought just like humans. She saw them everywhere. □

GRANTA

HOW TO WRITE
ABOUT AFRICA
Binyavanga Wainaina

Kenya

Always use the word 'Africa' or 'Darkness' or 'Safari' in your title. Subtitles may include the words 'Zanzibar', 'Masai', 'Zulu', 'Zambezi', 'Congo', 'Nile', 'Big', 'Sky', 'Shadow', 'Drum', 'Sun' or 'Bygone'. Also useful are words such as 'Guerrillas', 'Timeless', 'Primordial' and 'Tribal'. Note that 'People' means Africans who are not black, while 'The People' means black Africans.

Never have a picture of a well-adjusted African on the cover of your book, or in it, unless that African has won the Nobel Prize. An AK-47, prominent ribs, naked breasts: use these. If you must include an African, make sure you get one in Masai or Zulu or Dogon dress.

In your text, treat Africa as if it were one country. It is hot and dusty with rolling grasslands and huge herds of animals and tall, thin people who are starving. Or it is hot and steamy with very short people who eat primates. Don't get bogged down with precise descriptions. Africa is big: fifty-four countries, 900 million people who are too busy starving and dying and warring and emigrating to read your book. The continent is full of deserts, jungles, highlands, savannahs and many other things, but your reader doesn't care about all that, so keep your descriptions romantic and evocative and unparticular.

Make sure you show how Africans have music and rhythm deep in their souls, and eat things no other humans eat. Do not mention rice and beef and wheat; monkey-brain is an African's cuisine of choice, along with goat, snake, worms and grubs and all manner of game meat. Make sure you show that you are able to eat such food without flinching, and describe how you learn to enjoy it—because you care.

Taboo subjects: ordinary domestic scenes, love between Africans (unless a death is involved), references to African writers or intellectuals, mention of school-going children who are not suffering from yaws or Ebola fever or female genital mutilation.

Throughout the book, adopt a *sotto* voice, in conspiracy with the reader, and a sad *I-expected-so-much* tone. Establish early on that your liberalism is impeccable, and mention near the beginning how much you love Africa, how you fell in love with the place and can't live without her. Africa is the only continent you can love—take advantage of this. If you are a man, thrust yourself into her warm virgin forests. If you are a woman, treat Africa as a man who wears a bush jacket and disappears off into the sunset. Africa is to be pitied, worshipped or dominated. Whichever angle you take, be sure to leave the strong impression that without your intervention and your important book, Africa is doomed.

Your African characters may include naked warriors, loyal servants, diviners and seers, ancient wise men living in hermitic splendour. Or corrupt politicians, inept polygamous travel-guides, and prostitutes you have slept with. The Loyal Servant always behaves like a seven-year-old and needs a firm hand; he is scared of snakes, good with children, and always involving you in his complex domestic dramas. The Ancient Wise Man always comes from a noble tribe (not the money-grubbing tribes like the Gikuyu, the Igbo or the Shona). He has rheumy eyes and is close to the Earth. The Modern African is a fat man who steals and works in the visa office, refusing to give work permits to qualified Westerners who really care about Africa. He is an enemy of development, always using his government job to make it difficult for pragmatic and good-hearted expats to set up NGOs or Legal Conservation Areas. Or he is an Oxford-educated intellectual turned serial-killing politician in a Savile Row suit. He is a cannibal who likes Cristal champagne, and his mother is a rich witch-doctor who really runs the country.

Among your characters you must always include The Starving African, who wanders the refugee camp nearly naked, and waits for the benevolence of the West. Her children have flies on their eyelids and pot bellies, and her breasts are flat and empty. She must look utterly helpless. She can have no past, no history; such diversions ruin the dramatic moment. Moans are good. She must never say anything about herself in the dialogue except to speak of her (unspeakable) suffering. Also be sure to include a warm and motherly woman who has a rolling laugh and who is concerned for your well-being. Just call her Mama. Her children are all delinquent. These characters should buzz around your main hero, making him look good. Your hero can teach them, bathe them, feed them; he carries lots of babies and has seen Death. Your hero is you (if reportage), or a beautiful, tragic international celebrity/aristocrat who now cares for animals (if fiction).

Bad Western characters may include children of Tory cabinet ministers, Afrikaners, employees of the World Bank. When talking about exploitation by foreigners mention the Chinese and Indian traders. Blame the West for Africa's situation. But do not be too specific.

Broad brushstrokes throughout are good. Avoid having the

African characters laugh, or struggle to educate their kids, or just make do in mundane circumstances. Have them illuminate something about Europe or America in Africa. African characters should be colourful, exotic, larger than life—but empty inside, with no dialogue, no conflicts or resolutions in their stories, no depth or quirks to confuse the cause.

Describe, in detail, naked breasts (young, old, conservative, recently raped, big, small) or mutilated genitals, or enhanced genitals. Or any kind of genitals. And dead bodies. Or, better, naked dead bodies. And especially rotting naked dead bodies. Remember, any work you submit in which people look filthy and miserable will be referred to as the 'real Africa', and you want that on your dust jacket. Do not feel queasy about this: you are trying to help them to get aid from the West. The biggest taboo in writing about Africa is to describe or show dead or suffering white people.

Animals, on the other hand, must be treated as well rounded, complex characters. They speak (or grunt while tossing their manes proudly) and have names, ambitions and desires. They also have family values: *see how lions teach their children?* Elephants are caring, and are good feminists or dignified patriarchs. So are gorillas. Never, ever say anything negative about an elephant or a gorilla. Elephants may attack people's property, destroy their crops, and even kill them. Always take the side of the elephant. Big cats have public-school accents. Hyenas are fair game and have vaguely Middle Eastern accents. Any short Africans who live in the jungle or desert may be portrayed with good humour (unless they are in conflict with an elephant or chimpanzee or gorilla, in which case they are pure evil).

After celebrity activists and aid workers, conservationists are Africa's most important people. Do not offend them. You need them to invite you to their 30,000-acre game ranch or 'conservation area', and this is the only way you will get to interview the celebrity activist. Often a book cover with a heroic-looking conservationist on it works magic for sales. Anybody white, tanned and wearing khaki who once had a pet antelope or a farm is a conservationist, one who is preserving Africa's rich heritage. When interviewing him or her, do not ask how much funding they have; do not ask how much money they make off their game. Never ask how much they pay their employees.

Readers will be put off if you don't mention the light in Africa.

And sunsets, the African sunset is a must. It is always big and red. There is always a big sky. Wide empty spaces and game are critical— Africa is the Land of Wide Empty Spaces. When writing about the plight of flora and fauna, make sure you mention that Africa is overpopulated. When your main character is in a desert or jungle living with indigenous peoples (anybody short) it is okay to mention that Africa has been severely depopulated by Aids and War (use caps).

You'll also need a nightclub called Tropicana, where mercenaries, evil nouveau riche Africans and prostitutes and guerrillas and expats hang out.

Always end your book with Nelson Mandela saying something about rainbows or renaissances. Because you care. □

STATEMENT OF OWNERSHIP, MANAGEMENT, AND CIRCULATION
1. Publication Title: Granta
2. Publication No.: 0000-508
3. Filing Date: 29 September 2005
4. Issue Frequency: Quarterly (4 times per year)
5. Number of Issues Published Annually: 4
6. Annual Subscription Price: $39.95
7. Complete Mailing Address of Known Office of Publication: 1755 Broadway, 5th Floor, New York, NY 10019-3780
8. Complete Mailing Address of Headquarters of General Business Office of Publisher: 1755 Broadway, 5th Floor, New York, NY 10019-3780
9. Full Names and Complete Mailing Addresses of Publisher, Editor, and Managing Editor: Publisher: Rea S. Hederman, 1755 Broadway, 5th Floor, New York, NY 10019–3780; Editor: Ian Jack, 2/3 Hanover Yard, Noel Road, London N1 8BE; Managing Editor: Matt Weiland, 2/3 Hanover Yard, Noel Road, London N1 8BE
10. Owners: Granta USA LLC, 1755 Broadway, 5th Floor, New York, NY 10019-3780; Rea S. Hederman, 1755 Broadway, 5th Floor, New York, NY 10019-3780; Robert M. Hederman, III, 625 N. State Street, Jackson, MS 39202; Sara Hederman Henderson, 625 N. State Street, Jackson, MS 39202; Jan Hederman, 625 N. State Street, Jackson, MS 39202; NYREV, Inc., 1755 Broadway, 5th Floor, New York, NY 10019-3780; Rea S. Hederman, 1755 Broadway, 5th Floor, New York, NY 10019-3780; Robert M. Hederman, III, 625 N. State Street, Jackson, MS 39202; Sara Hederman Henderson, 625 N. State Street, Jackson, MS 39202; Jan Hederman, 625 N. State Street, Jackson, MS 39202; Morningside Partnership LLP, 625 N. State Street, Jackson, MS 39202; Rea S. Hederman, 1755 Broadway, 5th Floor, New York, NY 10019-3780; Robert M. Hederman, III, 625 N. State Street, Jackson, MS 39202; Sara Hederman Henderson, 625 N. State Street, Jackson, MS 39202; Jan Hederman, 625 N. State Street, Jackson, MS 39202
11. Known Bondholders, Mortgagees, and Other Security Holders: None
12. Tax Status: Has Not Changed
13. Publication Title: Granta
14. Issue Date for Circulation Data: Summer 2005
15. Extent and Nature of Circulation: Average No. Copies Each Issue During Preceding 12 Months:
a. Total No. of Copies: 40,845
b. Paid and/or Requested Circulation: 0
1. Paid/Requested Outside-County Mail Subscriptions Stated on Form 3541: 27,489
2. Paid In-County Subscriptions Stated on Form 3541: 0
3. Sales Through Dealers and Carriers, Street Vendors, Counter Sales and Other Non-USPS Paid Distribution: 4,833
4. Other Classes Mailed Through the USPS: 0
c. Total Paid and/or Requested Circulation: 26,676
d. Free Distribution by Mail:
1. Outside-County as Stated on Form 3541: 0
2. In-County as Stated on Form 3541: 0
3. Other Classes Mailed Through the USPS: 320
e. Free Distribution Outside the Mail: 0
f. Total Free Distribution: 266
g. Total Distribution: 26,942
h. Copies not Distributed: 13,903
i. Total: 40,845
j. Percent Paid and/or Requested Circulation: 99.0%
Extent and Nature of Circulation: No. Copies of Single Issue Published Nearest to Filing Date:
a. Total No. of Copies: 32,768
b. Paid and/or Requested Circulation:
1. Paid/Requested Outside-County Mail Subscriptions Stated on Form 3541: 16,135
2. Paid In-County Subscriptions Stated on Form 3541: 0
3. Sales Through Dealers and Carriers, Street Vendors, Counter Sales and Other Non-USPS Paid Distribution: 4,590
4. Other Classes Mailed Through the USPS: 0
c. Total Paid and/or Requested Circulation: 20,725
d. Free Distribution by Mail:
1. Outside-County as Stated on Form 3541: 0
2. In-County as Stated on Form 3541: 0
3. Other Classes Mailed Through the USPS: 256
e. Free Distribution Outside the Mail: 0
f. Total Free Distribution: 256
g. Total Distribution: 20,981
h. Copies not Distributed: 11,787
i. Total: 32,768
j. Percent Paid and/or Requested Circulation: 98.8%
16. Publication of Statement of Ownership will be printed in the Winter 2005 issue of this publication.
17. Signature and Title of Editor, Publisher, Business Manager, or Owner: I certify that all information furnished on this form is true and complete. Rea S. Hederman, Publisher

BUSINESS REPLY MAIL

FIRST-CLASS MAIL   PERMIT NO. 115   JACKSON, MS

POSTAGE WILL BE PAID BY ADDRESSEE

GRANTA

P O BOX 23152
JACKSON MS 39225-9814

BUSINESS REPLY MAIL

FIRST-CLASS MAIL   PERMIT NO. 115   JACKSON, MS

POSTAGE WILL BE PAID BY ADDRESSEE

GRANTA

P O BOX 23152
JACKSON MS 39225-9814

GRANTA

THE OGIEK
Geert van Kesteren

Geert van Kesteren

The Mau Forest, on the escarpments of the Great Rift Valley in Kenya, was once Africa's second largest forest. The Ogiek people have lived inside it, and in harmony with it, for thousands of years. Famous as honey-gatherers, only relatively recently, in the 1950s, did they begin to keep livestock and grow crops, out of necessity rather than choice. Over the past century they have been repeatedly evicted from their ancestral territories and settled on government reserves while the forest has been cut down around them. Now eighty per cent of its 900,000 acres has been destroyed.

Despite their ancestral claims, the Ogiek have no legal rights to their lands. The British colonial government never acknowledged native land rights, and since Independence in 1963, subsequent Kenyan governments have taken advantage of this gap in the law and given away sections of the Mau Forest to political friends and fellow clan members. These new landowners have sold off the trees and turned the deforested areas into agricultural land.

Today, of the estimated population of 20,000 Ogiek, most live in government reserves, working as dirt farmers, but some still return to the forest and to their traditional way of life. I joined a group of them as they searched for honey, deep within the forest and watched as they scrambled up the trees to reach the hives. The strongest of the hunters, a twenty year old known simply as Williamson, screamed to himself, a sound like 'brrrrr, brrrrr', as he thrust his bare hands into the honeycomb and the bees swarmed around him, attacking his face and arms, but he seemed unafraid. 'We only take what we need to survive,' he told me when he was safely back on the ground. 'That way the forest gives us what we need in return.'

But this simple philosophy no longer applies. Later that evening, an older man in a ragged Kappa T-shirt pulled out some matches to light the fire, then climbed a tree to get a better signal for his cellphone. The Ogiek have lived isolated from other people for centuries, but now they are being forced to communicate with them in a bid to survive.

Charles Sena is an Ogiek lawyer who works from a scruffy office in Narok, about 200 kilometres west of Nairobi. When I arrived he was shouting down his phone, 'You can't fuck with my people!' It turned out he was talking to a government official. 'Soon there will be nothing left,' he told me later. 'I know you can't stop globalization, but we are losing our language, our culture, our identity.'

The Ogiek

Wilson Memusi, an Ogiek elder, watched from a hillside as an ancient tractor dragged a load of tropical wood across the devastated ground. It had been cut illegally by men from another tribe. They earn less then the equivalent of fifty eurocents a tree. 'What can I do?' Memusi said. 'They're just some poor guys.' The guys who run the Kenyan companies they work for—Timsales, Raiply Timber and Pan African Paper Mills—are not poor. For the past twenty years they have been cutting down the forest at top speed. Massive yellow-and-black sawing-machines with gigantic tyres drive up and down the forest. Legal employees are paid two dollars a day. 'We are people from yesterday,' Memusi said. 'The forest has been our school since immortal times. Now we are chased out. We look like fools because we know nothing about the world. But tell me, who is primitive—we the illiterate, or the others, the literate, who are organized into groups so they can destroy nature?'

The National Rainbow Coalition, which succeeded President Daniel arap Moi in 2002, regards the Ogiek as squatters. Joseph Towett, founder of the Ogiek Welfare Council (the Ogiek also have their own website: www.ogiek.org), wants the government to bring in a new constitution that acknowledges the land rights of the Ogiek and other indigenous peoples; to stop logging, replant trees, and relocate the people who have settled illegally in the forest. 'You can't leave forestation to corrupt politicians,' Towett said. 'They don't understand our ecosystem.'

The combined efforts of deforestation and farming mean that water sources have been drastically reduced. Because of the logging, a swamp at the heart of the Mau forest has dried up. It supplied seven rivers which run through famous wild life resorts such as Masai Mara National Park and Lake Nakuru. Bernard Kuloba, a research scientist at Lake Nakuru National Park told me 'The lake is dying. Flower farmers use fertilizer. When the rains come, the fertilizer flows from the eroded hills into the rivers. The rivers run into the lake and the fertilizer makes the algae grow too fast. The algae suffocates and putrefies. Each day we collect thirty dead flamingos. They need fresh water to survive.' He gives the lake a few more years before it dries up completely. 'The only thing that can save us now is another natural disaster. El Niño. Only El Niño can refill the lake with water.' □

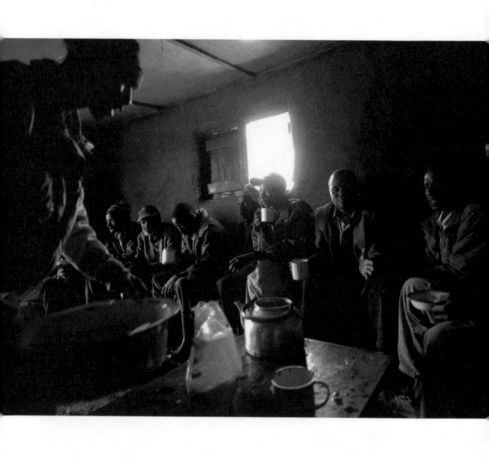

GRANTA

JOBURG
Ivan Vladislavic

South Africa

When a house has been alarmed, it becomes explosive. It must be armed and disarmed several times a day. When it is armed, by the touching of keys upon a pad, it emits a whine that sends the occupants rushing out, banging the door behind them. There are no leisurely departures: there is no time for second thoughts, for taking a scarf from the hook behind the door, for checking that the answering machine is on, for a final look in the mirror on the way through the hallway. There are no savoured homecomings either: you do not unwind into such a house, kicking off your shoes, breathing the familiar air. Every departure is precipitate, every arrival is a scraping-in.

In an alarmed house, you wake in the small hours to find the room unnaturally light. The keys on the touch pad are aglow with a luminous, clinical green, like a night light for a child who's afraid of the dark.

Johannesburg is a frontier city, a place of contested boundaries. Territory must be secured and defended or it will be lost. Today the contest is fierce and so the defences multiply. Walls replace fences, high walls replace low ones, the highest walls acquire electrified wires and spikes. In the wealthier suburbs the pattern is to knock things flat and start all over. Around here people make the most of what they've got; the walls tend to grow by increments. A stone wall is heightened with prefab panels, a prefab wall is heightened further with steel palisades, the palisades are topped with razor wire. Wooden pickets on top of brick, ornate wrought-iron panels on top of plaster, blade wire on top of split poles. These piggyback walls (my own included) are nearly always ugly. But sometimes the whole ensemble achieves a degree of elaboration that becomes beautiful again, like a page in the *Homemaker's Fair* catalogue.

There are vanished gateways everywhere. On any street, you may find a panel in a wall where the bricks are a different colour or the courses poorly aligned, indicating that a gap has been filled in. A garden path leads to a fence rather than a gate, a doorstep juts from the foot of a solid wall. Often, the addition of a security fence or a wall has put a letter box beyond reach of the postman.

The tennis courts at the corner of Collingwood and Roberts are on a terrace. Once, a flight of stairs cut into the stone-faced slope led up from the pavement, and then a few paces would bring you to a gate in a low wire fence. Now a curtain of stone has been drawn across the stairway halfway up and a tall palisade fence has been raised on the edge of the terrace. Through it you can see the old fence posts, like sentries standing guard on a fallen frontier.

Set into brick or stone gateposts, too difficult or costly to remove, metal hinges remain behind to mark the places where the old gates swung, before they were taken down and replaced by security doors or remote-controlled barriers.

Gold was discovered on the Witwatersrand in the winter of 1886. Until then the veld had offered little more than grazing for cattle farmers, but soon it was dotted with wagons, tents and reed huts, as gold-seekers poured into the area. Within three or four years a town of brick houses, offices, hotels and government buildings sprang up, and within a generation Johannesburg was home to half a million people.

Commissioner Street, the backbone of the city, follows the old wagon track between two of the first mining camps, from Jeppestown in the east to Ferreirasdorp in the west. So the city's spine was fused to the Main Reef, the subterranean gold deposit that called it into life. Today, going down Commissioner into the high-rise heart of Africa's richest city, I am reminded that here we are all still prospectors, with a digger's claim on the earth beneath our feet.

When my grandfather died in the early Sixties, he left me a handful of lapel badges. One of them showed the chevrons of the Citroën marque, another the outline of the African continent on a long pin. All the rest had been issued, at the rate of one a year, by the Railway Recreation Club at Berea Park, where he was a member. There were around three dozen of these ornate little enamelled shields, with gilt edges and the initials of the club and year of issue inscribed on scrolls, and not much to distinguish one from another except the dates. But once or twice in the Fifties, some creative temperament on the committee had asserted itself (I imagine) and a badge with an unusual shape or colour was produced. There was one in the shape of a fish, coloured the pale sea-green of salmon scales. It must have delighted the club's anglers.

The box in which I kept these badges had belonged to my mother when she was a schoolgirl. It was a wooden casket half the size of a pencil case, decorated with forest scenes made of inlaid segments of stained wood, now faded to a perpetual autumn. There was a secret mechanism for opening the drawer, a wooden switch concealed beneath a small tile that could be slid aside—it fitted so perfectly you could not even insert a fingernail into a crack, you had to moisten the tip of your finger and pull gently. Pressing the switch caused the drawer to spring open.

I liked to spread the badges out, arranging them by shape and colour, or more often by date. The older ones from the Thirties and Forties had a butterfly stud at the back, but modern jackets did not always have a buttonhole in the lapel and so the more recent badges had pins. My grandfather came to life in these small things, which evoked his hands, resting on a sheet of paper and holding a pen. When I grew up, I realized that they were also signs of his belonging in the world, the world of the railway goods yard, the pub, the working-man's club. I imagined him wearing them when he went down to the Berea to watch the football on a Saturday afternoon or when, on any day of the week, he walked up to the Vic in Paul Kruger Street for a pint. They were badges of identity, simple markers of a life story. The mere gesture of spreading them out, with a casual sweep of the hand, produced a plot. My grandfather's absence during the war years, his time 'up north', was never clearer to me than in the missing chapters in the story told by the badges.

Two boys came to my door one day begging for food, a teenager and his smaller brother, both in rags and looking pitiful. While I was fetching bread and apples from the kitchen, they slipped into my flat and pilfered what they could stuff in their pockets. They did not run away. When I came back with the food they were waiting dejectedly on the doorstep, and they accepted the packet with thanks and quietly withdrew. A day or two passed before I noticed the small absences: a stapler, a travel clock, my grandfather's badges.

Later, I came across the splinters of the box at the foot of an oak in Saunders Street, not far from my home. A few sticks of wood and a rusty spring. Frustrated by their inability to open the box, they had smashed it. Instead of the coins it must have promised when they shook it, the box had coughed up a handful of trinkets. I searched in the roots of the kikuyu on the verge, and scuffed through leaves and litter in the gutter, convinced that something must have been left behind, but whether or not they were disappointed with their haul, they had carried off every last one.

A single badge finally did turn up in my wardrobe, pinned since the previous winter to the lapel of a sports coat. Nothing special, just a variation on a theme: a small gilt shield, with a red banner at the top saying SOUTH AFRICAN RAILWAY RECREATION CLUB and two white banners at the bottom: PRETORIA and BEREA PARK. In the middle, in gold on a black shield, is a winged wheel and the date, 1951.

Johannesburg is justly renowned for its scenic waterways. The finest body of water in my part of town is generally held to be the pond at Rhodes Park, established when the city was young on the site of an existing *vlei*, but I have always preferred Bruma Lake, which replaced the old sewage treatment works on the banks of the Jukskei. When the lake was first excavated in the Eighties, as the focal point for a new shopping centre, there were teething troubles: the Jukskei kept washing down garbage and clogging the drainage system. Not long after the grand opening they had to drain the water to make modifications to the filters, and the system has worked well ever since. In 2000 and 2001, when the Bruma serial killers were at work in the eastern suburbs, the bodies of several men were discovered in the water, and the police had the lake drained to search for clues. It was a salutary reminder that the lake was artificial, that it was nothing but a reservoir lined with plastic.

In Johannesburg, the backdrop is always a man-made one. We have planted a forest the birds endorse. For hills, we have mine dumps covered with grass. We do not wait for time and the elements to weather us, we change the scenery ourselves, to suit our moods. Nature is for other people, in other places. We are happy taking the air on the Randburg Waterfront, with its pasteboard wharves and masts, or watching the plastic ducks bob in the stream at Montecasino, or eating our surf 'n turf on Cleopatra's Barge in the middle of Caesar's.

When Bruma Lake was brimming again and the worst of the stench had dispersed, I had supper down on the quay at Fishermen's Village. Afterwards I had a stroll over the little pedestrian replica of the Golden Gate Bridge, with its stays and cables picked out in lights, and watched the reflections dancing on the dead water.

Herman Wald's *Leaping Impala* sculpture was installed in Ernest Oppenheimer Park in 1960. Eighteen animals in full flight, a sleigh-ride arc of hoof and horn twenty metres long, a ton and a half of venison in bronze. In the Sixties and Seventies, fountains splashed the flanks of the stampeding buck, while office workers ate their lunch-time sandwiches on whites-only benches. Although the park deteriorated along with the inner city in the following decades, until it came to be used primarily as a storage depot by hawkers, the herd of impala seemed set to survive the century unscathed. But towards the end of 1999, poachers started carving away at it, lopping heads and legs with blowtorches and hacksaws. At the end of October, a civic-minded hawker, who arrived at the park to find a man stuffing two severed heads into a bag, called the police. They arrested the thief, but he was subsequently deported as an illegal alien and the heads disappeared without trace. A fortnight later, an entire impala was removed from the park by four men, who told security guards they were transporting it to another park. Stock thieves. A week after that, another ten heads were lopped. Police later rescued one of these heads from a Boksburg scrap-metal dealer. A leg was found in a pawnshop in the central business district.

Johannesburg has an abundance of wildlife, and the poachers have taken full advantage of the open season. They've bagged a bronze steenbok from Wits University; a horse from outside the library in Sandton (first docking the beast, to see if anyone would mind, and then hacking off its head like Mafiosi); a pair of eagles nesting near the Stock Exchange; and another steenbok in the Botanical Gardens at Emmarentia. This little buck, which had been donated to the Gardens by the sculptor Ernest Ullmann in 1975, was taken in 1998. The head turned up afterwards in a scrapyard and was returned to the scene of the slaughter, where it was mounted on a conical pedestal like a trophy, along with a plaque explaining the circumstances of its loss and recovery. But before long the head was stolen for the second time and now the pedestal is empty.

Of course, urban poachers are not just hungry for horseflesh: any old iron will do. They are especially fond of the covers on manholes and water mains. When Kensington Electrical Suppliers took over the Tile City hardware store they painted the covers on their pavement bright yellow to deter thieves, but the logic was flawed: now thieves could spot them from a hundred metres. Elsewhere in the city, the council has begun to replace the stolen iron covers with blue plastic ones. These bits of plastic tell the scrap-metal thieves to go ahead and help themselves, as the authorities have given up on protecting their resources. The council could wrest back the initiative by lifting all the remaining iron at once and selling it off. They could apply the same argument the Botswana government uses for the controlled sale of ivory: get the jump on the poachers by selling the booty yourself.

The man who paces up and down outside the Gem Supermarket like a creature in captivity begs from time to time, in an offhand way, as if it does not really matter to him. He'll beg for a while, breaking off his walking to ask for money in a low voice, and then he becomes more and more engrossed in his own rhythm, carried away by it, until he stops accosting people altogether.

One Sunday morning, I was spying on him when he asked a young couple for money, and the woman emptied the change from her purse into his palm. He examined her offering curiously. Before she could walk off, he began to pick through it and give the smaller denominations back to her. After a moment's puzzlement, she held out her hand to accept the rejects. She seemed fascinated by the exchange: his raw fingers picking the coppers out of the pile and laying them on her soft white palm, occasionally dropping a ten- or twenty-cent piece that took his fancy into the breast pocket of his shirt. I imagine that he would have winnowed the entire handful, but the woman's companion, who had been edging impatiently towards his car at the kerb, suddenly realized how improper it was, how ungrateful and insulting, strode back, struck the man's wrist so that coins flew everywhere, grabbed her arm and hurried her away.

A stoep in Good Hope Street. The deep-blue garden walls hold a precise measure of the twilight still. The smell of grass is quenching after a summer day, the dusk lays a cool hand on the back of your neck. We are talking, my friends and I, with our bare feet propped on the wall of the stoep, our cane chairs creaking. We have been talking and laughing for hours, putting our predicaments in their place, finding ways to keep our balance in a tide of change. We could fetch fresh beer glasses from the door of the fridge, but these warm ones, stickily fingerprinted and smelling of yeast, suit this satiated conversation better. We speak the same language.

This is our climate. We have grown up in this air, this light, and we grasp it on the skin, where it grasps us. We know this earth, this grass, this polished red stone with the soles of our feet. We will never be ourselves anywhere else. Happier, perhaps, healthier, less burdened, more secure. But we will never be closer to who we are than this.

The women come back from the pool at Jeppe Girls' High with their hair still wet, with the damp outlines of their swimming costumes showing through their cotton dresses. (Sally teaches history at the school and has a key to the gate.) The kids are crunching potato chips from the corner shop. They smell of salt and vinegar, and chlorine. The suns of our own childhoods fall on their freckled arms.

'Look!' says Nicky, feigning surprise, as they come up the steps. 'Three drunk men.'

'*Wise* men,' says Chas.

'We've been exploring the limits of our disgruntlement,' I say.

But Dave says that's unfair. I make it sound as if we're going in circles, when in truth we're going forward. And he tells the story about Little Jannie—in Dave's stories the schoolboys are always called 'Little Jannie'—who arrives late for class one morning.

'Why are you late, Jannie?' the teacher wants to know. 'And it better be good.'

'Well, Sir, for every two steps I took forward, I went three steps back.'

'Really!' the teacher says with a laugh of triumph. 'Then how did you ever get to school at all?'

'I turned around, Sir, and tried to go home.'

I came to the Johannesburg Public Library to read up on Max the Gorilla, our zoo's most famous resident, and instead I'm absorbed in a trivial mystery. Besides the usual traffic between the reference library and the reading room where I'm working, I see people coming and going through an antechamber that used to be out of bounds. In fact, the sign that says STAFF ONLY is still propped on the librarian's desk. Is there a toilet back there now? Or a new wing? It hardly seems likely when the municipal budget won't stretch to the basics like new acquisitions. What are they doing in there?

Ivan Vladislavic

I return a bound set of the *Sunday Times* to Basil, who runs the stacks, and steel myself in the magazine corner. Then I stroll into the antechamber. It is like finding a secret passage behind a shelf of books. I half expect the voice of authority to boom, demanding the password. I go down some stairs into grey air furred with the animal scent of old books. Scuffed Marley tiles make the place feel like a kitchen, and indeed here on a landing that ends at a closed door is a table just big enough for a kettle and a hotplate. I go down another flight and come to a barred gate through which I can see the stacks, long pent-up reaches of shelves full of books and binders. I retrace my steps to the floor above and try the door on the landing. It opens. I step out into the Harry Hofmeyr Parking Garage. This vast basement, where in years past you'd have been lucky to find a bay, is all but empty. A dozen cars are clustered around the secret entrance where I'm standing; I assume they belong to the staff and other initiates, the visitors I've seen coming and going. My own car is in a distant corner near the steps that lead up to Harrison Street. Shutting the door behind me, a featureless grey panel in a cement wall, and making a note of its location in case I ever need it again, I set out across a damp, echoey space as long as a football field.

Every new building in Johannesburg has secure, controlled, vehicle-friendly entrances and exits. The well-heeled—who naturally are also the well-wheeled—should be able to reach point B without setting foot in the street. The malls are hemmed in by parking garages. Complexes of apparently independent buildings, designed to simulate the neighbourhoods of a conventional city, are undermined by huge, unitary garages that destroy the illusion. Superbasements. Older buildings have to adapt to the new requirements. The Johannesburg Art Gallery has turned its back on the public space it was designed for: instead of strolling in through Joubert Park, visitors leave their cars next to the railway line and hurry in through the back door. Elsewhere, walls have been broken through or tunnels and walkways opened up from existing basement parking garages into lobbies and reception areas. Usually these angular additions conceal their motives beneath a coat of paint, but the makeshift reversal at the Public Library is refreshingly ingenuous: while the black schoolchildren who are now the main users of the facility stroll arm-in-arm up the broad staircase from the library gardens or gather in the grand lobby to giggle and whisper, the few white suburbanites who still venture here park underground and slip in up the back stairs.

Blenheim Street, where Minky and I live, is a thoroughfare from Roberts to Kitchener, and people coming down the hill from the shops drop their peels and papers in our gutters. But when my old neighbour Eddie lived at No. 19 the pavement outside was always perfectly clean. He tidied up in his own way, by punting the litter downhill. The street rises steeply there, and so a cool-drink tin usually needed just one stiff kick to send it trundling off his turf. A milk carton might have to be harried all the way to the border. Eddie's law was precise: as soon as a piece of rubbish crossed into a neighbour's territory, it ceased to concern him.

Although Eddie has sold his house and moved away now, gravity and summer thunderstorms still ensure that most of the litter in Blenheim Street washes up on my doorstep further down the hill. There is no point in being angry with the forces of nature. From time to time, I go out with a garbage bag in one hand and a gardening glove on the other and pick everything up. In my lazy moments, I follow Eddie's example and boot a crust of bread or an orange peel or an empty *mageu* carton down the storm-water drain.

After a storm, everything is transformed. The cannas burst into wet flames, the dark scents of the earth seep out. Eddie's gladioli, the ones grown from the bulbs he gave me, pop magically from the clean cuff of the air. The sound of water rushing in the storm-water drains makes me grateful that I am neither on top of the hill, nor down in the valley, but somewhere in between.

Every month for the past fifteen years, on the second Thursday of the month, I have met my brother Branko for coffee at the Carlton Centre. I could chart the life and death of this great complex by the sequence of coffee shops which came to serve as our regular meeting-place over the years: from the Koffiehuis, where the waitresses were got up as Dutch dairymaids in clogs and lace caps, to the Brazilian Coffee Shop, where the cups and saucers arrived and departed on a conveyor belt.

When we first began meeting, the multi-storey car park in Main Street, opposite the hotel, was always full. You would have to wind up the spiral ramp to the fourth or fifth floor to find a bay. Little arrows and neon signs saying FULL and UP, in red and green respectively, kept you circling higher until a floor would accept you. There were attendants too, the obligatory middlemen between motorists and machinery, waving you on. The shiny concrete gave unexpected squeals of delight beneath the tyres. When you finally came to rest, you had to memorize the colour of the floor and the number of the bay or you would never find your way back. There were four lifts, large enough to park a Volkswagen in. Even here, in the car park, the slightly unsettling smell of food which circulated reminded you that pleasurable consumption lay ahead.

Then, in the mid-Nineties, the car park began to shrink. The demand for parking fell, level by level, like a barometer of change in the city centre. The people with cars were clearly going elsewhere. You could find parking on the fourth floor now, and after a while on the third, and then always on the second or first. Finally the illuminated arrows were switched off.

In May 1998, when I turned into Main Street there was a chain slung across my usual entrance. The middleman, who had always been there at the boom to catch the ticket the machine spat out and hand it to me through the window, was nowhere to be seen. Instead a sign urged me down an unfamiliar ramp into the basement. A long tunnel, with odd twists and turns in it, peculiar level landings and sudden lurching descents, took me down below the ground. I soon lost my sense of direction. Eventually I found myself in a crowded corner of the basement where the cars were all huddled like refugees. An armed guard oversaw my arrival. I made my way to the nearest lift, but there was a label pasted across the crack between the doors, as if to prevent them from opening: HOTEL CLOSED. It reminded me of a crime scene in an American TV series. The guard appeared at my shoulder and directed me to a distant lift, which brought me out in an unpopulated alley of the centre.

As we sat drinking our espressos at the little counter in the office block, which has the knack of making you feel like you're in New York, my brother told me that he couldn't face the city any more. It's too dangerous, he said, and unpleasant anyway, what with empty shops and echoing corridors and the smell of piss in the doorways. We should move our monthly meetings to Rosebank or Illovo. There are coffee shops in the suburbs where you can still read your paper and eat your biscotti in peace. What about Eastgate?

When I resurfaced into the chilly air a little later, a fierce white light caught my eye. Welders in overalls were sealing off the canopied entrance to the Carlton Hotel behind a palisade fence.

The grand old cinemas, the bioscopes, were driven out of business years ago by the multiplexes. Most of the defunct bioscopes have been appropriated by people who own junk shops. Perhaps they were the first to arrive at the Plaza or the Regal or the Gem when the curtain fell, hungry for spills of red velvet and rows of seats joined at the hip, and so much echoing space proved irresistible. You can trundle a piano through the wide doorways and pile things to the rafters, or even put in a mezzanine to double the floor space, as they've done at the Plaza. If there are windows at all, they are small and high, and do not even need bars.

The junk shops, like other businesses in the neighbourhood, take the names of the old establishments, as if it is important to preserve the association. The Plaza Pawn Warehouse in Primrose specializes in outmoded office furniture, a film-noir decor of grey steel desks and filing cabinets, wooden in- and out-trays, adding machines, fans, typists' chairs with chrome-plated frames and imitation-leather cushions. Regal Furnishers opposite the Troyeville Hotel sells plywood bedroom suites and kitchen cabinets. Gem Pawn Brokers buys and sells anything of value, as its sign declares. In its heyday, when the Gem was the grandest bioscope in the eastern suburbs, a back door gave on to a small landing, where the usher could loaf between features smoking a Lucky Strike, gazing over the tiled roof of the Second Church of Christ, Scientist, to the lights in the suburbs of Bez Valley and Bertrams, one ear tuned to the mutter of the spooling picture. Now this doorway is a frozen frame bricked in to keep out thieves.

The alliance of dark cinemas and second-hand goods is a happy one. In this deconsecrated space, objects that would appear lifeless in an ordinary shop throw flickering shadows. The profusion of goods evokes a storehouse rather than a market. These are the cast-off properties of people's lives, mementos of their hopes and failures, and the signs of use that should be off-putting seem poignant. A piano stool with a threadbare cushion, a dented toolbox, a Morris chair with cigarette-burned arms, a vellum lampshade dotted with postage stamps, a soda siphon, a bottle-green ashtray in the shape of a fish—there is nothing so tawdry that it is powerless to summon a cast of characters.

Here he is, the security guard at Gem Pawn Brokers, relaxing outside. It is the end of the working day and I'm heading to the Jumbo Liquor Market for some beer. He has already helped his colleagues to carry in the jumble of pine tables and metal shelves displayed on the pavement today as 'specials', but a single chair has been left behind in which he can lounge until the doors are shut. When the manager comes out with the key, the guard will carry in this last item, a fat, balding Gomma Gomma armchair, and oversee the locking and barring.

He always ignores me, though I can tell that he recognizes me, passing by, just as I recognize him, sitting there. It irks me, this denial of the everyday pleasantries that set people at ease. Why won't he acknowledge me? Is it the neighbourhood that makes people so guarded? I have been shopping in the Gem Supermarket for years and still no one greets me at the till. Any hint of friendliness is met with brooding suspicion, as if it must be a prelude to asking for credit. After ten years of patronizing the Jumbo, I once found myself short of a couple of rand on a bottle of wine. I offered to make up the balance the next day, but the cashier wouldn't hear of it. The manager was summoned. Grudgingly, he produced a two-rand coin from his wallet and put it in my hand, informed me that I was now indebted to him personally rather than the business, as if that would guarantee my honesty, and went away with a long face. The shopkeepers have reason to insult us, I suppose, for people are quick to take advantage. But what could I possibly want from the security guard at Gem Pawn Brokers?

An experiment. I greet him one afternoon, putting my heart into it. He returns the favour. *Hello! Hello.* It is no more than an echo, but it gives me some pleasure. *Hello! Hello.*

After a month of this game, a follow-up experiment becomes necessary and is made one afternoon. I don't say anything; he keeps silent too. The next day I try to catch his eye as usual, but he looks away, bewildered and resentful. He thinks I'm up to something. I had no idea my experiment would produce this irrevocable reversal. Now, when he sees me coming, he draws back into himself and glazes over. Even if I throw out a cheery greeting, he pretends he hasn't heard.

Occasionally, when my friend Louise was teaching at the Twilight Children's Shelter in Esselen Street and I was working as an editor at Ravan Press in O'Reilly Road, we would meet for lunch at the Florian in Hillbrow. If the weather was good, we sat outside on the first-floor balcony. Then she would slip her arms out of her paint-stained overalls and tie the sleeves in a big bow across her chest, so that she could feel the sun on her bare shoulders. Despite the chocolate-dipped letters of its Venetian name, the Florian offered English boarding-house fare: chops and chips, liver and onions with mashed potatoes, mutton stews and long-grained rice. We drank beer, although it was sure to make us sleepy, watched the traffic in the street below, and stayed away from work longer than the lunch hour we were entitled to.

The discovery of something unexpected about the world always filled her with an infectious wonder. Once, she tugged me over to the balcony railings at the Florian to point out the iron covers on the water mains set into the pavements. Did I know the spaces below these covers, where the meters were housed? Well, the poor people of Joburg, the street people—we did not call them 'the homeless' in those days—the tramps, car parkers and urchins, used them as cupboards! They stored their winter wardrobes there, and the rags of bedding they used at night, they preserved their scraps of food, their perishables, in the cool shade, they banked the empty bottles they collected for the deposits. It tickled her—she laughed out loud, just as if the idea had poked her in the ribs—that such utilitarian spaces should have been appropriated and domesticated, transformed into repositories of privacy for those compelled to live their lives in public. Any iron cover you passed in the street might conceal someone's personal effects. There was a maze of mysterious spaces underfoot, known only to those who could see it. And this special knowledge turned them into the privileged ones, made them party to something in which we, who lived in houses with wardrobes and chests of drawers, and ate three square meals a day, could not participate. Blind and numb, we passed over these secret places, did not even sense them beneath the soles of our shoes. How much more might we be missing?

The food came. While we ate, I began to argue with her about the 'cupboards' and what they represented, as if it were my place to set her straight about the world.

'It's pathetic,' I said, 'that people are so poor they have to store their belongings in holes in the ground.'

'No it's not. It's pathetic when people don't care about themselves, when they give up. These people are resourceful, they're making a life out of nothing.'

'It's like a dog burying a bone,' I said.

'Oh, you'll never understand.'

When we'd finished our lunch and were walking down Twist Street, I wanted to lift up one of the covers to check the contents of the cavity beneath. But she wouldn't hear of it. It wasn't right to go prying into people's things.

'What about the meter-readers?' I asked. 'Surely they're always poking their noses in?'

'That's different,' she said. 'They're professionals. Like doctors.'

'They probably swipe the good stuff,' I insisted.

'Nonsense. They have an understanding.'

Then we parted, laughing. She went back to the children and I went back to the books. This parting, called to mind, has a black edge of mourning, because she was walking in the shadow of death and I am still here to feel the sun on my face.

Ten years later, the domestic duty of a tap washer that needs replacing takes me outside into Argyle Street to switch off the mains. There is a storm raging in from the south, the oaks in Blenheim Street are already bowing before its lash, dropping tears as hard as acorns. I stick a screwdriver under the rim of the iron cover and lever it up. In the space beneath I find: a brown ribbed jersey, army issue; a red flannel shirt; a small checked blanket; two empty bottles—Fanta Grape and Lion Lager; a copy of *Penthouse*; a blue enamel plate; a clear plastic bag containing some scraps of food (bread rolls, tomatoes, oranges). Everything is neatly arranged. On one side, the empties have been laid down head to toe, the plate balanced across them to hold the food; on the other, the blanket has been folded, the shirt and jersey side by side on top of it, the magazine rolled up between. In the middle, behind a lens of misted glass, white numbers on black drums are revolving, measuring out a flood in standard units.

I kneel on the pavement, like a man gazing down into a well, with this small, impoverished, inexplicably orderly world before me and the chaotic plenitude of the Highveld sky above.

The range of steering locks available in South Africa is impressive—the Wild Dog, the MoToQuip anti-theft lock, the Twistlok, the SL2 Auto-Lok, the Eagle Claw by Yale, the Challenger… All these locks work on the same principle: they are attached to the steering wheel and immobilize the vehicle by preventing the wheel from being turned.

The locks also have the same basic design. There is a hardened steel shaft and an extendable bar. The two parts are connected by a locking ratchet mechanism and each part is furnished with a U-shaped hook or 'claw'. To engage the lock, you place the shaft diametrically across the steering wheel, with the bar retracted and the shaft claw around the rim. Then you extend the bar until the second claw fits around the opposite side of the rim. The ratchet engages automatically and locks the bar in place. If an attempt is made to turn the steering wheel now, the protruding bar strikes the passenger seat, windscreen or door. To disengage the device, you insert the key in the lock and retract the bar, freeing the claws on both sides.

In some devices, the U-shaped hook on the shaft is replaced by a corkscrew hook, which is twisted around the rim of the steering wheel before the bar is engaged. The Twistlok, for instance, has such a hook, which is called the 'pigtail end'.

The selling points of the various locks are similar. They are made of hardened steel which cannot be drilled, sawn or bent, and they are coated with vinyl to protect the interior fittings. They are easy to install, thanks to the automatic locking system, and highly visible to thieves; to heighten their visibility, and therefore their deterrent value, they are often brightly coloured. They have pick-resistant locks and high-security keys: the MoToQuip has 'cross point' keys; the Challenger has a 'superior circular key system'; and Yale offers a 'pin tumbler locking system' with 10,000 different key combinations, and exerts strict control over the issuing of duplicates.

Some of these products draw explicitly on the symbolism of the predatory animal. The Eagle Claw, for instance, suggests a bird of prey, a raptor with the steering wheel in its clutches. The logo of the Wild Dog depicts a snarling Alsatian, more rabid and vicious than the conventional guard dog. The association with wild animals known for their speed, strength or ferocity is also found in other areas of the security industry: tigers, eagles and owls appear on the shields of armed response companies, and rhinoceroses and elephants in the logos of companies that supply electrified fencing and razor wire.

We have left the security arrangements for my birthday party until the last minute, resisting the imposition of it, hoping the problem will resolve itself. Once, your responsibilities as host extended no further than food and drink and a bit of mood music; now you must take steps to ensure the safety of your guests and their property.

'I think it's irresponsible of us to have a dinner party at all,' I say to Minky. 'There should be a municipal by-law that only people with long driveways and big dogs are allowed to entertain. We should call the whole thing off.'

'It'll be fine,' she says. 'Just stop obsessing.'

The last time we had people over, I had to keep going outside to check that their cars were still there. It spoiled my evening.

'We'll get a guard,' she says. She phones the armed response people. It is too late, all their guards are booked. But they recommend the Academy of Security, where trainees are registered for on-the-job experience. She phones the Academy. Yes, they do supply security guards for single functions. A dinner party? Sevenish? Can do. That will be the half-shift deal, unless you want him to stay past midnight, and pay the full-shift rate? Being inexperienced, the guard cannot be armed, of course, but he will be under constant supervision. They could arrange an armed guard from another company, probably—but at such short notice, it will be more expensive, you understand? We settle for inexperienced, unarmed, half shift.

'The security costs more than the food,' I say, 'and he's still an appie. We should have gone to a restaurant.'

The apprentice security guard is called Bongi. So far, he has only acquired the top half of a uniform, a navy-blue tunic that is too short in the sleeve. The checked pants and down-at-heel shoes are clearly his own. By way of equipment, he has a large silver torch and a panic button hanging around his neck. My theory is that he is earning the uniform item by item, as payment or incentive. After six months or so, he'll be fully qualified and fully clothed.

'I knew this was a bad idea,' I say to Minky. 'He's just a kid.'

Bongi is standing under a tree on the far side of the road. He looks vulnerable and lonely. It is starting to drizzle. Minky takes him an umbrella from the stand at the door, the grey and yellow one with the handle in the shape of a toucan, which once belonged to her dad. With this frivolous thing in his hand, Bongi looks even more poorly equipped to cope with the streets.

'This is unforgivable,' I say, 'this is a low point. I'd rather live in a flat than do this.'

'What difference would that make?' says Minky, who always sees through my rhetoric. 'People have still got to park their cars somewhere.'

'A complex, then, I'd rather live in a complex. Some place with secure parking.'

The guests begin to arrive. Bongi waves the torch around officiously, and then stands on the pavement under the toucan umbrella, embarrassed.

When dinner is served, Minky takes out a plate of Thai chicken and a cup of coffee. 'Poor kid's starving,' she says when she comes back.

Excusing myself from the table, on the pretext of fetching more wine from the spare room, I sneak outside and gaze at him from the end of the stoep. He's squatting on the kerb, with the plate between his feet on the tar, eating voraciously.

'He's a sitting duck,' I say to Minky in the kitchen, when we're dishing up seconds. 'What the hell is he expected to do if an armed gang tries to steal one of the cars, God forbid. Throw the panic button at them? This whole arrangement is immoral. Especially our part in it. Our friends are insured anyway, if someone steals Branko's car, he'll get another one. What if this kid gets hurt while we're sitting here feeding our faces and moaning about the crime rate?'

With a plate of food under his belt, Bongi is looking better. We exchange a few words. He comes from a farm near Marikana, out near the Magaliesberg, and he's been in Joburg since June. His uncle found him this job, his uncle has been a 'full-time security' for five years. He looks quite pleased with himself. Perhaps he's thinking this is not such a bad job after all.

But we cannot see it that way. At ten-thirty, Minky calls him inside to watch the cars from the stoep, over the wall. When the supervisor arrives an hour later, there's a hullabaloo. You've got to maintain standards, he says, especially when you're training these guys. You can't have them getting soft on the job.

That's it, we say to one another afterwards. No more parties. Never again.

As I'm coasting down the ramp to the Harry Hofmeyr Parking Garage, I remember the back way into the reading room, which I discovered the last time I came to the library. Should I use that door? I'm not sure I'll be able to find it. Anyway, I should resist this scurrying about underground, this mole-like secretiveness: I park as usual near the cashiers' booth, take the tiled tunnel under Harrison Street and go up the steps that come out beside the City Hall. I like the walk, never mind the broken paving stones and hawkers' clutter. I want to approach the library along a city street like an ordinary citizen, passing from the company of people into the company of books. I won't go sneaking up the back stairs like a thief.

I cross over Harrison and pass the cenotaph. The library gardens are full of people. It looks like a rally of sorts. Men, men in uniform, thousands of them, a ragtag army in blue, black and grey fatigues, wearing berets of every colour, combat boots, flashes on their sleeves.

'What's happening?' I ask the man next to me at the Simmonds Street crossing.

'Strike,' he says. 'Security guards' strike.'

Cut-off whitey, he's thinking to himself, doesn't know what's going on. Actually, I've read about the strike, and I know the library gardens have long been a rallying point for popular causes, but I wasn't aware the strikers were gathering here. Probably wouldn't have made the trip if I'd known. There's a current of tension in the air and it swirls round me as I approach the hawkers' stalls, a mood as pungent as the smoke from the braziers where women are roasting *mielies* and frying thick coils of *wors* in a froth of yellow fat. Up ahead, on the plaza in front of the library, between the lawns and the stairs ascending grandly to the main doors, a man is speaking through a megaphone. Perhaps the tension is rippling out from him? He could be announcing a breakthrough or a deadlock in the negotiations. Who are they negotiating with? One can guess at the issues: wages, benefits, conditions of employment. I climb up on a bench so that I can see the man with the megaphone over the heads of the crowd. There's a statue to the left of the plaza, a family group in bronze, and he's joined them on the pedestal, hooking a comradely arm through one of theirs. A knot of men at the pond on the right. What are they doing? Some sort of tussle going on in the water, it looks like a baptism or a drowning. All these berets. You can tell by their headgear which of the companies are run by military men, the out-of-work soldiers of the old SADF: these guards wear their berets moulded tightly to their heads, scraped down over their right ears, whereas the guards employed by businessmen have soft, spongy berets, mushrooms and marshmallows no real soldier would be seen dead in.

Familiar faces on all sides. There are security guards everywhere in Joburg, and now they all look like people I've seen before. If I had time I could probably spot Bongi, the apprentice security guard from my faraway birthday party. He must be a seasoned pro by now and uniformed from boot to beret. Strangers keep catching my eye, casing my white features. No doubt they're wondering what the hell I'm doing here. This thought could make me apprehensive, except that no one focuses on me for long, their attention keeps being tugged to the left, to the Market Street side of the gardens.

What will the crowd do next, disperse or attack?

Before I can follow the thought there's a loud bang, a shotgun report, I think, and the crowd bursts apart like shrapnel from the heart of a blast. Some of them rush away in an anticlockwise whorl like water down a drain, others surge at me and carry me back towards President Street. I am running too, without thinking, and then stopping, as the wave subsides and wheels back intuitively towards the sound. We all turn, crouching, or huddled together, or craning boldly as if the whole range of attitudes has been choreographed. I am crouched between two men in front of the hawkers' stalls with the mesh of a gate pressing against my back.

Tumult on the opposite side of the gardens, men in blue pouring in from both ends of the row of stalls. Riot policemen. They are also policemen of a kind, the security guards, but in their berets and boots they look more like soldiers. The front lines clash, men go sprawling over the low walls on to the grass, there are more reports, bouncing back off the office blocks all around, rubber bullets or shotgun pellets, I don't know. But I do know, with every bone and muscle, that I am in the wrong place. I shouldn't be within a day's hike of this madness, I cannot get myself shot in a security guards' strike. Especially not with a rubber bullet. No amount of irony could erase the ignominy.

A tear-gas canister comes arching over the green roofs of the stalls. The frozen moment thaws in an instant into flight. We scramble through a gap in a curving wall, buffeting one another. I plunge out of the stream on to the pavement beyond and crouch behind the wall, among hawkers trying to defend spills of oranges and apples, relieved to have brick and mortar between my soft flesh and the guns. My fingers sink into orange pulp on the stone, my feet scatter Quality Street toffees and little building-blocks of Chappies bubblegum. All around there is a strange blend of fear and hilarity, faces wincing and laughing. Impossible. I cannot stay here. The sensible thing would be to go east along President, there's a staircase into the parking garage close by. But when I look over my shoulder, the intersection is a blur of men and vehicles and gas—it's drifting downwind! So I must go the other way, crouching behind parked cars, feeling absurdly like a child playing a game. To my right a lane runs through to Pritchard Street, but there are armoured vehicles at the end of that too, beyond the frivolous jet of a fountain, and policemen with helmets and shields.

I peep around the corner of the last stall. The police have taken the plaza, which is almost empty. Three dripping, bedraggled men, scabs the strikers were teaching a lesson about solidarity, are sitting on the edge of the pond with their hands in the air, coughing up water. Blood and slime beard their chins.

While I'm deciding what to do, a head pops up between the parked cars ahead of me, closer to the library building, and then another. Half a dozen people step gingerly into the open. Innocent bystanders, my kind of people: a pensioner, a middle-aged woman, a couple of schoolchildren. The adults shepherd the youngsters across the plaza and up the stairs. The policemen at the pond glance back idly but do nothing to stop them. A quick knock on the door, which opens to admit them, and they're gone.

I scoot over to the same gap between the cars. From here I have a better view of the plaza and the gardens. Apart from the group at the pond, and a thin cordon of armed men along the periphery, the place is nearly empty. The action has surged away across Simmonds Street and on into the city, leaving behind a trail of litter and placards, jerseys and shoes. I cross the pavement and go up the stairs, hurrying but not running, feeling more and more like a play actor. The stairs are low and wide and it is a long way to the top. I push at the first door but it's locked. Panicky, I hammer on the second one and it opens a crack. Two faces appear, one above the other, a grey-haired librarian and a shaven-headed security guard. Satisfied that I pose no threat, they roll aside a book-laden trolley and let me in.

If I was looking for sanctuary, an oasis of calm and quiet, I've knocked at the wrong door. The lobby looks and sounds like a marketplace. A hubbub as if every unread book had begun to speak at once: children laughing and talking, acting out their narrow escapes for one another, librarians hurrying upstairs with armfuls of precious papers or manning the barricades, grimly amused or stoical.

'You can't go in there, sir, we've had to close the reference section for the safety of the books. But the reading room is open.'

Basil is on duty in the reading room as usual and he fetches the bound issues I'm after. Some men are talking at the windows, watching the drama on the pavement in President Street where the police have their command centre. The air seeping in from outside is still soured with conflict. I find a space at a desk and settle down to work. Later, I'll go upstairs to a window with a view of the gardens and see whether it's safe to leave. If necessary, I'll take the back way out, although I'd rather not. What's the hurry? I can read until it quietens down.

When I lick my finger to turn the page it tastes of orange juice.

A man rattles the metal catch on our back gate every third or fourth day. When I lift the curtain at the bedroom window to see who's there, he shows his face between the iron bars of the gate like an identity card. He used to say his name, but now he has fallen back on this visual shorthand. Even in the gloom, I recognize his white peaked cap. I go out and let the money fall into his cupped palm. He squints at me through the bars and drops a little curtsey. Neither of us says a word. We have been reduced to a simple mechanism of supply and demand. Occasionally, I spy on him as he leaves counting the coins, stepping out quite confidently. I think he is pretending to be a backward rustic to keep my sympathy.

Ivan Vladislavic

I'm coming home along Roberts Avenue, when I see my old neighbour Eddie dithering on the pavement by the substation near the Black Steer steak house. He's looking up and down Blenheim Street, walking a step or two downhill and then hurrying back up again.

It must be six months since he sold his house and moved, and this is the first time I've caught sight of him in the old neighbourhood. I'm pleased to see him, and yet I don't feel like talking to him. Even in the moment, this impulse strikes me as uncharitable, but I cannot suppress it. So I stop in the shade of the fig tree on the corner to watch. He hasn't seen me and he doesn't seem likely to either; he's too engrossed in his own dilemma. Up and down, up and down. His pacing is like paging; he has lost his place in the world. Finally, he goes downhill decisively towards his old house. I've seen him do this countless times, hobbling back from the Gem with a loaf of bread under his arm, going up the garden path. But he doesn't live here any more. When he's one door away from his old home he veers across to the other pavement and stops, watching from a distance, on the bias. He cannot face it. He starts coming back up the hill again.

Now a meeting is unavoidable, and I'm suddenly delighted to see him. He's just as pleased to see me: he seizes upon me like a bookmark. But he also looks guilty, as if he's been caught out doing something discreditable. Before I can ask, he starts telling me how much he enjoys it in Germiston. Just around the corner from Joburg, he says, but it feels like a small town. Been gone eight months already, can you believe it? His daughter had business in town today, so she dropped him off. He's been visiting with George at the Black Steer and old Mrs Ferreira. Looking around. George is closing down, did you know that? Mrs Ferreira used to own half the block. Now she's reduced to her place and the place next door, and not even a decent tenant for that.

I let him tell me yesterday's news. Then I ask: 'What's it like to be back? Have we changed?'

We both turn and face down the hill.

'My garden's not looking so good,' he says.

'No.'

'New chap's not much of a gardener.'

'It's a pity.'

'This has always been a beautiful part of town,' he says. 'The streets are so wide, and the oaks are grand, and the houses are set back just right, don't you think? You notice it when you've been away for a while. I was saying to my daughter this morning: There isn't a finer street in Joburg than Roberts Avenue.'

The plane takes off. I am looking forward to seeing Joburg from the air. It is always surprising to discover how huge and scintillating the city is, that it is one place, beaded together with lights. As the aircraft lifts you out of it, above it, it becomes, for a moment, comfortingly explicable. Personal connections dissolve, and you read your home from a distance. The South African writer Lionel Abrahams, flying over Joburg by night, saw the 'velvet obliteration' of all his landmarks: 'Everything familiar had been forgiven.' But there is another, more intimate comfort in the vastness: it assures you that someone, inevitably, is looking back. At one of those millions of windows, on one of those thousands of stoeps and street corners, someone must be standing, looking up at the plane, at the small, rising light that is you, tracing your trajectory, following your flight path.

We have hardly lifted into air when the plane banks to the left and the lights dip below the horizon of the window ledge. It is sudden enough to be alarming, this lurch and slide, but I am merely annoyed. I look across the dim sloping interior, but the dull-witted economizer in the window seat opposite has pulled down the shade. Through the other windows I catch the briefest sparkles and flares. The plane continues to bank. We are going to spiral out of here, I can just see it, rising like a leaf in a whirlwind until the entire city has been lost in the darkness below. Disappointment wells up in me, disproportionate and childishly ominous. This failure to see Johannesburg whole, for the last time, will cast a pall over the future. Tears start to my eyes. And then just as suddenly the plane levels out and the city rises in the window, a web of light on the veld, impossibly vast and unnaturally beautiful. □

GRANTA

LEGACIES
Adewale Maja-Pearce

Nigeria

Adewale Maja-Pearce (right) with his mother and
brother in Lagos

I returned to Lagos in 1993 to claim the property I inherited from my father. Although my father was a wealthy man I hadn't expected to inherit anything from him. To say that I was estranged from him assumes a relationship between us that we didn't have. When my parents were still together, he was a distant figure to me; he would sometimes come to the beach with us on Sunday afternoons and fussed whenever we wanted to go for a dip, even though my mother had already taught us how to swim. The only time we did anything together was when the circus came to town every year to mark Nigeria's independence from British rule. He never called me 'son' and rarely talked to me on my own. The only piece of advice he ever gave me was soon after I turned fifteen. He was driving me back to my boarding school in Lagos and suddenly stopped in the middle of the road to say something to a man walking by. As we drove away, he said that they had been at university in Dublin together but that the man had flunked out because he had spent all his time chasing women. He said that I should study hard and pass my exams and then I could have as many women as I liked. His message to me was clear: I was doing badly in school and had only been promoted to the next class 'on trial'. I had also caught my first bout of clap and the school doctor had obviously made good his threat to tell my father.

When I was ten, my mother, unable to cope any longer with my father's sadistic treatment of her, returned home to Britain, taking my younger sister with her and leaving me and my two younger brothers behind. I spent the next five years pleading with my mother to send me a plane ticket so I could join them because otherwise, I felt, I would go under: my father was a tyrant who made me dread my holidays from boarding school. I finally went to live with my mother in London when I was sixteen. My father was a stranger to me after that; I saw him only three more times.

I was at university, thanks to a government grant, the first time I saw him again. I had written to him when I first got my place, to tell him that I was going to read history; when I was at school in Nigeria he had made me drop history, a subject I loved, for physics, one I hated. He replied to congratulate me and enclosed a cheque for £10. I was pleased because I hadn't expected to hear from him at all. I wrote to him again the next year, this time complaining that I was broke. Again he sent me £10 and warned me not to 'incur such expenses and expect me to help you out like that'. He advised me to live at home with my mother during the vacations to save on costs and to take a holiday job as well. Being prone to impulse, always to my own cost, I returned the cheque and vowed never to talk to him again. My vow lasted exactly one year. In the middle of my finals, I got a telegram from him saying that he was in London and would very much like to see me. My first instinct was to ignore the summons but in the end I went because I was pathetically grateful that he still remembered who I was, a humiliating condition that afflicts all spurned sons.

The meeting itself turned out to be a mistake but then it couldn't have been otherwise. My brothers Richard and Michael were also over from Lagos. We all met up in my mother's cramped maisonette on a west London housing estate. My mother hit on the idea that he should take us to Ronnie Scott's, the jazz club—in order to make him spend lots of money, which he did. He chuckled inanely to hide his irritation every time my mother ordered another bottle of the most expensive wine 'and a little something to go with it'. The guest musician was Elvin Jones, the drummer who had played with John Coltrane and Miles Davis, but I was yet to discover jazz and I didn't appreciate it. Everybody was tense but only my sister expressed it. She had never lived with my father and she giggled openly when the Lagos Big Boy who employed a cook and a steward and a driver and a gardener deferred to our impatient white waiter. Later, when we got back home, he and my mother retired to the makeshift bed in the sitting room—as though his nightly beatings all those years ago were now to be considered of no account by those who had been forced to endure them in silence down the hall.

The next morning, none of us could look at each other as my father sipped tea in the narrow kitchen with the fold-down table and thin walls. He didn't stay long and could hardly hide his impatience; his other family, his new family, was waiting for him in their cozy little flat in the West End. He asked me about my plans. I said that I was going to Canada, where I had won a scholarship to do another degree. He promised to give me his brother's address in New York but he never did. Only my sister acted honestly; she locked herself in her room and refused to come out until he was gone.

Years later, after my father's death, I asked my mother why she had slept with him that night. She was silent for a moment and then burst into tears. She said she had done it because she thought we might be a family again. But I doubt even she believed that.

The next time I met him was ten years later when I went to see him in hospital in London. He was dying. It was odd seeing him in that setting because he was a doctor and now he was a patient recovering from surgery. I knew that he had been diagnosed with prostate cancer some years previously but thought that he had been cured. At first I didn't even recognize him. He was incredibly thin and looked much older than his sixty-six years. He reminded me very much of Papa, his own father, whom I had last seen when he was ninety, just before I left for England. Even his hands looked like Papa's hands; they trembled when he raised them to complain about the pain in his head. He didn't believe that he was dying. He said that he was actually feeling much better, and hoped to return home soon. I didn't stay long. My mother had insisted on coming with me and her presence disturbed him. He became even more uncomfortable when, not long afterwards, my stepmother turned up with her eldest son. They sat across from us so that he was sandwiched between the two women: two predators looking for satisfaction. My mother could ignore a person for as long as it took (her ability to do so had distressed me no end as a child); my stepmother seemed to be gloating over her imminent victory. My father pretended to be asleep but his illness meant that he had to get up to pee all the time. At a signal, my stepmother pushed her son forward but my father had hardly started on his painful journey to the lavatory when his flaccid penis popped out of his pyjama trousers. My half-brother didn't notice and my father was too weak to help himself. Both women turned away, and so did I.

I went to see him again in hospital, but this time by myself and at midday to avoid my stepmother who, I had gathered, never visited before late afternoon. He smiled weakly when he saw me and again said that he was feeling better although he didn't look any different to me. He looked worse, if anything, but then I still wasn't used to his appearance. He was now an old man, not the robust, middle-aged man I remembered, with a slight paunch and a habit of chewing his tongue with his back teeth when he was concentrating. He said that his doctor would be visiting him soon and that I should wait to hear what he had to say. He kept drifting off, sometimes in the middle of a sentence. Eventually the specialist arrived, a handsome, vigorous man with a white moustache and a female junior doctor in tow. He asked my father how he was. My father lifted his hand to his head and complained about the pain which wouldn't go away, he said. The specialist looked baffled and said something to the young woman and then left, promising to return.

I sat with my father for another hour. He could hardly raise his arm, much less strike anyone. His mouth hung open as he slept and I noticed that most of his back teeth were missing. When he next opened his eyes, he took a few seconds to remember that I was there. I told him that I was going but that I would come and visit him again. He smiled weakly and said that he wanted to give me some money. I told him not to worry but he insisted, indicating his wallet in the bedside cabinet. When he opened it, his hands shaking, he found only two, one-pound coins. He looked puzzled. 'I rely on them to get me what I need,' he said apologetically. He meant my stepmother and her children. On my way out, I used the money to buy some flowers for my mother. I didn't visit my father again. Four months later, he was dead in Lagos.

I was living in Birmingham when I received the news. I went for a walk one Sunday and stopped at a public phone box to call my mother. My sister answered and said, 'Your father's dead.' She said that an English friend of my mother's who lived in Lagos had phoned a couple of days before to tell them the news. She added breathlessly: 'I was hoping that we might have got closer. I went to visit him, you know, just before he flew back. I asked him for some money but he said he didn't have any. And *she* was there the whole time. She wouldn't leave me alone with my own father, even for a minute.' When my sister had finished, I blurted out, 'Well, it's too late now, isn't it?'

In his will, my father left to me and my brothers and sister a block of four flats on the Mainland, with an adjoining 'BQ'—Boys' Quarters—for Michael to mark his status as the favourite. This was a change from the will he had written two years before. In this earlier will he left two of the flats to the children of his first marriage. We were to share the other two. My mother was actually my father's second wife. My father's first wife, a Nigerian, was with him in London with their two children when he met and married my mother. My father had told my mother he was divorced but he wasn't, which made him a bigamist and me a bastard.

My parents met in London at the end-of-year dance at Moorfields Eye Hospital in London. My mother was an eighteen-year-old Scottish girl and a trainee nurse. She had been watching my father admiringly because he was a beautiful dancer with a charming smile; when it was the turn of the ladies to ask the men she went straight up to him. He turned out to be twenty years older than her. A few weeks later, they eloped to Gretna Green because she was underage and her parents were against the marriage. I was born nine months later. My mother said that I cried every day for the first three months of my life. I stopped crying only when we boarded the boat for the two-week voyage to Lagos. She said that just before they set sail, her father had asked her if she knew that she was going to the white man's grave. Six months later, she said, she was shivering under a mosquito net and wondering whether his prediction was about to come to pass.

When I was ten years old, my father hit my mother so hard that she suffered permanent damage to her right ear. It was a Sunday. My father had come in late the night before and there had been the inevitable row when he insisted on waking the cook to prepare a meal he had no intention of eating. The row continued the following morning until we went to church, leaving my father behind. We returned to find an agitated steward on the verandah who told my mother that 'Master' wanted to see her upstairs. Shortly afterwards, I heard her scream and then she came running down the stairs and out of the house. She was gone for some time. On her return, she sat in the parlour sobbing into a handkerchief. I asked about going to the beach but she just shook her head. It was a hot, still day, perfect for diving into the cool water and letting the waves wash over you. Now we were condemned to an afternoon of boredom. I wandered to the bottom of the garden and climbed over the low wire fence and sat by the edge of the lagoon. I spent a lot of time by that lagoon watching the gentle ripples caused by the passing canoes that disturbed the tiny crabs by the water's edge. The sun was high overhead and everywhere was quiet. I wandered back to the house and sat with my brothers on the veranda with the big-leaved cocoyam plants my mother called elephants' ears.

By and by, my father came downstairs. I remember that he wore brown linen trousers and a white singlet and carried a file of papers. He walked past my mother to the desk by the French windows and put the file in one of the drawers. And then he stood there for a while looking towards the lagoon. I remembered that only a year earlier, he had stood in that same spot while my mother trimmed his moustache. He must have been going out because he was smartly dressed and they were both laughing; he was nervous that she would cut his lip and she was mock-scolding him to hold still otherwise he would only have himself to blame. Everything had changed since then. She no longer trimmed his moustache and they didn't laugh about anything. The happy days were over. Suddenly, my father made for where my mother was sitting with her back to him, and punched her so hard that her head hit the glass-fronted bookcase which contained the leather-bound collected works of Dickens and the *Reader's Digest Atlas of the World*.

Many years later, after he was dead, my mother told me in a long letter that that was the moment she decided he would never hit her again. She reported the incident at the local police station. Unfortunately, the constable on duty was 'completely out of his depth' and could only phone his superior who in turn phoned my father for reassurance that his wife could return home safely. And that was it. In the same letter she recalled the night when he came home to find her sleeping in the spare room and 'went mad and dragged me out and proceeded to kick and punch me'.

As a foreigner, a white woman, she was defenceless, with no relatives of her own to turn to. My father, by contrast, had any number only too willing to take the side of their illustrious uncle and brother. They would descend on the house after every argument to explain to this stubborn *oyibo* woman that, whatever went on in London or in America, wife-beating was the style here and if she didn't like it she could go back to where she came from. And this is what she did. She left Nigeria with £20 in her purse 'and a suitcase full of cotton dresses'.

I got the news from our cook when I came back from school one day. I ran upstairs to their bedroom and saw that it was true. Her wardrobe was wide open and empty and all the jewellery on her dressing table was gone, too. A week or two later, the cook showed me a blue airmail letter she had written him asking him to help look after her children. I remember we were standing by the desk near the

French windows and the cook kept turning the letter over in his hands as if unsure what to do with it. Eventually he showed it to my father, perhaps because he thought it was the only way he could hope to carry out my mother's impossible request, perhaps because he thought that her desperate letter was actually meant for my father. Either way, it was a mistake. Early the next morning, my father charged into the kitchen and started beating him up. The cook was actually bigger than my father but he didn't try to hit back, just defended himself as best he could, even after his arm went through the glass-fronted kitchen door. Later that day, I returned from school to find that his room in the BQ was empty. His young wife had only recently had a baby but my father was evidently unmoved by this.

The only person who stuck up for my mother and, after she left, for me, was my father's father. Papa, as we called him, was a Methodist minster. Although long retired, he baptized me and my brothers and my sister in turn. He was already old then, older than my father was when he died, but I remember him as a kind, gentle, upright man. Once, I even overheard him asking my father what his in-laws would think when they heard how he was treating their daughter; they had entrusted her to his care in a faraway land. In those days you had to book a phone call to London a week in advance and then shout into the receiver—as we used to do every Christmas. Papa was ashamed for his son. You could see it in the way he looked at him. Papa didn't speak much and was hard of hearing but he gazed steadily at my father who kept wandering out to the first-floor wooden balcony overlooking the busy street, jangling his car keys. I think that was the last time we ever visited him.

Papa hardly ever came to our house but one day after my mother had left and my stepmother had moved in, he suddenly turned up an hour or so before my father was due back from the hospital. He sat in the parlour and refused even the glass of water offered by the bewildered steward, his hands resting on his wooden walking stick, his mouth set in firm disapproval. My father barely concealed his fury when he came in. Without greeting Papa, he ordered me upstairs. On my way, I heard Papa say, 'So you want to tell me that you don't believe in God. Is that what you are telling me?' My father didn't answer. Soon afterwards, Papa's car drove off. The grapevine hadn't taken long to tell the Methodist minister about his son's belief in juju.

A *babalawo* came to our house every Sunday afternoon, an elderly man with a servile manner, who wore a grubby *agbada* and dangled a white cock in his left hand. My father would look slightly shamefaced as he invited him upstairs, there to pluck out the entrails of the offering. Afterwards my father would give us some black powder wrapped in a piece of newspaper, and a ball of black soap. The powder was tasteless and probably just charcoal, and the soap, which we usually threw into the lagoon, was equally innocuous—it was available in any local market, although we didn't know it at the time. To me, it was just part of my stepmother's malevolent influence. My father took to blessing any new possession—a Toyota car with an icebox in the boot for long journeys we never made, a hunting gun he never fired because he never went hunting—with the sacrificial blood of the fowl, the *babalawo* muttering incantations all the while.

I went back to Nigeria, for the first time after twelve years, in 1983. The oil boom had happened shortly after I had left but the place didn't feel very different to me: the same heavy heat, the same open gutters, the same unrelenting poverty. When I was a child, the poverty had been both real and not real to me. I grew up in Ikoyi, a wealthy suburb of Lagos. The only poor people I knew were our servants who lived in the BQ that was screened from the house by a high hedge. Later, when I went to boarding school and became obsessed with the local prostitutes, I never made the connection between the poverty of the brothel's dirt-courtyard surrounded by corrugated tin hovels, and what it meant in daily terms for the women being screwed in them; now, as I sat in a shared taxi weaving its slow way through Lagos Island, I watched a woman with a baby on her back hawking plastic shopping bags—'Buy nylon', she was calling—in a way which suggested that she didn't believe she was going to sell very many of them in the course of the long, hot day. I was also shocked by what seemed like callousness on the part of my fellow passengers; they echoed my father in condemning the beggars for their shiftlessness. I couldn't see what an uneducated cripple was to do for themselves in such a society but I was yet to appreciate the remorseless logic of poverty: your misfortune is your own fault and possibly a sin.

I felt estranged from the country. Even now that I have settled in Nigeria, I am daily reminded that I am not properly Nigerian. As a half-caste, I am an *oyibo*, a white, like my mother. I don't look African. Nigerians were quick to congratulate me on this, telling me with approval that my mother's blood must be strong. But it was my upbringing, above all, that made me feel out of place. We came down every morning in my father's house to sausage and egg and toast and jam. Sunday lunch was a roast with all the trimmings. We poured brandy over the Christmas pudding and lit it with a match and got excited about who would find the silver sixpence. On Guy Fawkes Night, my father would come home with Catherine wheels and rockets and make us stand at the far end of the back garden while he cautiously let them off one by one, taking all the fun out of it, his bifocals perched on the end of his nose as he laboriously read the instructions. My first school, a short walk from the house, was staffed exclusively by English expatriates who taught us to dance round the Maypole and formed us into Cub and Brownie packs; my brother Michael nicknamed me 'Scout' when he saw me in my Cub uniform. This colonial fantasy suited my mother whose feelings about being lower middle class were assuaged by a houseful of servants in a country where her white skin already conferred higher status on her; she was a conspicuous figure as she drove her green-and-white sports car to the foreign import-only department stores. We always spoke English at home and the only time I heard Yoruba was when my father was on the phone to one or other of his relatives. I made no attempt to learn the language, even when I went to boarding school and should have picked it up, and my father never encouraged me to do so.

The Mainland was only somewhere my father took us to be measured for school uniforms or to have a haircut. He himself was quite natural in this setting, chatting away with the barber in Yoruba, insisting that the barber cut my widow's peak. I disliked having my hair cut, just as I disliked crossing the wooden plank over the open gutter while the local children chanted '*oyibo* pepper, if you eat pepper you go yellow more more'. Other than that, we used to make an annual pilgrimage inland to Abeokuta, my father's home town, which was a three-hour drive from Lagos. Here my mother's presence would attract even more chanting as we sat in an overstuffed parlour drinking warm Coke. She always had a headache by the time we returned to Lagos.

163

Adewale Maja-Pearce

I made a second trip to Lagos in 1985. I went to see our old house in Ikoyi. It was now occupied by strangers as my father had built himself a house in another part of Ikoyi after I left for England. I was unable to get in, let alone take a look at the lagoon. As soon as I got out of the car I was approached by a soldier stationed at the front gate who asked me, in halting English, what I wanted. When I said that I had lived here many years before and wanted to take a look he shook his head and said that it was a military area and that we should move. I thanked him and left. From the brief glimpse I had, the house seemed smaller than I remembered but I had forgotten the guava tree just over the fence from where I stood. I had climbed that tree and eaten its fruit and it was under there that I unwrapped the charcoal and the black soap that my father gave me to help me pass my exams.

It was during that second trip that I went to check on my inheritance, the flats on the Mainland. I hadn't even known about the property. The building itself, which faced you side-on as you approached, was in the middle of a horseshoe-shaped close of a dozen such buildings, which meant that there was no through-traffic in an otherwise busy part of the city. Its location alone made it valuable but it looked uncared-for: it hadn't been painted in years; the mosquito netting covering the windows was torn and filthy; the compound itself was jammed to capacity with half a dozen cars, two of which were propped up on breeze blocks and covered with jute sacking and looked as if they had been in that condition for some time. There was not a scrap of green anywhere. A sagging clothes line cut the compound in half so that you had to duck under its flapping load to get to the downstairs back flat as well as the BQ. Worse still, the lobby leading to the upper two flats had been cordoned off by a makeshift plywood structure, leaving only enough space for the staircase.

I went to visit my stepmother to get the title deeds for the property. Seeing her again was a strange experience. I wasn't even sure where her house was and the taxi driver was starting to get annoyed before I finally spotted the number in the gathering dusk, having passed it twice already. The compound itself was surrounded by a high fence and I had to bang hard on the iron gate before the watchman emerged from his bunker. He asked for my name and told me to wait while he went to tell madam. When he finally returned, he walked me to the veranda and pointed to the plastic table and chairs. The house had reflecting windows so that you couldn't see inside. As a building, it meant absolutely nothing to me as my father had built it after I left. It had a big garden with a badminton net in the middle, although it didn't look as if anybody had used it recently. A servant came from around the back and asked me what I wanted to drink. I was halfway through the bottle of beer when my stepmother finally emerged. She used a walking stick to support her bad leg. Her hair was roughly plaited and there was a lot of grey in it. She had also put on weight. I gave her the book I had just written. She read the blurb which said that the author was 'ruthless in exposing the human rights violations perpetrated by African rulers'. She smiled. 'You should be careful,' she said. 'These military boys don't take nonsense.'

She asked after my brothers and then, to my surprise, said that I didn't know it but she was from an illustrious Abeokuta family and she was even related to Fela Kuti, the musician. It only occurred to me afterwards that she was trying to get my approval. She actually cared that I might think her a money-grubbing interloper and perhaps she had felt my disdain as a child. Once, not long after she had moved in, she almost lost her leg in a motor accident and I was only sorry that she hadn't died. Unfortunately, her accident meant the end of her job as a matron and she became a full-time housewife instead. I was yet to begin my adventures in the local whorehouses but I had just discovered the joys of masturbation. My stepmother was in her early thirties and must have been amused by my furtive glances at her rising chest whenever she berated me for something or other—this was our only form of communication. When I was fourteen years old I tried to seduce the housegirl, a busty young woman only slightly older than me who declared my clumsy move 'isopotoijury' (she meant 'insult upon injury') and told my stepmother, who gleefully reported me to my father. My father didn't beat me that time, just quietly told me that he would throw me out of his house if I didn't 'buck up my ideas'. I had no reason to doubt him given his abandonment of his older children.

My stepmother humiliated me in front of my friends. One day during the holidays, three classmates stopped by to ask me to make up a fourth at lawn tennis. A year or so earlier, my father had bought me a racquet. We were in the department store where my mother had an account and he was laughing and joking with the manageress when he suddenly bought me the racquet, an expensive one, a Slazenger, that the other boys were forever borrowing, especially the older ones: 'Pearce, where is your racquet.' I soon became one of the best players in the school so it made sense for the other boys to ask me to join them. However I was mortified when I saw them approaching. They were in long trousers and I was in shorts; they were footloose and fancy-free and I was a prisoner waiting to be punished for my latest crime. We hung awkwardly on the balcony with the potted elephants' ears until my stepmother, hearing strange voices below, asked loudly, in an unwelcoming voice, who was there; they left without being offered so much as a glass of water. Years later, after I had settled back in Nigeria, I re-established contact with one of them, now a lawyer, who told me how sorry they had all felt for me that day.

There was also what my stepmother didn't do. For instance, she never bought me clothes. My father's duty on that score began and ended with my school uniform. The rest was nothing to do with him. It was what the wife did, except that his wife didn't. This was the reason I never had enough underpants. The ones I did have were torn and grubby and I always had to hide them, especially in boarding school. Once, when I was with the swimming team, some of the other boys got curious and went to investigate while I was still in the pool. They were laughing when I walked into the dressing room, one of them holding my pants between his thumb and forefinger. A German once picked me up in a blue Beetle car when I was walking home early one afternoon. He smiled in puzzlement when he unzipped my trousers to see a brown flap of my torn underpants covering the object of his desire. I was sipping a bottle of Coke at the time. I smiled back and he played with me for a little like we did with each other in boarding school and then he zipped up my trousers and dropped me near the house.

But the most upsetting thing for me was how well my father treated my stepmother. He didn't beat her; I never even heard him shout at her. He was hysterical with concern when she had her accident and insisted that I go and commiserate with her in hospital, her leg in plaster, her dark nipples showing through her nightie. Why didn't he beat her like he beat my mother? Was it because my mother was a white, or because she was a foreigner, or because she was a victim?

I had never liked my stepmother and now, all these years later, she seemed anxious that I think well of her. In fact, sitting there in the surrounding darkness, I didn't think about it very much. Mostly, I felt soiled by the past and wanted to forget it, although she insisted on a little ceremony in which I produced the power of attorney my siblings had given me and her son drafted a letter attesting to the handing over of the title deeds. As I prepared to go, she suddenly asked after my brother Michael. I thought that she was genuinely concerned, especially when she confided how my father had sat up in bed one night and cried and cried when he heard that Michael was in trouble with the police in London. She had never seen him cry like that before. When I said that he was okay but having personal problems, she nodded in satisfaction. It was what she had wanted to hear.

Michael was my father's favourite child. 'My Michael' was a constant refrain in the house, especially after my mother left. He was like a man besotted, as if Michael, with his delicate, almost girlish features, was his lover and not his son. Once, I remember, he promised to buy him some chocolate on the way back from the hospital but forgot. Michael, who had been waiting expectantly in the driveway, promptly threw a tantrum. My other brother Richard and I were startled, thinking that he would get a beating, but my father just smiled indulgently and got back in his car. There were no supermarkets nearby so he would have had to drive some distance. When he returned, he took Michael upstairs with him so that Michael could scoff the chocolate all by himself. Michael was gifted in physics and invariably came top of his class. I followed my mother in reading novels and Richard wasn't academically inclined. Each time our reports came, my father would deliberately wait until Richard and I were seated at the dining table and then proceed to mock our efforts, all the while looking with approval at Michael, who would snigger contemptuously. Contempt was a trait that my father exhibited in his dealings with anyone he thought beneath him, which was most people, at least in Nigeria. I was always shocked at the way he shouted at staff and patients whenever I visited him, in the hospital of which he was now the head, to screw money out of him. Michael copied this trait, much to my father's amusement.

This was the pattern of our life until I left to join my mother and my sister in London, soon to be followed by Richard. I didn't see Michael again until they all came over and we went to Ronnie

Scott's. Michael later dropped out of a British university in his final year because, he said, his father had forced him to study engineering when he wanted to study mathematics, and had then reneged on his promise to send him to flying school in America.

The title deeds showed that my father had bought the land for £499.6d in February 1960, just months before independence and everything started to unravel. This was what I had come for. Before I returned to London, I called on each of the tenants in the flats. They weren't surprised to see me because my stepmother had already put them on notice. I gave them each one year rent-free in the hope that they would go quietly. They didn't. I was back again the following December only to discover that my lawyer had done nothing in my absence. The problem was that I didn't know any lawyers. I should have been able to use one of my old classmates, a number of whom had studied law but I was yet to re-establish contact. I had met the one I was using through my work with *Index on Censorship* as he was interested in human rights, but I didn't know him at all well. It turned out that he didn't like going to court and wasn't au fait with what he himself called 'simple landlord and tenant cases'. It became clear to me that I would have to take a more personal interest in the case myself. I had no idea it would take me the next ten years to get back what was mine.

I moved to Lagos and found it exhilarating. Britain was not strange to me but it was a place I found difficult to connect with. This had a lot to do with my mother's own responses to her country. To her, Britain was a drab, austere place she had grown up in during and after the Second World War, a bombed-out country where oranges and bananas were an expensive rarity and where she was forced into nursing because of a dip in her family's fortunes. She described many times how, coming off the boat in Lagos after the two-week voyage from Liverpool, she was dazzled by the array of brightly-coloured tropical fruits on sale for pennies, some of which she had never seen before. She was also excited about sleeping under a mosquito net from reading Somerset Maugham novels about a similar climate in another part of the world, and she never had any problems with the weather. She spent hours under the sun whenever we went to the beach and I never remember her falling sick until her last days in Lagos, when she suspected my father of trying to kill her by refusing her medical attention.

Forty years after she left Lagos for good my mother went back to visit. I had invited her for Christmas. She was seventy-one. I hadn't seen her for several years because I had become tired of listening to her going on about what a terrible fellow my father was. She had married him, after all, in those far-off days in London and there were limits to what I could usefully say.

I was pleased to see that she was in good health, as she had assured me she was when we were making arrangements for her to travel. I had initially hoped that my brother Richard would accompany her but he had to cry off at the last minute. It was typical of my mother that she thought nothing of undertaking a journey that anyone else her age might have approached with trepidation; but then this was a woman who, half a century ago, had thought nothing of moving to an unknown continent because she had fallen in love with a man who came from there and believed everything he said, a character flaw of which even he failed to cure her.

As we drove around over the next three weeks, she remarked on how much the city had changed. All the expressways were new, as were the bridges linking the Mainland to the Island, including the one replacing the single-lane Carter Bridge that she used to drive across in her sports car. She now found the heat bothersome and broke out in a rash within days of arriving. I said that I thought she had always liked the sun; I remembered her lying for hours on the beach on Sundays while we played in the water. She laughed and said that it had been the fashion at the time to have a tan but now people knew it was dangerous. Nevertheless, when I took her to the beach she rubbed cream on her face and sat directly under the sun.

During her stay we talked about my father. 'Do you remember that Sunday afternoon when he hit me and I went to report him to the police?' my mother asked.

'Like yesterday.'

'The police were useless but it worked. He never hit me again after that.'

I could just imagine how it would have played at the Island Club or the Yoruba Tennis Club or the Ikoyi Club (the three big clubs in

Lagos) when he found himself face-to-face with the policeman who had politely asked him if his wife could safely return home. He was ashamed, that was all. Later, when my mother fled back to England, she was forced to write to the Chief Justice of the Federation, who was a friend of my father's, because my father refused to send the allowance he had promised to provide for my sister. The payments resumed but not for long. I remember how it was when I joined them five years later. There was never any food by Thursday evening and we were always cold in the winter, with just a paraffin stove in the bathroom to stave off the cold.

I asked her if she remembered that last time we saw my father in the London hospital as he lay dying.

'I was surprised because I never thought I would outlive him,' she said. 'I thought that he would always be around to haunt me.'

I asked my mother how she felt when she heard that my father was dead.

'Relieved,' she said.

'Only that?' I asked. 'Nothing more?'

'Nothing,' she said. □

GRANTA

BEETHOVEN
WAS ONE SIXTEENTH
BLACK

Nadine Gordimer

South Africa

'Beethoven was one sixteenth black,' the presenter of a classical music programme on the radio announces along with the names of musicians who will be heard playing the String Quartets No. 13 Op. 130 and No 16 Op. 135.

Does the presenter make the claim as restitution for Beethoven? Presenter's voice and cadence give him away as irremediably white. Is one sixteenth an unspoken wish for himself?

Once there were blacks wanting to be white.

Now there are whites wanting to be black.

It's the same secret.

Frederick Morris (of course that's not his name, you'll soon catch on I'm writing about myself, a man with the same initials) is an academic who teaches biology and was an activist back in the apartheid time, among other illegal shenanigans an amateur cartoonist of some talent who made posters depicting the regime's leaders as the ghoulish murderers they were and, more boldly, joined groups to paste these on city walls. At the university, new millennium times, he's not one of the academics the student body (a high enrolment robustly black, he approves) singles out as among those particularly reprehensible, in protests against academe as the old white male crowd who inhibit transformation of the university from a white intellectuals' country club to a non-racial institution with a black majority (politically-correct-speak). Neither do the students value much the support of whites, like himself, dissident from what's seen as the other, the gowned body. You can't be on somebody else's side. That's the reasoning? History's never over; any more than biology, functioning within every being.

One sixteenth. The trickle seemed enough to be asserted out of context? What does the distant thread of blood matter in the genesis of a genius. Then there's Pushkin, if you like; his claim is substantial, look at his genuine frizz on the head—not some fashionable faked Afro haloing a white man or woman, but coming, it's said, from Ethiopia.

Perhaps because he's getting older—Morris doesn't know he's still young enough to think fifty-two is old—he reflects occasionally on what was lived in his lifeline-before-him. He's divorced, a second time; that's a past, as well, if rather immediate. His father was also not a particular success as a family man. Family: the great-grandfather, dead long before the boy was born: there's a handsome man, someone from an old oval-framed photograph, the strong looks not passed on. There are stories about this forefather, probably related at family gatherings but hardly listened to by a boy impatient to leave the grown-ups' table. Anecdotes not in the history book obliged to be learned by rote. What might call upon amused recognition to be adventures, circumstances taken head-on, good times enjoyed out of what others would submit to as bad times, characters—'they don't make them like that any more'—as enemies up to no good, or joined forces with as real mates. No history book events: tales of going about your own affairs within history's fall-out. He was some sort of frontiersman, not in the colonial military but in the fortune hunters' motley.

A descendant in the male line, Frederick Morris bears his surname, of course. Walter Benjamin Morris apparently was always called Ben, perhaps because he was the Benjamin indeed of the brood of brothers who did not, like him, emigrate to Africa. No one seems to know why he did; just an adventurer, or maybe the ambition to be rich which didn't appear to be achievable anywhere other than a beckoning Elsewhere. He might have chosen the Yukon. At home in London he was in line to inherit the Hampstead delicatessen, see it full of cold cuts and pickles, he was managing for another one of the fathers in the family line, name lost. He was married for only a year when he left. Must have convinced his young bride that their future lay in his going off to prospect for the newly-discovered diamonds in a far place called Kimberley, from where he would promptly return rich. As a kind of farewell surety for their love, he left inside her their son to be born.

Frederick surprises his mother by asking if she kept the old attaché case—a battered black bag, actually—where once his father had told him there was stuff about the family they should go through sometime; both had forgotten this rendezvous, his father had died before that time came. He did not have much expectation that she still kept the case somewhere, she had moved from what had been the home of marriage and disposed of possessions for which there was no room, no place in her life in a garden complex of elegant contemporary-design cottages. There were some things in a communal storeroom tenants had use of. There he found the bag and squatting among the detritus of other people's pasts he blew away the silverfish moths from letters and scrap jottings, copied the facts recorded above. There are also photographs, mounted on board, too tough for whatever serves silverfish as jaws, which he took with him, which he didn't think his mother would be sufficiently interested in for him to inform her. There is one portrait in an elaborate frame.

The great-grandfather has the same stance in all the photographs whether he is alone beside a photographer's studio palm or among piles of magical dirt, the sieves that would sift from the earth the rough stones that were diamonds within their primitive forms, the expressionless blacks and half-coloured men leaning on spades. Prospectors from London and Paris and Berlin—anywhere where there are no diamonds—did not themselves race to stake their claims when the starter's gun went off, the hired men who belonged on the land they ran over were swifter than any white foreigner, they staked the foreigners' claims and wielded the picks and spades in the open-cast mining concessions. Even when Ben Morris is photographed sitting in a makeshift overcrowded bar his body, neck tendons, head are upright as if he were standing so immovably confident—of what? (Jottings reveal that he unearthed only small stuff. Negligible carats.) Of virility. That's unmistakable, it's untouched by the fickleness of fortune. Others in the picture have become slumped and shabbied by poor luck. The aura of sexual virility in the composure, the dark, bright, on-the-lookout inviting eyes: a call to the other sex as well as elusive diamonds. Women must have heard, read him the way males didn't, weren't meant to. Dates on the scraps of paper made delicately lacy by insects show that he didn't return promptly, he prospected with obstinate faith in his quest, in himself, for five years.

He didn't go home to London, the young wife, he saw the son only once on a single visit when he impregnated the young wife and left her again. He did not make his fortune; but he must have gained some slowly accumulated profit from the small stones the black men dug for him from their earth, because after five years it appears he went back to London and used his acquired knowledge of the rough stones to establish himself in the gem business, with connections in Amsterdam.

The great-grandfather never returned to Africa. Frederick's mother can at least confirm this, since her son is interested. The later members of the old man's family—his fertility produced more sons, from one of whom Frederick is descended—came for other reasons, as doctors and lawyers, businessmen, con men and entertainers, to a level of society created from profit of the hired fast-runners' unearthing of diamonds and gold for those who had come from beyond the seas, another kind of elsewhere.

And that's another story. You're not responsible for your ancestry, are you?

But if that's so, why have you marched under banned slogans, got yourself beaten up by the police, been arrested a couple of times, plastered walls with subversive posters. That's also the past. The past is valid only in relation to whether the present recognizes it.

How did that handsome man with the beckoning gaze, the characteristic slight flare of the nostrils as if picking up some tempting scent (in every photograph), the strong be-ringed hands (never touched a spade) splayed on tight-trousered thighs, live without his pretty London bedmate all the nights of prospecting? And the Sunday mornings when you wake, alone, and don't have to get up and get out to educate the students in the biological facts of life behind their condomed cavortings—even a diamond prospector must have lain a while longer in his camp bed, Sundays, known those surges of desire, and no woman to turn to. Five years. Impossible that a healthy male, as so evidently this one, went five years without making love except for the brief call on the conjugal bed. Never mind the physical implication; how sad. But of course it wasn't so. He obviously didn't have to write and confess to his young wife that he was having an affair—this is the past, not the sophisticated protocol of suburban sexual freedom—it's unimaginably makeshift, rough as the diamonds. There were those black girls who came to pick up prospectors' clothes for washing (two in the background of a photograph where, bare-chested, the man has fists up, bunched in a mock fight with a swinging-bellied mate at the diggings) and the half-black girls (two coffee one milk the description at the time) in confusion of a bar-tent caught smiling, passing him carrying high their trays of glasses. Did he have many of these girls over those years of deprived nights and days? Or was there maybe a special one, several special ones, there are no crude circumstances, Frederick himself has known, when there's not a possibility of tenderness coming uninvited to the straightforward need for a fuck. And the girls. What happened to the girls if in male urgencies there was conception? The foreigners come to find diamonds came and went, their real lives with women were Elsewhere, intact far away. What happened? Are the children's children of those conceptions on-the-side engendered by a handsome prospector who went home to his wife and sons and the gem business in London and Amsterdam— couldn't they be living where he propagated their predecessors?

Frederick knows as everyone in a country of many races does that from such incidents far back there survives proof in the appropriation, here and there, of the name that was all the progenitor left behind him, adopted without his knowledge or consent out of— sentiment, resentment, something owed? More historical fallout. It was not in mind for a while, like the rendezvous with the stuff in the black bag, forgotten with his father. There was a period of renewed disturbances at the university, destruction of equipment within the buildings behind their neoclassical columns; not in the Department of Biology, fortunately.

The portrait of his great-grandfather in its oval frame under convex glass that had survived unbroken for so long stayed propped up where the desk moved to his new apartment was placed when he and his ex-wife divided possessions. Photographs give out less meaning than painted portraits. Open less contemplation. But *he* is there, he is—a statement.

One sixteenth black.

In the telephone directory for what is now a city where the diamonds were first dug for, are there any listings of the name Morris? Of course there will be, it's not uncommon and so has no relevance.

As if he has requested her to reserve cinema tickets with his credit card he asks his secretary to see if she can get hold of a telephone directory for a particular region. There are Morrises and Morrisons. In his apartment he calls up the name on the Internet one late night, alone. There's a Morris who is a theatre director now living in Los Angeles and a Morris a champion bridge player in Cape Town. No one of that name in Kimberley worthy of being noted in this infallible source.

Now and then he and black survivors of the street marches of blacks and whites in the past get together for a drink. 'Survivors' because some of the black comrades (comrades because that form of address hadn't been exclusive to the communists among them) had moved on to high circles in cabinet posts and boardrooms. The talk turned to reform of the education system and student action to bring it about. Except for Frederick, in their shared seventies and eighties few of this group of survivors had the chance of a university education. They're not inhibited to be critical of the new regime their kind brought about or of responses to its promises unfulfilled.

Trashing the campus isn't going to scrap tuition fees for our kids too poor to pay. Yelling freedom songs, toyi-toying at the Principal's door isn't going to reach the Minister of Education's big ears. Man! Aren't there other tactics now? They're supposed to be intelligent, getting educated, not so, and all they can think of is use what we had, throw stones, trash the facilities—but the buildings and the libraries and laboratories and whatnot are *theirs* now, not whitey's only—they're rubbishing what we fought for, *for* them.

Someone asks, your department okay, no damage?

Another punctuates with a laugh—They wouldn't touch you, no way.

Frederick doesn't know whether to put the company right: the students don't know and if they do, don't care about his actions in the past, why should they, they don't know who he *was*, the modest claim to be addressed as comrade. But that would bring another whole debate, one focused on himself.

When he got home rather late he was caught under another focus, seemed that of the eyes of the grandfatherly portrait. Or was it the mixture, first beer then whisky, unaccustomedly downed?

The Easter vacation is freedom from both work and the family kind of obligation it brought while there was marriage. Frederick did have children with the second wife but it was not his turn, in the legal conditions of access, to have the boy and girl with him for this school holiday. There were invitations from university colleagues and an attractive Italian woman he'd taken to dinner and a film recently, but he said he was going away for a break. The coast? The mountains? Kimberley.

What on earth would anyone take a break there for? If they asked, he offered, see the Big Hole, and if they didn't remember what that was he'd have reminded it was the great gouged-out mouth of the diamond pipe formation.

He had never been there and knew no one. No one, that was the point, the negative. The man whose eyes, whose energy of form remain open to you under glass from the generations since he lived five years here, staked his claim. One sixteenth. There certainly are men and women, children related thicker than that in his descendant's bloodstream. The telephone directory didn't give much clue to where the cousins, collaterals, might be found living on the territory of diamonds; assuming the addresses given with the numbers are white suburban rather than indicating areas designated under the old segregation which everywhere still bear the kind of euphemistic flowery names that disguised them and where most black and colour-mixed people, around the cities, still live. And that assumption? An old colour/class one that the level of people from whom came the girls great-grandpapa used must still be out on the periphery in the new society? Why shouldn't 'Morris, Walter J. S.' of 'Golf Course Place' be a shades-of-black who had become a big businessman owning a house where he was forbidden before and playing the game at a club he was once barred from?

Scratch a white man, Frederick Morris, and find trace of the serum of induced superiority; history never over. But while he took a good look at himself, pragmatic reasoning set him leaving the chain hotel whose atmosphere confirmed the sense of anonymity of his presence and taking roads to what were the old townships of segregation. A public holiday, so the streets, some tarred and guttered, some unsurfaced dirt with puddles floating beer cans and plastic, were cheerful racetracks of cars, taxis and buses, avoiding skittering children and men and women taking their right and time to cross where they pleased.

No one took much notice of him. His car, on an academic's salary, was neither a newer model nor more costly make than many of those alongside, and like them being ousted from lane to lane by the occasional Mercedes with darkened windows whose owner surely should have moved by now to some such Golf Course Place. And as a man who went climbing at weekends and swam in the university pool early every morning since the divorce, he was sun-pigmented, not much lighter than some of the men who faced him a moment, in passing, on the streets where he walked a while as if he had a destination.

Schools were closed for the holidays, as they were for his children; he found himself at a playground. The boys were clambering the structure of the slide instead of taking the ladder, and shouting triumph as they reached the top ahead of conventional users, one lost his toe-hold and fell, howling, while the others laughed. But who could say who could have been this one that one, give or take a shade, his boy; there's simply the resemblance all boys have in their grimaces of emotion, boastful feats, agile bodies. The girls on the swings clutching younger siblings, even babies; most of them pretty but aren't all girls of the age of his daughter, pretty, though one couldn't imagine her being entrusted with a baby the way the mothers sitting by placidly allowed this. The mothers. The lucky ones (favoured by prospectors?) warm honey-coloured, the others dingy between black and white, as if determined by an under-exposed photograph. Genes the developing agent. Which of these could be a Morris, a long-descended sister-cousin, whatever, alive, we're together here in the present. Could you give me a strand of your hair (his own is lank and straight but that proves nothing after the Caucasian blood mixtures of so many following progenitors) to be matched with my toenail cutting or a shred of my skin in DNA tests? Imagine the reaction when I handed in these to the laboratories at the university. Faculty laughter to cover embarrassment, curiosity. Fred behaving oddly nowadays.

He ate a *boerewors* roll at a street barrow, asking for it in the language, Afrikaans, that was being spoken all around him. Their mother tongue, the girls who visited the old man spoke (not old then, no, all the vital juices flowing, showing); did he pick it up from them and promptly forgot it in London and Amsterdam as he did them, never came back to Africa? He, the descendant, hung on in the township until late afternoon, hardly knowing the object of lingering, or leaving. Then there were bars filling up behind men talking at the entrances against Kwaito music. He made his way into one and took a barstool warm from the backside of the man who swivelled off it. After a beer the voices and laughter, the beat of the music made him feel strangely relaxed on this venture of his he didn't try to explain to himself that began before the convex glass of the oval-framed photograph. When his neighbour, whose elbow rose and fell in dramatic gestures to accompany a laughing bellowing argument, jolted and spilled the foam of the second beer, the interloper grinned, gave assurances of no offence taken and was drawn into friendly banter with the neighbour and his pals. The argument was about the referee's decision in a soccer game; he'd played when he was a student and could contribute a generalized opinion of the abilities, or lack of, among referees. In the pause when the others called for another round, including him without question, he was able to ask (it was suddenly remembered) did anyone know a Morris family living around? There were self-questioning raised foreheads, they looked to one another: one moved his head slowly side to side, down over the dregs in his glass; drew up from it, when I was a kid, another kid...his people moved to another section, they used to live here by the church.

Alternative townships were suggested. Might be people with that name there. So did he know them from somewhere? Wha'd'you want them for?

It came quite naturally. They're family we've lost touch with.

Oh that's how it is people go all over, you never hear what's with them, these days, it's let's try this place let's try that and you never know they's alive or dead, my brothers gone off to Cape Town they don't know who they are any more...so where you from?

From the science faculty of the university with the classical columns, the progeny of men and women in the professions, generations of privilege that have made them whatever it is they are. They don't know what they might have been.

Names, unrecorded on birth certificates—if there were any such for the issue of foreign prospectors' passing sexual relief—get lost, don't exist, maybe abandoned as worthless. These bar-room companions, buddies, comrades, could any one of them be men who should have my family name included in theirs?

So where am I from?

What was it all about?

Dubious. What kind of claim do you *need*? The standard of privilege changes with each regime. Isn't it a try at privilege. Yes? One up towards the ruling class whatever it may happen to be. One sixteenth. A cousin how many times removed, imagined from the projection of your own male needs on to the handsome young buck preserved under glass. So what's happened to the ideal of the Struggle (the capitalized generic of something else that's never over, never mind history-book victories) for recognition, beginning in the self, that our kind, humankind, doesn't need any distinctions of blood percentage tincture. That fucked things up enough in the past. Once there were blacks, poor devils, wanting to claim white. Now there's a white, poor devil, wanting to claim black. It's the same secret.

His colleagues in the faculty coffee room at the university exchange Easter holiday pleasures, mountains climbed, animals in a game reserve, the theatre, concerts—and one wryly confessing: trying to catch up with reading for the planning of a new course, sustained by warm beer consumed in the sun.

—Oh and how was the Big Hole?

—Deep.

Everyone laughs at witty deadpan brevity. □

GRANTA

THE WITCH'S DOG
Helon Habila

Nigeria

They had just turned twelve, and today was their first day at secondary school. School was over and they were in the mango grove, reluctant to go home. Their father was away on one of his business trips, and their aunt Marina wouldn't be back from the farm until late in the evening when the sun hung over the hills, low and burning red. The dog's loud barking gave Mamo the idea. They were up in a tree, their legs dangling in the air, their mouths yellow with mango juice. He stopped gnawing on the mango seed and said, 'You know, dogs can see spirits and ghosts.'

LaMamo looked at him. 'How do you know that?'

'I read it somewhere, in a book.' LaMamo couldn't read, so he didn't argue. Mamo went on, 'You can see spirits too if you rub dog's rheum in your eyes.'

LaMamo was immediately captivated by the idea.

'Let's get Duna,' he suggested. Duna was the old witch's dog, and because it was perhaps the most vicious dog in the whole village, they knew without discussing it that to get its rheum they'd first have to kill it. They got down from the tree and picked up their school bags where they had dropped them in the grass and set off for home, immersed in trying to find the best way to kill a dog. Halfway home Mamo hit on a solution.

'Batteries!'

'What batteries?' LaMamo asked, puzzled.

'We poison it...with the black stuff in radio batteries.'

'How do we...?'

'Come.' Mamo was running, his bag flying from its strap behind him, his spindly legs jumping high over the thick grassy undergrowth. Their compound was a few metres from the edge of the grove. They found used radio batteries in the garbage pit behind the outhouse. TIGER HEAD BATTERY, FOR LONG LIFE. They spread out old newspaper pages on the ground and cracked open the batteries on them. The black carbon powder poured out on to the paper—it was a disappointingly small amount.

'More, it is a big dog,' Mamo said, pushing another battery on to the paper. When they had enough they carefully poured the black powder into leftover bean cakes. This stage was easy, by now the outer skin of the akara was tough and membranous, it didn't crumble when they made a tiny hole in it and hollowed out the inside. The

185

Helon Habila

tricky part was to make sure the carbon did not touch the skin on the outside, otherwise the dog would be repelled by the strong smell before it had a chance to swallow the cake. They overcame this by putting in a pinch at a time.

Soon they were back in the grove. The old witch, Nana Mudo, lived alone with her dog on the other side of the grove. Her house was a tiny mud hut fenced in by a wall of straw and sticks; she spent the daylight hours seated on a log under a tamarind tree outside her house. The tamarind trunk was human shaped, people said it was her husband, trapped in there by her witchcraft. A footpath leading to the market passed before her house, and though she was blind she could tell from the footfalls who was passing and would call out their names and harangue them with gossip. Duna was always beside her, a huge black mongrel that loved to growl and chase after passers-by, children especially, while the old woman encouraged it gleefully, 'Go, catch them, Duna, get them. Ha! Ha!'

Many a parent had come to complain, his tearful, dog-bitten child in tow, only to be greeted by her wild cackles, her sightless eyes shining, her toothless gums pink and crooked. 'Tell your child to stop calling me "Old Witch"!' Nana Mudo would scream at the parent.

As the twins approached the old woman's house they perfected their plan. 'You will play bait,' Mamo, the elder twin, said to his brother. 'Stand so the dog sees you. Wave and throw stones at it, when it gives chase, run and climb up the tree where I'll be waiting. It will stand barking under the tree, and that is when I'll throw down the akara. Any questions?'

'What if it doesn't come after me?' LaMamo was smiling, his eyes shining with anticipation; his brother looked the opposite, his feet dragged, his hand which held the spiked akara was sweaty and limp.

'It will,' Mamo said shortly. They chose a tree in the centre of the grove. It was small but leafy, easy to climb and a fair running distance from Nana Mudo's house. LaMamo did a few test runs, jumping from the ground and grabbing a lower branch with both hands, then swinging up into the tree.

'Easy, let's do it.'

First they reconnoitred to make sure they were alone in the grove—but this was July, the mango season had ended in May, and not many people came to the grove when the mango season was over. In the muddy ground beneath their feet last season's mango seeds had already begun to sprout tender shoots. Insects and tiny frogs flew out of the undergrowth as they passed. It was hot, the moisture hung in the air, trapped beneath the mango leaves. Mamo sweated profusely; he used his sleeves to wipe his forehead every minute or so.

'There she is.'

She was seated in her usual place, on the log under the gnarled tamarind tree. Her faithful dog was stretched on the ground beside her, its huge tongue lolling out of its mouth.

'You...you know what to do?' Mamo asked. His mouth was dry and he kept licking his lips.

'Stand in view, throw stones at the dog, make sure it sees me, then run.'

Mamo returned to the tree to wait. He did not wait long. A few minutes later he heard deep barking, then the sound of feet racing through the grass, then LaMamo appeared running, almost flying over the undergrowth, dodging trees. The dog was a blur behind him, a black ball moving faster than the eye could register. Then with a sinking feeling Mamo saw that LaMamo had missed the tree—the trees all looked the same anyway—he was running round in circles, his eyes searching desperately, the dog snapping at his heels.

'Here... here... here!' Mamo croaked, shaking with nerves. Without thinking he dropped out of the tree and started jumping about, waving his arms frantically. LaMamo saw him and made straight for him, breathing hard through his mouth; they both jumped as if on springs and grabbed at a branch and they were up and safe. The enraged dog rushed at the tree and stood on its hind legs, scratching at the trunk with its front paws, jumping up, all the time barking, its fangs bared, saliva dripping out.

'Where is the akara, where is the akara?' LaMamo shouted at his brother, breathing hard, laughing, high on adrenaline. But Mamo couldn't get his hands to move, they were shaking uncontrollably. He was staring down into the dog's wild, yellow eyes, mesmerized.

'There,' he croaked, pointing with his mouth at the parcel in the crook of a branch above his head. LaMamo reached up and took the parcel and threw it down at the dog. Duna charged at the parcel, its body quivering with rage, then, scenting food, it stopped barking and poked its snout into the parcel. The twins leaned down from their perches, eyes fixed on the dog. Suddenly the dog looked up and growled at them, once, then it lowered its head into the parcel and began swallowing the bean cakes hungrily. As soon as the parcel was empty it resumed barking up at the tree, but the poison acted swiftly—the barking grew progressively weaker, and soon the dog seemed to have lost all interest in them. It turned and headed for home, staggering from side to side as it went. Then they heard the old woman's voice, it sounded close. She was calling the dog. 'Duna! Come here, you crazy dog. Duna!'

The dog made for the voice, wagging its tail weakly, but it did not get far. It stretched out in the grass, and after a few thrashes and turns it went quiet. The twins looked at each other. 'Do you think it is dead?'

'It should be. It finished all the akara.' They spoke in whispers.

They cautiously descended from the tree. Now the old woman came into sight, tapping in front of her with her walking stick, all the time calling, 'Duna, Duna.'

'She can't see,' Mamo whispered to his brother needlessly. Soon she was out of sight, her voice growing fainter as she went. They ran to the motionless dog and stood over it; they were undecided what to do next. They were shocked and momentarily scared by the sight of the dog, dead on its side in the grass.

LaMamo knelt down and felt the dog's black coat with his hand. It was still warm.

'Let's get the rheum and go.'

'How?'

Mamo hesitated, then he said, 'Rub it into our eyes.' He shrank as his brother reached for the dog's eye and scraped the rheum from the edge with his index finger then carefully rubbed it into his eyes. LaMamo looked up and saw the expression on his brother's face.

'Come on, let's hurry and get out of here,' he said impatiently as he scraped the rheum from the other eye. Mamo knelt beside his brother and presented his eyes.

The rheum turned out to be a disappointment—initially. They did not wash their eyes that night while taking their bath before going to bed, so as not to reduce the rheum's potency. Their house was a big, L-shaped, rambling structure; their father, Lamang, had built it incrementally. Originally, before the twins were born, the compound had consisted of two mud huts, which still stood. He had built the shorter part of the L when he was getting married, fourteen years ago. It was squat and rectangular, consisting of two rooms and a living room, with square zinc windows and heavy wooden doors: the effort of local builders more used to working in clay and thatch. But in its time it had stood out among the surrounding thatched structures as a piece of architectural magnificence. Then five years after his wife's death Lamang had added the longer part of the L; the children were growing up fast and they needed more room. Also, he had reinvented himself as a businessman and he could easily afford the expense now. The new house had louvres on the windows, and netting to keep out mosquitoes.

So the house stood, the old linked to the new: the living room was the juncture where the two met. The children and Auntie Marina occupied the new section, while Lamang preferred the old section, with his dead wife's picture and memories hanging over the bedpost like a guardian spirit.

The children's room was next door to Auntie Marina's: it was her job to keep them quiet when their father wanted some peace, to wake them up when they overslept, and to make them sleep when they stayed up too late.

But on the night of the dog rheum there wasn't much noise from the children's room. They shut their door soon after the evening meal, and each went to his bed and lay shivering with anticipation—they left the lantern on, low. Mamo was the first to drift off into a fitful slumber, he muttered in his sleep, tossing and turning. LaMamo was the one who heard the gentle tapping on the window, the one overlooking the grove. *Tap... tap... tap...* It came again, and again, regular, insistent. He froze under his sheet, his eyes fixed on the window.

'Mamo...' he said. 'Can you hear that...'

But Mamo was asleep. Eyes still fixed on the window, LaMamo got out of bed and crossed the room to his brother's bed. He grabbed his brother's arm and shook him awake.

'Can... Can you hear that?' They listened: faraway, dogs howled into the night, voices of drunks coming back late from the market rent the air in raucous notes, then the tapping came again: *tap... tap... tap...* The glass louvres amplified the sound until it seemed to be coming from somewhere inside their heads.

'It...is only a branch knocking against the window,' Mamo said, trying to conceal the tremor in his voice. He was glad when LaMamo slipped into the bed beside him, but they did not go to sleep immediately—they lay in the gloom of the lamp, their eyes tightly shut, their limbs stiff as if with rigor mortis, their ears focused on the tapping on the window.

When they finally fell asleep they dreamed that it was raining outside—which indeed it was—and as the rain fell the world grew darker until not a ray of light could be seen, save when bright fissures of lightning lit up the air suddenly, followed immediately by thunder. In the mango grove the water was shoulder high: bodies floated past the window, their dead eyes glowing like lamps. First was their mother, her mouth opening and closing as she passed by. She was trying to say something but water kept filling her mouth, drowning the words. She struggled against the strong tide, but it took her away, her eyes still fixed on them, glowing, turning the muddy water translucent and silvery. Next came the old woman with Duna on a leash, she was cackling dementedly, struggling with the leash, fighting the water to get to the window, and all the time the dog barked and barked, the sound blood-curdling. Now she was at the window, she hammered at it with her walking stick, *tap... tap... tap*, until gradually the glass began to crack under the insistent hammering.

The twins woke up screaming. The scream became louder when they found out they could not see. They scrambled out of bed, kicking their legs out of the sheets, knocking against each other, knocking into the table, beds, chair, each other, the walls, in their desperate search for the light. And all the time their eyes were wide open, blinking.

'Mamo, I can't see!'

'Me too!'

Then they heard Mama Marina's voice outside the door. They threw themselves at her, sobbing with relief when she opened the door and they saw the morning sunrays behind her, clear and strong, as she stood on the threshold. ☐

GRANTA

POLICEMAN TO THE WORLD
Daniel Bergner

Mark Kroeker, May 2004

Policeman to the World

In Liberia, the Mamba Point Hotel is the place where the Westerners stay. There is a wide, graceful veranda facing the sea and a walled garden hinting at jungle. Just up the road, late in the spring of 2004, a machine-gunner peered out from the sandbagged booth of a United Nations checkpoint. Close by in the other direction, perched on a UN tank, a turret-gunner protected the neighbourhood with his right hand on his sizeable weapon and his left hand clutching a purple parasol.

The neighbourhood, a spit of beachfront shared by the hotel, the American embassy and the headquarters of the European Commission, didn't feel much removed from the anarchy of the rest of Liberia's capital, Monrovia, in the aftermath of fourteen years of civil war. The cityscape of looted and abandoned buildings started right next door to the hotel. And when Mark Kroeker, the UN's police commissioner in Liberia, drove over to meet me for breakfast one morning at the Mamba Point, he said that as he'd been eating lunch there several weeks earlier, one of Monrovia's impromptu mobs of vigilantes had run past along the road, yelling 'Rogue! rogue!' and chasing a man who'd stolen a pair of jeans. Mobs were a regular means of law enforcement in the capital. They commonly burned or beat their captives to death.

Still, the Mamba Point felt just removed enough, just calm enough, to foster the belief that Kroeker could succeed in his mission—to create a functional Liberian police force, to begin to establish the rule of law in a country that could seem to have no law at all. He'd been a deputy police-chief in Los Angeles in the early 1990s, when deadly rioting had erupted in African-American sections of the city; later he'd run the department in Portland, Oregon. Now he was at the heart of the UN's effort at nation-building, at pulling Liberia away from horrific implosion and towards democracy. National elections were scheduled for just over a year away. Kroeker is a missionary's son; he speaks with a steady, sonorous faith. 'The place for bringing peace into the world,' he said at breakfast, 'it is here.'

A few days later he called me on my cellphone. There'd been a murder at the hotel, he said. He was headed there now. I happened to be in my room, taking an hour's refuge from the city. I walked across the gently overgrown garden and into the main building and met him where the body was.

193

Blood streaked the carpet and one wall of room number twelve. In a corner, the man lay on the floor on his back, naked to his white briefs, his legs forming a diamond, heels together and knees spread. Dried blood caked the hair on his arms, stained his underwear, painted his thighs. It coloured his chin below his moustache. He was white and thickly built, and, judging by all the splashes and sprays of blood, it looked like he'd put up a struggle.

Kroeker leaned into the room, careful not to step inside, not to disturb the crime scene. Six foot three and still solidly put together at the age of sixty, he wore his white uniform-shirt, silver stars pinned to the collar, a patch with the United States flag on one shoulder and the UN's baby-blue insignia on the other. He has a beakish pink nose and thin lips that make him look like a tall earthbound bird, more affable than imposing. He'd been at his job for six months. He had about 700 UN police officers, from thirty or so countries, working under him. With them, he meant to transform a national police department that was an embodiment of state terror, corruption, and ineptitude; while he carried out this remaking, he hoped to offer the Liberian people some interim sense of order, to persuade them that packs of vigilantes might not be necessary, and to give them reason to believe that a viable Liberian society has a decent chance of taking shape. He needed to train local officers, and to catch criminals and deter crime, and with the body on the floor he hoped to accomplish a bit of each.

But there was, for him, extra urgency to this investigation. The dead man was an American, a civilian contractor working with the US military; he'd been staying at the hotel along with around twenty American marines. They were in Liberia to assess whether the US might help in developing a new national army, one less prone to atrocity than Liberian armies of the recent past. 'This is the worst thing that could have happened,' a man from the American embassy was muttering in the hall outside the room, 'the worst thing.'

The corridor was tight with UN police in uniform and Liberian police in street clothes, some because they were detectives and some because uniforms were among the many things—cars, two-way radios, paper to write reports on—that the Liberian National Police couldn't afford. Kroeker stepped away from the open door, away from the throng. Talking with the hotel's Lebanese manager and a Liberian police colonel, he pieced together that, in the hours before dawn that morning, the killer had cut through the corrugated metal sheeting of the hotel's roof.

'So this is a guy with some tools,' Kroeker said.

'He doesn't need too much tools,' Colonel Flomo, a short, bald man in a tan sports jacket, said. 'Scissors will cut the zinc.'

The killer had dropped down, first, into the room of an American woman working with the military assessment team. While she slept, he'd taken $8,000 in cash, some jewellery, a cellphone. Then he'd climbed back into the crawl space, crept above the hall, and lowered himself again through a panel in the ceiling into another room. There he'd probably woken the man in his underwear. A maid had discovered the body a short while ago, about ten hours after the murder.

Marines in their fatigues were now coming into the hallway, returning to their rooms at day's end, confused by the sight of the crowd. The embassy rep told them to pack up; they were leaving the hotel and would wait for orders from behind embassy walls. By the look of things, Kroeker didn't think it likely that the killing had been planned—a way to frighten off the small military role that the US government was contemplating. Given the local yearning for any kind of American involvement, any form of American salvation, the likelihood seemed especially slim. He figured this was simply a burglary gone bad. But the fact that it had happened at the Mamba Point, with its expatriate guests and UN sentries nearby, made it a glaring sign of the country's lawlessness, the type of sign that helps to scare away outside aid and investment, and to ensure that a lost nation like Liberia, a country that is among the most destitute on the planet, remains a kind of netherworld.

In his deep, faintly gravelly voice, a voice I never heard him raise, Kroeker managed the crime scene. He tried to do this as a mentor, without offending Liberian pride, without seizing sole authority. He suggested to Flomo that he choose just two detectives to enter the room, that he order the rest of the milling Liberian officers to leave. He phoned his counterpart, the chief of the Liberian National Police, who was on his way. 'Director Massaquoi,' Kroeker said, 'I want you to know that things are moving along here. Colonel Flomo is in charge.' But while the colonel, the head of all LNP detectives, had been definite about the killer's tools, he didn't seem so expert about supervising the handling of evidence, including the body.

'He's talking about disposing of the remains,' Kroeker said quietly to one of his UN team, 'and he hasn't started processing the crime scene.' Where the wounds were and what the weapon had been were still unknown, because the dead man had been found, for some reason, with a bunched floral blanket covering much of his torso. 'He's going to need some help here,' Kroeker muttered.

A UN forensics specialist, a young Filipino with a brush cut, was called in. Was there any fingerprint powder? he asked. Any way to process blood? Any baggies for collecting evidence?

There wasn't. The LNP had no forensics equipment. The UN's vast bureaucracy hadn't provided Kroeker with any, either. And he didn't have the money to purchase anything for the Liberians. Twenty million dollars had been pledged (about half of it by the United States); none had yet materialized. 'We will improvise,' the forensics officer said. He asked the hotel manager for some plain white paper, and led the two Liberian detectives in folding small pouches to hold bits of evidence. He was meticulous in the folding, like a grandfather making a newspaper hat. He was painstaking, too, in teaching the detectives how to sketch the scene and how to label a pouch after they'd found a strand of hair on the bed and how exactly to navigate their way through the room toward the body which, it turned out, had been stabbed through the middle of the chest.

'Reception is right there,' the squat, frazzled manager said to Kroeker at the end of the hall, pointing down the one flight of stairs to the front desk, which was manned every night. 'But no one heard anything. Too much noise. Too much rain.'

The first scattered downpours of the rainy season had arrived, building toward the diluvial months that keep the country lush, with vines in lavender bloom climbing over checkpoint sandbags. Last night the rain had beat so hard against the metal roof above my room it had almost drowned out the thunder.

Now, at nightfall, Kroeker convened a case meeting in a dim conference room next to the hotel's empty bar. The Mamba Point's guests, aid administrators as well as marines, were starting to check out. The bar's stereo blared 'Strawberry Fields'. An LNP detective told Kroeker and Massaquoi, a handsome, dignified man in a uniform of deep blue and a cap adorned in gold brocade, that a suspect had emerged. That morning, someone in the neighbourhood had noticed a well-known criminal named Emmanuel Mulbah carrying a grey bag; the details matched a rucksack that had been taken from the woman's room. Mulbah was already suspected of cutting through the roofs of nearby homes, including the apartment of a UN policeman. (Apartments rented by UN officers, who were plainly among the best paid people in the city, were being burglarized, one way or another, at a rate of close to one each week.) Kroeker praised the fast police work and suggested that the Liberians start an immediate search for Mulbah, who went by the nicknames Boye and Uncle Sam. It was a basic suggestion, but there was a basic problem: transportation. The detectives hoped to move discreetly, so Boye's associates wouldn't warn him off. The UN's shiny red and white SUVs were too conspicuous, and the entire Liberian police force had three vehicles— white pickup trucks recognized by all Monrovians from the years when the police used them to raid neighbourhoods, conscripting fresh government soldiers at gunpoint and loading them in. Across the conference table, Kroeker asked the hotel's manager if he would pay for a taxi or two for the night.

'Anything,' the manager said.

So the manhunt began.

At a Christian university just outside Los Angeles, Kroeker had once been a music major, playing trumpet and dreaming of composing choral and classical music. He'd flunked out, and soon turned to police work, joining the LA force in 1965. A month into his career, he found himself taking cover behind a fire truck, with guns raging and buildings burning during the Watts riots. He made his way up through the ranks in LA and eventually, as deputy chief, he was put in charge of instilling community faith in the police after officers beat a speeding African-American driver, Rodney King, in 1991, and after the acquittal of the cops sparked riots that left neighbourhoods in cinders and more than fifty dead.

Along the way, Kroeker had become more of a student; he'd earned an undergraduate degree in criminal justice and, inspired by his international childhood as a missionary's son, a masters in international public administration, though he had no coherent idea how he might use his advanced degree. Then, in 1994, a chance meeting at a law enforcement dinner led to his going several times to Haiti for the US Department of Justice, to help design a programme of police reform. The department later sent him on an assessment trip to Rwanda, where he met a Tutsi major who had lost his children, wife, and parents in the genocide. The man was now guarding *génocidaires* in jail. With me, Kroeker recalled the man's stoicism, his restraint—and Kroeker remembered the man's words: 'The only thing that I have, and the only thing I intend to hang on to, is the law.' That, Kroeker told me with veneration, 'is the ultimate rule-of-law story.' He served for a year as a deputy commissioner with the UN police in Bosnia, in 1997, trying to integrate law enforcement units among Bosnians, Croats and Serbs, and trying to limit their human rights abuses. Then, after four years as chief in Portland, he signed back on with the UN in Liberia.

But when he talked about his work in Liberia, he was less likely to refer to his long professional past than to quote from the poets—Shakespeare, Hugo, Wordsworth, Housman—whose lines he memorized and often recited to himself. 'It helps me to sort some things out,' he said. In literature he was self-taught. The funeral scene in the movie of *Out of Africa* had led him to Housman; a wounded officer, reading poetry in his hospital bed, had steered him, years ago in LA, to Wordsworth's 'Character of the Happy Warrior':

> Whence, in a state where men are tempted still
> To evil for a guard against worse ill...
> He labours good on good to fix, and owes
> To virtue every triumph that he knows...
> And, through the heat of conflict, keeps the law
> In calmness made, and sees what he foresaw;
> Or if an unexpected call succeed,
> Come when it will, is equal to the need...

His pronouncement of these lines to me—and he quoted them more than once in his narrow office in the grounds of the UN's compound—might have seemed a terrible burst of self-congratulation, a nomination of himself as the poet's ideal. Yet his voice was so filled with enthusiasm, with open awe, for the words themselves, that he seemed to rely on them for inspiration. They seemed to buoy him above despair.

In 2004, the UN had 15,000 peacekeeping soldiers spread throughout Liberia. The civil war had killed perhaps 200,000 people, while displacing more than half of Liberia's three million population between 1989 and 2003. Many of the deaths were indirect, with starvation and disease soaring as the war kept people from planting crops or getting medical care. But plenty of the killing was immediate, and most of the victims were civilians. 'The factions,' a US State Department report declared in 1997, during an interlude when peace seemed to be taking hold, 'committed summary executions, torture, individual and gang rapes, mutilations, and cannibalism. They burned people alive; looted and burned cities and villages; used excessive force; engaged in arbitrary detentions and impressments, particularly of children under the age of eighteen...' The factions had only the vaguest pretence of political ideology. Partly they were built around tribal loyalty, but mainly on personal greed. Conscripted boys as young as eight or nine, stoked on alcohol and narcotics, and regarding their commanders as fathers, took part in the fighting and atrocities. Liberian society was ravaged by the conflagration.

Liberia was founded—as a settlement on the coast of West Africa in 1822 and as the continent's first independent republic in 1847—by freed slaves shipped back to Africa from the United States. They were sent by an organization of white Americans (Henry Clay, Francis Scott Key and Daniel Webster among them) that aimed both to reverse the cruel uprooting of the past and to reduce the number of free blacks who might stir trouble for slaveholders. The African-American settlers named their capital after the US President, James Monroe. They established a senate and a house of representatives, designed a red, white and blue flag, and proceeded to subjugate the indigenous people who came under their rule, denying them the vote, bounding them within tribal homelands, and putting down their rebellions. This gradually eroding hierarchy lasted until 1980, when an army sergeant of indigenous descent, Samuel Doe, led a small squad of soldiers over the iron gate of the executive mansion. They disembowelled the president, and Doe declared a coup. He executed thirteen of his predecessor's ministers and family before a crowd of thousands on the beach. He nurtured a Cold War alliance with the United States (the country most Liberians, descendants of freed slaves and indigenous alike, view with reverence as a fatherland). He announced that only God could tell when his term in office would end.

In 1990, a rebel commander, Prince Yeduo Johnson, killed him. First, the commander supervised as a string of fetishes was torn from Doe's waist and both ears were sliced from his head. Johnson drank beers and made sure that the event was videotaped.

National anarchy came next, followed by the rule of Charles Taylor. A former government official who had escaped from a Massachusetts prison (where he was being held for extradition, on charges of embezzling from the Liberian treasury), Taylor had returned home to lead an insurgent army specializing in SBUs—Small Boy Units. Taylor was eventually forced into exile by a rebel invasion of Monrovia in the summer of 2003, and the UN, at the time of my visit a year later, was trying to sustain a transitional power-sharing government. Under a UN-sponsored accord, rebel leaders and remnants of Taylor's regime had divided the ministries between themselves. This seemed to be less transitional governance than division of spoils, shares in corruption. Meanwhile the UN, with more peacekeeping troops on the ground in Liberia than in any other country in the world, was planning for national elections in October of 2005; it was aiming to anoint a viable nation. Prince Yeduo Johnson had recently announced his candidacy for senate. 'If Liberia is going to have a chance in hell of surviving,' Corinne Dufka, a West Africa expert at Human Rights Watch, had told me before I travelled there, 'It's going to be because of the rule of law component in the UN mission.' The component was meant to draw the culture away from ingrained fatalism, from the presumption of chaos and the pull of self-destruction.

Kroeker took strength from Wordsworth's spirited lines. But he quoted, too, from the American poet John Bennett:

> The sea of care will surge in vain
> Upon a careless shore

It wasn't that he thought the Liberian people didn't care, didn't long for change, not at all. It was only that he couldn't help wondering if he would be able to accomplish much of anything in this place. 'Futility,' he whispered to me in his office. 'It's right there at the edge, always.'

One morning, a few days before the Mamba Point killing, I rode out to a police station at the northern edge of the city with Josaia Rasiga, a Fijian working under Kroeker. We headed away from the bombed-out hulls of the bank and ministry buildings downtown, away from the displaced civilians and former soldiers, newly if incompletely disarmed by the UN, who lived by the thousands in the skeletal remains. The red and white SUV dropped us off on a road of shacks. The station, a cement block about fifteen feet square, had been stripped almost bare during the war, though it was hard to know exactly how different it had been beforehand. It was missing portions of its roof. It was only slightly more decrepit than the other stations I visited. All of them grew lightless at sundown. The city had no public electricity, just as it had no running water.

But there was a glimmer of purpose at the outpost where Rasiga had just begun advising. Rasiga had bought a book of lined paper, so the Liberian officers could record any arrests they made. By the week's end he would pay, from his salary, for the roof to be fixed. He would mount a battery-powered clock on the wall, and encourage the men to note the time of any activity on the new lined pages, which were already starting to disintegrate in the damp. And this morning he was trying to figure out how to move forward with the case of Teta Jamal, a nineteen-year-old girl who said that three neighbourhood boys had attacked her, taking turns holding her down and raping her, when she'd gone to use the bathroom—a thicket of palms, vines, and ferns—behind the beach.

One of the suspected rapists had been arrested, then taken by LNP officers from Rasiga's station to a larger one equipped with a holding cell. The arrest was somewhat extraordinary, given that Teta hadn't paid the police to make it. At the larger station, with a Liberian lieutenant arbitrating, Teta and the suspect had reached a settlement. He paid her about two dollars and was set free. Rasiga, learning this the next day, was stunned. 'In Fiji, a rape is a rape,' he said. He had a delicate voice; his outrage came quietly. 'There would be a full investigation. The file would fill pages and pages. There would be nothing like this arrangement.' The settlement had been reached five days ago; since then Rasiga had tracked down Teta and sent her off in a taxi to get a medical exam at a public hospital downtown. He wanted a doctor's evidence. He wanted to reopen the case. He had a witness: a friend of Teta's had been with her on the beach and wound up chasing the boys off. But this morning Teta had returned to the station, without any exam. The problem, it seemed, was that the doctor at the public hospital had wanted a private payment for his services, so now Rasiga sent her off again with a few dollars for the physician's bribe.

It wasn't that he didn't have his doubts. The suspect who'd been arrested had told the police that Teta was a prostitute, that he'd come upon her having sex with a UN soldier, that the soldier had run off, and that she had accused him only because he'd cost her the price of a trick. And Teta, who favoured a glossy crimson shirt that draped low off one shoulder and revealed a good deal of breast, and who lived alone in a surfside shanty, next door to several other single girls and down the road from a UN garrison, did fit the part. I had my doubts, too. But the suspect had also told the police a different, conflicting story, and Teta insisted that she was merely a secondary school student. She had the blue school dress and the recent tests to prove it, with fill-in-the-blank spelling problems like 'h_mbu_ger' and 'b_ _kb_g'. She was proud, when I visited her, to show off a mark of ninety-five per cent, and, giggling behind a bright smile, she quickly snatched away a math test with a score of fifty. With the two dollars, she told me, she'd been able to afford medicine in case the rapists had carried disease. 'For infection, to shove in me,' she said, showing me the tablets she'd bought. One possibility, as the station's chief detective pointed out, was that she was both a prostitute, or someone's paid mistress, and a student, that she sold sex to pay her school fees. 'I think she is frustrated,' he said. 'She is ambitious, she wants to learn, so she is looking for someone to cater.' He could well have been right; the aid organization Save the Children later published a study: sixty to eighty per cent of secondary-school girls in the country were selling sex as a way to finance their education.

But it didn't settle the question of whether Teta had been raped. The question wasn't going to be settled. The chief detective wasn't much driven to answer it. He went to the crime scene once, briefly— mostly, it appeared, because Rasiga encouraged it and because I paid for a taxi that took the detective and me the two miles from the station. Teta led us into the jungly patch behind the beach, where she said the assault had happened. The detective, a mild-mannered, almost frail man of fifty-seven, a police veteran of thirty-eight years, a husband and father whose family had lived for years in a refugee camp in the Ivory Coast, asked her only, 'So where you all did the fucking?'

Too much time had passed for the medical exam to be conclusive. It came back negative: it showed no evidence of violent intercourse. Rasiga seemed to give up, to give in, for the moment, to the place whose realities he was starting to understand. If Teta had been raped, justice, for her, would have to be two dollars.

'Is anybody above the law?' Kroeker stood at the head of the classroom, in front of twenty or twenty-five graduating trainees. The police academy had been looted during the war; most of the rooms held nothing within their chipped concrete walls. This one was equipped with ancient school chairs.

'No, Sah!' the graduates called out in unison.

Kroeker gestured with his hands, encircling the room. There was his tall, sturdy body, fit from daily running, and there were the bird-like features, at once comical and handsome. And beneath the physical there was the deep, steady voice. 'The law is above all of us. We don't enforce our opinions. We don't enforce our emotions. We don't enforce the will of politicians. We enforce the law.... Our number one value is what?'

'Compassion!' They sat straight. They had mustered up dress shirts and ties. One wore a tuxedo.

'Number two?'

'Courage!... Respect!... Integrity!' they gave the series of answers.

'Yes. Yes,' he said, his style as much soothing as declamatory, as though he were coaxing, rather than commanding, the graduates to heed him. 'If you don't have integrity, you wander in an ocean, lost, not knowing what to do. You sacrifice your ideals for a few dollars on the street... Number five?'

'Excellence!'

'Number six?'

'Service!'

'Yes. Yes. Every day for a policeman begins with compassion and ends with service.' The graduates were police veterans, many of ten or fifteen years. Until now, few had received any formal training. It had been a long time since the government had run an academy class—no one I asked, including Massaquoi, could say exactly how long. In the ragged field outside the academy's entrance, a bust of the late Joseph Tate, commander in his cousin Charles Taylor's rebel army, and then director of police during Taylor's regime, stood resplendent, its gold patina still mostly intact. Until his death in a plane crash, Tate had presided over a department that drew heavily from Taylor's army. The police had been better known for torturing political detainees and mugging vendors in the markets than for enforcing any written laws.

The applause when Kroeker had finished speaking echoed and swelled in the stark room. The trainees were called up, one by one, to shake his hand and receive a new identity card. It seemed they wanted ardently to show their good intentions. They executed meticulous heel turns in the aisle, marched up to the commissioner, and gave salutes so rigid their fingers bent backward. He smiled, big-toothed, beaming, and returned their salutes. Then everyone went out to the academy's front steps and gathered close around Kroeker for a photograph, opposite Tate's statue.

In the months since he'd arrived, Kroeker's work had involved guiding the LNP leadership, overseeing the outreach at the stations, and running two-week interim programmes like the one the graduates had just completed. Soon full training of officers would begin: three months at the academy with UN instructors, followed by six months of UN supervision on the job, then another month back in the classroom. Some 3,500 officers would pass through. The force would be rebuilt almost from scratch. Current policemen would have to apply alongside new candidates. Applicants would be vetted for human rights abuses. A high-school diploma and proof of literacy—in a country where less than half of all adults could read—would be required. At the academy, all instruction, all teaching of technique, would be interlaced with lessons on sensitivity and ethics and honour—lessons that would be part of every course, Kroeker stressed one evening as we talked in his two-room apartment. The apartment was in a gated riverside community of expatriates, an enclave of luxury by local standards: the walls were smooth, the whitewash on the cement was fresh, a UN soldier guarded the gate. 'Most police academies in the US are learning that if you have a tactician to teach tactics and you have a community policing person to teach community and a gender awareness person to teach gender awareness, then the cops are all going to listen to the tactician because they relate to it. You know, smoking guns, swinging from ropes, all that stuff.... But then this other person goes in and they tune out. So you have to integrate the training....

'The core values,' he said—compassion, integrity, service—'will be hammered in, hammered and hammered and hammered, because I'm the boss.' He laughed to undercut the word 'boss'. 'And that's what will breathe a whole new air into the thing. I think it can be done. You either believe that or you go home. And I believe that, so that's what I'm working on. So I'm here. I think it's doable.... Sometimes I'm a little bit too optimistic. But I'd rather be a little bit too much that way than the other way.'

'We will follow you people. We will follow in your footprint,' a young man told me outside a station, after turning in his application for the academy. And in the interim programme I watched the trainees laugh raucously, appreciatively, during an interrogation class, as an African-American sergeant from Detroit played a cocky armed robber, slinging insults, while a student tried desperately to get a confession. Eagerly the students learned to protect themselves during a session on riot control. Then, in a legal issues class, a trainee raised her hand, saying, 'But excuse me, Sir,' and asked a question that spoke of the distance between the country Kroeker came from and the one he'd come to. The student, a middle-aged policewoman, didn't seem able to accept that a thief shouldn't be beaten, whether by the community or the police wasn't clear by her wording. The correct handling of a thief, the Liberian lawyer teaching the course reviewed, was 'not to flog him or put the tyre around his neck'. ('Flog' is the term Liberians use for all types of beating. A tyre is used in 'necklacing': the hands of an alleged 'rogue' bound behind his back, a tyre set around his shoulders, kerosene poured on the rubber, the fuel set aflame, the accused burned to death.)

'Don't you worry that—' I started to ask Kroeker once.

'Yes,' he said before I'd finished. It didn't matter what my question was going to be; he worried about it all. He worried about the vetting, about how to weed out the applicants with the worst histories of abuse before they made it into the new force. He planned to go over candidate lists with human-rights groups, but this could catch only a fraction of the problem, especially since a good number of police had previously been soldiers. He was haunted by a Human Rights Quarterly report on how commonly and brutally Liberia's soldiers had raped—the figure was that more than ten per cent of fighters had raped at least ten times. Recalling his command of the Hillside Strangler investigation, a case of serial rape and murder in LA, he was sometimes seized by the thought, 'Am I going to be putting Hillside Stranglers in police uniforms?'

He worried, too, about issuing handguns at the end of the full academy training, though he knew he couldn't leave the police without firearms, as they were now under the UN's disarmament programme. Their lack of guns lessened the chance that they would do anything to stop a crime or arrest a suspect or even carry out a patrol. Yet in giving them pistols, he asked, 'Am I creating the perfect shakedown department?'

And he worried that corruption so permeated every level and every part of the legal system that his imbuing of core values would mean nothing. We stared, one afternoon, at a giant cube of cocaine wrapped in white plastic and sitting on a table in the three-storey wreck of the LNP headquarters. A UN and Liberian team had just made the bust. Kroeker guessed it was worth several million dollars. 'If we weren't here,' he said, as we walked away down the dark stairwell, 'this would all be taken care of for a few hundred dollars.' The country's chief prosecutor was already working to release one of the two suspected traffickers. Soon both would disappear. There seemed to be no keeping things under control. 'Liberia's most significant drug arrest in many years,' Kroeker sighed a few weeks later, 'has vanished into thin air. In the US, a place largely law-abiding, you target a corrupt official, you run a sting, you go to the US attorney, he's eager to make the case. Here, you'll have to dismantle the entire system.'

But he worried, almost above all, that he and the UN would lose credibility with the Liberian police if he didn't supply something tangible—quickly—to go with the advising and training. 'I need some stuff now. I need some real things to give them. I need some real police station building, I need some real uniforms, I need a crime lab, I need some cars for them and fuel.... "You're going to come here and consult,"' he summarized the potential for LNP resentment, "'and you go home to your nice house and you make plenty of money and you can't give us anything? What's wrong with you guys?"'

Massaquoi, talking with Kroeker and his senior staff, with the LNP building seeming ready to collapse around them, asked how he could run a department with only three vehicles that might soon, he added, be repossessed. And how long would the UN guarantee that his officers got their meagre pay? I laughed with Kroeker about it later: the repo man was coming after the LNP! Kroeker's laughter was thin, brief. Even assuming that the twenty million dollars that had been pledged actually appeared, it probably wouldn't be enough. He couldn't help thinking about how much US nation-building money was evaporating in Iraq. He couldn't help thinking about what even a fraction of those dollars might accomplish here, where the culture was so much more receptive and the recent history of civilian anguish was, as he saw it, so much more severe. 'If you establish a criterion of human suffering,' he said, 'there's no comparison.' He tried not to dwell on Iraq, tried to scramble for what he could here. He was lobbying the Chinese embassy to supplement LNP pay with bags of rice at reduced cost.

Kroeker and Massaquoi were in agreement about the LNP's needs, partly. The Liberian director asked me, 'How do we get to the rule of law?' and answered himself, 'logistics... salaries... resources.' Yet Kroeker didn't see money as the true means of change. He talked more passionately about inculcating principles, about remaking the soul of the department. The man from the land of indigence dreamed in material terms; the man from the land of wealth dreamed in terms of the spirit.

Listening to Kroeker, I thought not only of him standing at the front of the classroom, giving his call-and-response graduation speech about core values. I thought, too, of him standing at the pulpit on the Sunday I'd gone with him to church.

He'd become a regular congregant at an orphanage. His wife volunteered as an administrator there. Most of the 400 children had lost their parents to the war. Each week, the same toddler climbed into his lap. And each week, after the singing of the orphan's choir and before the preaching of the pastor's sermon, Kroeker was beckoned up to the simple wooden podium to teach a hymn. The church, a long sturdy shed furnished with plain benches, had one adornment: a delicate swirl of cement cut across each square, glassless window, dividing the light into elegant curves. Kroeker sang alone, voice rich and low, before signaling the congregation to join him.

> *Shine!*
> *Shi—ii—ine!*
> *Let the light*
> *From the lighthouse*
> *Shine on me.*

He didn't look uneasy in his pastoral role. He was, in a way, a man who had come home. He had grown up in Africa until he was ten, outside the town of Idiofa in the middle of the Belgian Congo, where his father, a Canadian, had founded a Mennonite mission. From the time his family had left the Congo, in 1954, until his coming to Liberia a half century later, Kroeker had returned to Africa only once, briefly, on the trip when he'd met the Tutsi major guarding the *genocidaires*. But childhood memories shone through his life now: the way his father had polished his black dress-shoes every morning before setting out on the paths, village to village, to spread word of the new Mennonite health clinic, the new Mennonite school, and the Mennonite faith; the taste of the pepper sauce; the spectacular storms of the rainy season.

He saw his work now as linked to his father's. Kroeker no longer called himself a Mennonite. For one thing, he was not a pacifist; for another, he didn't have much interest in theological boundaries. 'I don't belong to any denomination,' he said. 'I'm a believer. My label is my life. We are His possession, and we should carry out His ministry. Serving other people. Doing things that count.' He thought of his policework the way his father had once described it, as his 'mission field'.

On the coffee table squeezed into Kroeker's tiny apartment was a three-inch stack of index cards, each with a biblical quotation to be memorized. '*God is our refuge and strength*,' he told me he would recite to himself from the psalm, when the obstacles in Liberia overwhelmed him. '*Therefore will not we fear, though the earth be removed, and though the mountains be carried into the midst of the sea.*' He paused. 'I mean, that's beautiful literature. And it's very calming. *Take it easy,*' he said, laughing at his own simple exegesis of the passage, 'everything is going to be ooookaaay.'

Then he went on: 'I am personally reaching out to Africa with my life now.... The investors, for the return on their investment, would say it's too risky, it's corrupt, there's a threat of another coup, you could get back to war, so we have an investment dollar, we'll put it somewhere else. But those who invest in terms of a return that is personal fulfilment, using some of your life to help people who really need you—this is the place to be.'

I asked if he ever worried that his work in Liberia, and the work of the UN with its Western imprimatur, was a kind of re-enactment of a nineteenth-century drama, a drama scripted in part by missionaries: the white man, the West, coming to save Africa, to civilize it. I asked if he ever worried about reinforcing an old message of moral superiority and racial hierarchy. Perhaps I was unclear, but he understood my question only the second or third time I rephrased it. The question may have seemed academic. He acknowledged the worry I spoke of, but it was far from the first concern on his mind. He talked about the 'world abandonment' of Africa. He talked about the continent's civil wars, the 'starvation and mutilation and disease', the three million dead in the Congo. 'Africa,' he said, 'is on the verge of the abyss.'

The killing of the American contractor at Mamba Point had happened in the pre-dawn hours of a Monday. By Tuesday morning a teenaged girl was cooperating—a tiny girl, barely five feet tall, in blue jeans and a red T-shirt that said BIGFLIRT—telling Kroeker and Massaquoi and Flomo that she'd been with Boye and his friends on Monday night. They'd been partying, spending plenty of Boye's money. 'They were on good joy last night,' she said. Boye hadn't talked about the robbery or the killing, but she'd seen him with a grey bag like the one that had been stolen.

Above her bangs, Bigflirt had little bow shapes woven into her copper-tinted hair. She wore a small glittery star-shaped pendant at her throat. She might have weighed less than ninety pounds. She sat on the only chair in Flomo's barren office, a half dozen UN and LNP officers standing above her, talking back and forth over the little copper bows, struggling to figure out what to do next. Then she interrupted.

Calmly, she said she could call Boye on his cellphone. She was a close friend of his girlfriend's, she said; he might agree to meet her.

Her motives weren't completely clear. She hoped, it seemed, for LNP leniency on some unrelated traffic accident. It was only clear that Bigflirt wasn't cowed by anyone, not Boye, not the LNP brass, not Kroeker. When Massaquoi suggested that she entice him with the promise of a tip about the police investigation, she gazed back at him blankly and told him no—that would only make Boye suspect that she was with the police. When she reached Boye by phone, and they agreed to meet at a spot called the Star Hotel, Kroeker wanted one of his men, an African-American, to go there right away, undercover, and wait for Boye to reveal himself when the girl arrived. Bluntly, in her raspy voice, she dismissed this, too—Boye might have friends hanging around the hotel, and there was no way any African-American was going to pass for Liberian, not if he had to open his mouth.

On his legal pad, with Flomo and an American captain hunched close, Kroeker started to sketch out plans to make sure Boye wouldn't escape. Two plans were discarded. Time was slipping away; they needed to send the girl. Kroeker diagrammed another. An LNP officer would pose as a taxi driver. Bigflirt would be in the back seat, on the left side. They would turn off the main road and pull over near the Star. Bigflirt would lure Boye into the taxi. He would get in next to her, on the right. The driver would turn back on to the main road and head quickly toward an SUV, parked on the right, filled with members of the rifle-wielding Jordanian protection unit attached to the unarmed UN police. The LNP would be waiting close by. Together they would take Boye into custody.

The American captain had misgivings. 'I don't like it,' he said. 'With the girl in there, we could have a moving hostage situation.'

Boye would have a weapon. The girl would be sitting next to him. He would spot the SUV up ahead; he would know he'd been tricked.

But no one could come up with a better plan. They didn't know exactly where he'd be waiting, watching for her arrival, whether he'd be in the hotel or somewhere nearby; the Star was in a crowded neighbourhood just outside downtown; they wanted her for bait and the taxi for a closed space to entrap him. Bigflirt didn't object. Kroeker drew an arrow on his diagram. The taxi, he instructed, should swerve to the right, grazing the side of the SUV; Boye would be pinned. 'That way he can't open that door and he's got to climb out over her,' Kroeker said. He turned to the girl. 'Keep your door locked.' It was the one time I saw him look straight past the humanity of any Liberian in front of him. 'In the States,' the captain said to me later, 'you'd never put a civilian at risk like that.'

But now everyone was focused on finding a taxi and on whether the LNP lieutenant who would drive it should be armed. One of the LNP produced a corroded handgun. 'Have you had any training?' Kroeker asked the lieutenant.

The man nodded. He took the gun. The clip was in. He checked out the weapon, waving it around in the process, pointing it, at a distance of four feet, at a UN officer. 'No!' Kroeker yelled. 'Hey, hey!' people shouted. 'It's loaded!' The UN officer flinched backward and bumped into a wall, then laughed at his helplessness and the slapstick of the scene.

It was decided that the lieutenant would go unarmed. Someone from the LNP hauled a taxi driver in off the street. 'My man,' Massaquoi told him, 'we got to use your taxi now. We pay you for it. Where the keys?'

The driver was led away. Massaquoi turned to Kroeker. The lieutenant, he said, needed to put some minutes on his cellphone, in case anything went wrong and he had to call in. Massaquoi asked Kroeker for five dollars for a phone card.

The girl left with the lieutenant, and twenty minutes later reports started reaching headquarters. The taxi had broken down just short of the hotel; the operation had collapsed. Seething quietly, Kroeker drove fast to the scene, pulling off the main road at the mouth of an alley, where police and a crowd were milling. Patchwork hovels leaned between the ramshackle Star and a similar establishment called the Think of Yourself Motel. Kroeker began piecing together what had happened. It seemed that the stalled taxi had been only an extra glitch. The driver of a UN vehicle, posted for back-up nearby, had misunderstood the entire plan and rushed in towards the hotel as soon as the taxi appeared—before Bigflirt could make contact with Boye, before anyone had seen him. No one knew where he was. Kroeker had no way to surround the vast neighbourhood of clotted passageways in time to keep him from stealing out. To search every shanty would take days. Then the killer started calling Bigflirt, saying he might surrender tomorrow. Kroeker asked for her phone, warned him of vigilantes, promised him safety, urged him to surrender today. 'You can surrender to me,' he coaxed, 'you'll see me in the white shirt.' Boye hung up. He didn't turn himself in that day or the next or in the days after that. He had escaped. Later there were reports that he had accomplices in the LNP. Three officers were arrested. It seemed possible that one of them had tipped off the killer about the girl. It seemed possible that Boye had never gone to meet her at all, that he had been somewhere else, calling just to keep the police confused, that the law had never had a chance.

A t dawn, in a fishing town just outside Monrovia, the blue canoes are paddled out to sea and, the next morning, glide in over the swells, their lacy yellow nets filled with cassava fish and shrimp and lobster. There the town commissioner, a plump, smiling woman in a white smock dress, told me enthusiastically about her 'vigilante forces', who protected her constituents—and who collected their own salaries from them—patrolling at night 'with cutlasses and sticks and planks'.

The colours were just as brilliant at one of Monrovia's biggest markets where, on another morning, I sidestepped women selling mounds of red peppers from iridescent plastic tubs set on the mud. I walked with Gene Allen, a young policeman from Waterville, Maine, who was part of Kroeker's force. He was telling me what had happened there a week earlier. It looked 'almost like a Roman movie,' he remembered. 'One of the movies you see where the thousands of people just clash, melded together.... Sticks up in the air, coming down *whack whack whack whack*, hitting and attacking.' It was an array of mobs swarming around alleged thieves. Allen and two Jordanians wedged themselves towards the centre of one mob. With poles torn from the stalls, the crowd struck at two teenaged boys who were on the dirt, clothes ripped and bloody. But the vigilantes gave way; Allen stood the boys up. One had been stabbed in the side. Allen put the boys in cuffs, 'to show the crowd that we're not there just to protect them, we're there to prosecute them as well.' He sat them in a gap between a stall and his SUV, guarded by a Fijian partner, while he and the Jordanians ran toward another mob. The young man trapped within it was bleeding from the head. The sight of the Jordanians' rifles cleared some ground, but people darted in to take their last licks. The man staggered and fell; Allen propped him upright. They made it to the SUV, where a throng was yelling that there had been a mistake. One of the two alleged rogues attacked by the first mob was in fact merely a biscuit seller, people said; he should be set free. Allen uncuffed him, after asking the boy if he would now be safe. The crowd erupted in cheers. Then Allen drove the remaining two suspects to the nearest police station, a few minutes away. The man caught by the second mob was dead by the time Allen pulled him from the back seat.

If progress for Kroeker was so difficult in and around the capital, could he succeed upcountry, in villages like the one I visited after feeding Charles Taylor's lioness? Taylor had kept two lions, gifts from the president of Niger, in a private upcountry zoo, but he'd stopped feeding them as rebels had closed in on Monrovia, and the male of the pair had starved to death just after Taylor went into exile. Kroeker had informally adopted the lioness, sending it food and arranging for veterinary care, and one day I drove up with a full flank of beef. The lioness was sickly, its stride permanently crippled by malnourishment. But it retained its underlying grace, like the village nearby, ravaged by war and besieged by poverty but still lovely, with a stream whose banks were so green they looked surreal. There the closest station of the LNP was a half day's journey on foot, the only means of transportation. The police had no relevance at all. A village official showed me the boulder that criminals were made to lie across, so they could be efficiently whipped and beaten.

And what chance did Kroeker have to foster a modern system of law enforcement in the true hinterlands? Just before I left Liberia, I flew with him by helicopter to the town of Zwedru. No matter how reluctant his officers were, he had started to post UN advisors in spots like this, where a day's walk on a jungle path would take you over the border into the Ivory Coast, and where a handful of American policemen were subsisting on rice and sauce and trying to work with the rebel militia that kept its hold on the town. Visiting an outlying village, Kroeker happened upon a recruiting poster for his LNP training; it had found its way into the village chief's mud hut. 'All the way out here'—I can still hear the pleasure of that discovery in his voice.

Daniel Bergner

He is gone from there now. He is based in New York, at the UN's headquarters. He is the new head of all the UN's police missions around the world, from the Congo to Kosovo, from Haiti to Liberia to Sudan. We talk from time to time. Boye, he tells me, is still at large. One of the officers arrested as his accomplice soon bought his own way out of detention, and disappeared. Mob justice may be starting to slow, but it continues in the capital. Director Massaquoi has resigned, accused of stealing an electrical generator worth $20,000 from the government and of ordering a government official flogged. Kroeker tells me that the LNP remains bereft of equipment—and that he is working to spur the UN's donor nations to start a kind of trust fund, so that future police missions can begin with a surge of tangible support to spark morale.

Yet his thoughts of Liberia aren't all despairing. He has talked of nascent changes, small signs, of establishing a foundation of morality. 'This week I feel very good,' he told me once, by phone from Monrovia. He'd just been out to the academy; he'd leaned into a classroom. 'They were talking about the officers' code of ethics, and they weren't just going through the motions,' he said. They were huddled together in the battered school chairs, searching for rules and comparing notes, turning through the photocopied duty manuals and new red plastic notebooks they'd been given. 'They were engaged in that arena, the arena of what does it mean to be a professional police officer.' He sounded as though, in this glimpse of the trainees, he had found a magnificent psalm. □

GRANTA

THE BLACK ALBUMS
Santu Mofokeng

In 1989, the South African photojournalist Santu Mofokeng
began to collect portraits of black people and families taken
between the end of the nineteenth century and the middle of the
twentieth. They presented a view of black South Africans that had
been ignored and suppressed under apartheid.

Santu Mofokeng

As far as I can recall there are no photographs of me as a baby. My first encounter with the camera happened in the early 1960s when I was seven or eight years old. The person behind the camera was an itinerant, journeyman photographer who plied his trade on a Lambretta motor-scooter. He came to our house in Soweto at the behest of my mother, to photograph me and my younger brother one cold morning. She wanted to memorialize the jackets she had sewn for us with bits of leftover material from the garment factory where she worked. She was proud of her handiwork. We were happy for the warmth we got from these coats of many colours, though we regretted they did not carry any store labels. Let me confess that envy is one of the motivations that steered me into the photography business. A few friends and peers at primary school had cameras. I noticed that they were very popular and had no problems approaching girls and chatting them up. They always had loose change jangling in their pockets.

The first camera I ever owned had probably fallen off a truck. I was seventeen years old and in high school. The camera was in a dismal state of disrepair, so I couldn't do anything to make it worse. I paid for it to be repaired with my own money, which I'd earned from a commission on a sale of a complete set of Collins encyclopedias during school vacation in 1973. I only had this camera for two years before my neighbour came to borrow it (in my absence) from my sister. I never saw it again.

In those two years, however, I cherished that camera. It helped me overcome my awkwardness around strangers. I got invited to parties. My social status was enhanced. Everywhere I went strangers would approach me to have their photograph made or simply to talk, all because I was lugging a camera. They asked me whether I could shoot colour or black and white or both, and whether the lens could see in the dark. I was often asked if I could shoot photographs inside a house, or when it was cloudy or windy or raining. Cameras carried a mystical fascination for a lot of people. It was as though the act of looking through the camera transformed and enchanted the landscape or person through the viewfinder.

Cameras in whatever condition were difficult to come by because they were said to be too expensive. They were considered rather complicated. When you did chance upon one it carried with it a kind

Ouma Maria Letsipa and her daughter, Minkie, c.1900s. Maria was born to a family of 'inboekselings' (loosely translated it means forced juvenile apprenticeship in agriculture) in Lindley, Orange River Colony now Orange Free State. They became prosperous farmers at the turn of the century. The image belongs to the Ramela family of Orlando East. This information was supplied by Emma Mothibe. Photographer: Scholtz Studio, Lindley, Orange River Colony.

of an invisible warning, like the zig-zag sign one might find on a power station. Ignorance about how they operated gave them an irresistible allure. Cameras were the preserve of specialists; the press, men on 'government business', a few rich families and educated people. This probably explains my artificial social elevation.

Looking back, I am still amazed that a schlemiel like myself made a career of photography. I have always been nervous around machines and part of my paralysis reflects the experience of an impoverished upbringing: 'Leave other people's things be', I'd be told. 'I cannot pay for the damned thing to be fixed.' And later, 'You think this lens was made in Soweto?'

I began to learn the trade as a street-photographer. As a roving portrait photographer you charged a deposit for every exposure you made for a client. You then hoped you had enough business to finish a roll of film, or as many rolls of film as you had in a weekend, so you could come back the next weekend with the finished prints and collect the balance. You had to sell all the exposures you made, including the duds. You could make enemies for life if you didn't return all the exposed prints you'd made of the subject.

Tardiness in returning photographs could cost you your reputation and business, perhaps even a beating. Most township people felt vulnerable and exposed when they gave you permission to take (or make) an image of them. Many felt that their 'shade' (the new anthropology term), *seriti/isithunzi* (in the vernacular), or 'soul' (the older missionary term) was implicated in the process. They feared that their essence could be stolen or their destiny altered by interfering with the resulting image or images: 'Camera-man, why are you taking so many photos of me. What are you going to do with the rest of them?' Often I found myself at pains trying to explain why I have to make many exposures. I imagine that this explains why I still use comparatively very little film on professional assignments.

If all went well, clients paid me the balance due and took their photos. Most of these images found their way into family albums. Photo albums in the townships are cherished repositories of memories. The images in them are similar to the images in albums the world over: weddings, birthday parties, school trips, portraits—special occasions of one sort or another. They are treasuries of family history, visual cues for the telling of stories. They are mostly of happy, smiling people, dressed to party and surrounded by food and drink. The more formal portraits are crafted to promote what might be called a petit-bourgeois or suburban sensibility: everyone and everything must look its best. Sometimes the moment memorialized is the presence of the camera! Going through township photo-albums can sometimes be a tortuous journey. But it is considered impolite to decline an invitation to look through them because it is a kind of induction into a family's history.

In spite of the popularity I gained by having a camera, I still did not consider photography as a career. The reasons were many; the main one being that I was not making a lot of money. 'Hey Santu! On the weekend of ... I/We are celebrating our wedding anniversary/twenty-first birthday/unveiling of a tombstone etc. etc., I/We would like to invite you to be there. Be sure to bring your camera and don't worry about film. I/We will provide the films and am/are going to pay for processing and printing myself/ourselves! You don't have to worry. Come and enjoy yourself, you can bring your girlfriend and some of your friends along!' The real meaning of the invitation was that I was not going to be paid. Pressing the shutter was not considered work.

As soon as I had matriculated, I went to work as a quality-control tester in a pharmaceutical laboratory. It took me four years before I decided to forego a career in pharmacy because of boredom. I took a job in a newspaper darkroom. This career move cost me a fifty-per-cent pay cut in wages. I began as a *donker kamer-assistente*, a dead-end position. Only white people could be apprenticed as photographers.

In South Africa at the time, 'technician' was a status reserved for whites or Coloureds. Occasionally a black person could be employed as a technician in the more progressive foreign companies. But as an *assistente* in a pro-government newspaper, I was a dogsbody to every photographer, freelance journalist or anyone else who was chummy with the department's secretary. In that newspaper there were no black photographers, only Coloured reporters who also made pictures in order to illustrate their stories. Government policy on the colour-bar was followed to the letter.

In the first few months as darkroom assistant I learned more about life in my country than in my twelve years of schooling. For instance, that 'black skin and blood make beautiful contrast'. This from a conversation overheard in the photography department office: 'Come check at this, China! Isn't this beautiful?' says one very famous South African photojournalist to an Indian account's clerk. He is referring to a colour transparency. The tranny depicts a corpse, an ANC cadre, bleeding in death, lying on asphalt near a curb; a casualty in what is now known as the Silverton Siege (Pretoria). 'I don't get it,' responds the clerk. 'I see nothing beautiful in this. This is ghoulish, man!' 'You know fuck all, China! This is a masterpiece. There is nothing as beautiful as black skin and blood! It makes beautiful contrast. There's nothing like it, China!'

Four years I wormed my way as a darkroom man at various newspapers in and around Johannesburg. I also began to do freelance work as a photographer, mainly covering sport and social events. I took the abuses and insults that came with the job.

All this time I was reading whatever books that were available to me in order to learn the photographic theory and technique. When I felt confident enough as a photographer and darkroom-technician, I left newspaper work in order to apprentice as a photographer's assistant in an advertising outfit.

Ironically, in the light of my professed black consciousness, the person who nurtured me as a freelance photographer was a white man, David Goldblatt. For reasons I could not explain, I enjoyed his documentary work above anything anyone else was doing at the time. This education was valuable, though it was short-lived when I lost all my camera equipment in a mugging incident. While I missed the camera and equipment I considered myself lucky to escape with my life. I went back to work as *donker kamer-assistente* in the same newspaper where I had begun. Within a few months I was fired because I was carrying too many books into the workplace.

I joined the Afrapix Collective in 1985. I had no work, no equipment and no resources. Afrapix gave me a home. It provided me with money to buy a camera and film in order to document Soweto and the rising discontent in the townships. Their confidence in me was, in some ways, misplaced seeing that I was less interested in the unrest than in the ordinary life in the townships. Nevertheless,

I became an Afrapix member and contributed to the education programme the group was preparing for unionized workers. A short time later I joined the *New Nation*, an alternative newspaper, as staff photographer. A photojournalistic career in those days was not without hazards, not all of which came from police bullets and batons. I was once nearly 'necklaced' by comrades at a night vigil in Emndeni (Soweto) after being branded an informer simply by asking permission to photograph the proceedings. At another time, while documenting the 1987 mine strike, I fell into the hands of scab workers. But for the insistence of Paul Weinberg, a photographer who refused to leave the mine without me, I would be dead.

A few months after this incident I left photojournalism to concentrate on documentary work. I was unhappy with the propaganda images that reduced life in the townships into one of perpetual struggle, because I felt this representation to be incomplete. So I joined the African Studies Institute (now called IASR), in the Oral History Project, at the University of the Witwatersrand.

This move was frowned upon by a few friends who considered it a sign of lack of commitment. My work at the institute involved documenting worlds that did not usually feature in the images of South Africa so beloved of American and European audiences. Instead it involved rural communities and marginal Coloured communities threatened with resettlement. I also continued with my documentation of township life; a long term project which I had begun as a 'metaphorical biography' in 1982, divided into small, manageable chapters or saleable photo essays. This work was vindicated in the early 1990s when the overseas market, weary of struggle images, began to ask for ordinary pictures of everyday life in the townships. Suddenly my pictures of quotidian African life: of shebeens, street soccer and home life, which had been considered unpublishable in the 1980s now found commercial favour. My credentials as a struggle photographer were restored.

It was not until I had my first solo exhibition that I really began to ponder my role as photographer. The exhibition explored not only the townships, where the focus of the struggles for liberation were well documented, but rural landscapes as well. I had some reservations about the way the show was received by the majority of people in the black communities. I soon realized that a lot of people in the townships could not relate to the realities that resided in my photographs. One comment from a visitor who signed his name as Vusi haunts me: 'Making money with Blacks'.

That simple comment forced me like nothing else ever had to question the value of my work. I began to understand that the messages I was trying to send, however different from others that came before, would always be overshadowed by the perceptions and assumptions about South Africa that viewers bring with them. The other thing that became clear to me as a result of Vusi's comment was that in my pursuit of the art I was not paying enough attention to the narratives and aspirations of the people I was photographing. I had either forgotten, neglected or disregarded my early beginnings. I had simply graduated into being a professional photographer without first thinking about my position. I had not thought about my own responsibility in the continuing, contentious struggle over the representation of my country's history.

I began to enlist the participation of the communities where I worked. Soon after, in another show, I juxtaposed images *of* the township (public/political) with images *in* the township (private/personal). I was looking at those pictures I had been making for the media and contrasting them with those I had been doing as a street-photographer, i.e. images people choose to treasure and pass on to their children. This is how I began to explore the politics of representation. And it was only then that I became aware of urban family portraits that were made at the beginning of this century.

These images are slowly disintegrating in plastic bags, tin boxes, under beds, on top of cupboards and kists in the townships. And because they lie outside the education system, including the museums, galleries and libraries in this country, I found them enigmatic. These solemn images of middle- and working-class black families, crafted according to the styles (in gesture, props and clothing) of Georgian and Victorian portrait painting, portray a class of people who, according to my history lessons, did not exist at the time they were made. My quest for an explanation for this omission made me appreciate the crime of apartheid, 'The struggle of man against power is the struggle of memory against forgetting' (Kundera). And as I examine old family albums, I feel I have come full circle. □

Bishop Jacobus G. Xaba and his family, c.1890s. Bishop Xaba was the presiding Elder of the African Methodist Episcopal Church in Bloemfontein, 1898–1904. The church participated strongly in the events leading to the formation of the South African Native National Congress in 1912. Photographer: Deale, Bloemfontein.

Unidentified, c.1880s. This print was found in a wooden box labelled (in Afrikaans), 'Aan M. V. Jooste van die persooneel van Die Vaderland.' In the box there were sixty-eight images including one of 'Their most Gracious Majesties, Edward VII and Queen Alexandra. In their robes of State.' This box belongs to Moeketsi Msomi, whose grandfather, John Rees Phakane, was a bishop in the A. M. E. Church. Photographer unknown.

Unidentified, c.1900. Found in box as opposite. Photographer unknown.

Elliot Phakane c.1900s. On the back of this photograph is written, 'My brother Elliot Phakane, Bethlehem Location, OFS Stand No. 1161 ...january, fEByaRiE, MaRich, APRiL, may, june, july, auGust. Septembur, octoBer, NovemBer, BecemBer'. It was found in the box owned by Moeketsi Msomi, whose grandfather John Rees Phakane was a bishop in the A. M. E. Church. Photographer unknown.

Cleophas and Martha Moatshe, c.1900s. Cleophas and his wife Martha came from Boshoek, where he was a moderator in the breakaway Anglican church. He died in 1923 from 'drie dae', influenza. This information comes from Moatshe from Mohlakeng, Randfontein. Photographer unknown, Boshoek.

Maliwase Langatshe, Nobusika Sibiya, Nomazinyane Mazibuko and Ntombinjane Makhubu, sisters, from Kwa-Mahamba in Swaziland, c.1900. They settled in the Orange Free State where they worked on farms. Maliwase married Stuurman a 'smous' (hawker) and worked as a washerwoman. My respondent, Mrs Alinah Modibedi, said that she kept the photograph as a memento but she had not thought it was going to cause her 'trouble', alluding to the interview with me. Photographer: Andrews, Harrismith.

Unidentified young men, c.1900s. Photographer unknown.

A. NAPIER, Corner Kerk & Joubert Streets, Johannesburg.

Unidentified, c.1880s. From the wooden box owned by Moeketsi Msomi, whose grandfather, John Rees Phakane, was a bishop in the A. M. E. Church. Photographer: A. Napier, Johannesburg.

Unidentified portrait, c. 1900s. Photographer unknown.

Mmamothupi Motsoatsoe, c.1910. Mmamothupi's family was dispossessed of their land in the Orange Free State by the 1913 Land Act. They moved to Ventersdorp, in the Transvaal. She worked as a domestic servant and was notorious for being a 'cheeky and proud maid'. This information from her daughters Sekeke and Evah Motsoatsoe of Orlando East. Photographer unknown, Potchefstroom.

GRANTA

WE LOVE CHINA
Lindsey Hilsum

The Bintumani Hotel, Freetown

I arrived in Sierra Leone in June 2005, at the height of the rainy season. Mud washed down the pot-holed streets of the capital, Freetown, and knots of beggars, some without arms or legs, huddled under trees and against battered shop-fronts. It was a fortnight before the G8 summit in Gleneagles, Scotland, where Bob Geldof and Bono were to celebrate a huge increase in aid to Africa, but in the Bintumani Hotel no-one spoke of this. Gusts of rain-filled wind blew through the hotel's porch to set the large red lanterns swinging. Cardboard cut-outs of Chinese children in traditional dress had been stuck on the windows. The management had just celebrated Chinese New Year.

It was my first visit to Sierra Leone in more than twenty years' reporting from Africa, and I was to make a film not about the normal issues covered by British television—orphans, war victims, corruption—but about something few outside Africa seemed to have noticed: the rapidly growing influence of China in the continent.

The hotel's manager, Yang Zhou, was pleased to show me round, helped by his spiky-haired young translator who introduced himself as Maxwell. While Chinese businessmen stick to their real names, Chinese translators in Sierra Leone give themselves English names to ease communication with Africans and visiting Europeans.

The Beijing Urban Construction Group, which is owned by the Chinese government, started to rebuild the Bintumani Hotel even before Sierra Leone's civil war ended in 2002. The wall opposite the manager's office had been decorated with glossy photographs of China's economic progress: one showed the Three Gorges Dam, another a group of pretty young Chinese women throwing their mortar boards in the air to celebrate graduation. The captions were in Chinese and English, as was the sign for the toilet which featured a girl with pig-tails sticking out horizontally from her head and the word LADIE's. The clocks above reception gave the time in Beijing, Freetown, London, Paris and New York. London was out by an hour.

'Africa is a good environment for Chinese investment, because it's not too competitive,' Yang Zhou said as he ushered me into the Presidential Suite, the hotel's best room. Shower: made in China. TV: made in China. Kettle: made in China. The doors to the rooms were designed *for* the Chinese as well as *by* them—the six-foot-four Danish cameraman with me had to stoop to get inside.

Lindsey Hilsum

Sierra Leone epitomizes the British Prime Minister Tony Blair's vision of Africa as a 'scar on the conscience of the world'. By most calculations it is the poorest country on earth, with seventy per cent of the population living in poverty. UN troops keep the peace, after a brutal conflict over power and resources in which child soldiers amputated people's arms and legs with machetes, and rape was widespread. Sierra Leone, a former British colony, is one of the largest recipients of British aid, but the benefit is hard to see. Few homes have electricity or running water, and sixty per cent of young men are unemployed.

Most European companies abandoned Sierra Leone long ago, but where Africa's traditional business partners see only difficulty, the Chinese see opportunity. They are the new pioneers in Africa, and— seemingly unnoticed by aid planners and foreign ministries in Europe— they are changing the face of the continent. Forty years ago, Chinese interests in Africa were ideological. They built the TanZam railway as a way of linking Tanzania to Zambia while bypassing apartheid South Africa. Black and white footage shows Chinese workers in wide-brimmed straw hats laying sleepers, and a youthful President Kenneth Kaunda of Zambia waving his white handkerchief as he mounted the first train. As an emblem of solidarity, China built stadiums for football matches and political rallies in most African countries which declared themselves socialist. In the 1980s and 1990s, the Middle Kingdom withdrew to concentrate on its own development, but in 2000 the first China–Africa Forum, held in Beijing, signalled renewed interest in Africa. Now, the Chinese are the most voracious capitalists on the continent and trade between China and Africa is doubling every year.

On the outskirts of Freetown, on the site of an abandoned centre for disabled refugees, the privately owned Chinese company, Henan Guoji, has created the Guoji Industrial Entry Zone, a small complex of workshops and factories. In the city centre, a new multi-storey government office-block, military headquarters, and refurbished stadium are all the work of the Chinese. The British say future aid will depend on Sierra Leone's progress towards democracy. China, which follows a policy of 'non-interference' in African politics, and is scarcely in a position to tell any other country to be democratic, has nonetheless built the modernistic, brown bunker tucked into a hillside which serves as the country's new parliament.

Xu Min Zheng (translator: Lucy), the Henan Guoji representative in Freetown, told me that his company was following the Chinese government's injunction to 'Go Global'. The first part of the twenty-first century is dubbed 'the period of strategic opportunity'. Chinese companies are preparing themselves to become multinationals, and Africa is their proving ground. 'The Chinese are very diligent,' said Mr Zheng, who wore a jacket and tie despite the humidity. 'We are good at learning, and our equipment and raw materials are cheap.' Many companies bring even their labour force from China. Africans watch in surprise as buildings are erected in weeks. ('The Chinese don't seem to rest,' Sierra Leone's Information Minister told me. 'We could learn from that.') Managers and translators live in barracks-style accommodation. No spouses, no children, none of the comfort and expense Western expatriates demand.

'I never thought my life would be so exciting,' Lucy the translator said. 'My mother wants me to go back to Beijing and get a boyfriend and have a child, but I want to be here for a few years. Then maybe I'll get to go somewhere else in Africa or even to Britain. With a company like Henan Guoji, if you speak English, you can go anywhere.'

When I first went to Africa in the early 1980s, it was rare to see a Chinese face, other than in embassies or Chinese restaurants. Now, the Chinese are everywhere—building the new State House in Uganda, starting joint businesses in South Africa and, most significantly, establishing themselves in countries with natural resources. Chinese companies are involved in mining, timber, fishing and precious stones. Above all, they are involved in oil.

Second only to the United States in its oil consumption, China needs Africa's resources to fuel its own phenomenal growth. In oil-rich countries like Angola, Chad, Nigeria and Sudan, the influence of former colonial powers is waning. The Chinese government imposes no political conditions on African governments before signing contracts for exploration or production. No Chinese pressure groups lobby Chinese oil companies about 'transparency' or environmental damage. Not surprisingly, African governments welcome these undemanding new investors.

I employed a young Sudanese journalist, Nima Elbagir, to find out how Chinese investment was changing Sudan, 2,500 miles from Sierra Leone on the other side of the continent. She got hold of the Sudanese energy ministry video archive of Chinese activities in the oil sector: earnest seismologists on their knees tapping the dry, brown desert for the latest oil find; the Sudanese President, Omar al-Bashir, and the head of the African division of the Chinese National Petroleum Corporation (CNPC) at a ribbon cutting ceremony for the new oil refinery at Al Jaily, north of Khartoum. She filmed billboards across the capital showing smiling Sudanese and Chinese oil workers in yellow hard hats shaking hands, with the legend—in Chinese, Arabic and English—CNPC: YOUR CLOSE FRIEND AND FAITHFUL PARTNER.

Sixty per cent of Sudan's oil goes to China; twelve per cent of China's oil comes from Sudan. No wonder the Sudanese government is untroubled by the oil sanctions which prevent American investment. 'With the Chinese, we don't feel any interference in our Sudanese traditions or politics or beliefs or behaviours,' Awad al-Jaz, Sudan's energy minister said when Nima interviewed him on camera in Khartoum. He smiled as if trying to suppress a laugh. 'Business is business. There is no other business but the business.'

In 2004, when Britain and the US pushed for a punitive UN Security Council resolution against Sudan for the mass killing of civilians in Darfur, China threatened a veto. The weaker resolution which passed with Chinese approval had little impact. Chinese companies have built three small-arms factories near Khartoum; most of the weapons used by government forces and militia in Darfur are manufactured there or in China.

Human rights workers have a new problem here. As their economic interest in Africa has declined, Europe and America have gone along with calls for 'good governance' and an end to human rights abuse in Africa. It is easy to moralize at regimes which you have no reason to cultivate. But such regimes will not cow to this new moralizing if China is offering practical support without conditions. In May 2005, President Robert Mugabe—regarded as a pariah by Europe and the United States—told the crowd celebrating twenty-five years of Zimbabwe's independence: 'We have turned east, where the sun rises, and given our back to the west, where the sun sets.'

When white farmers dominated commercial agriculture, Zimbabwe used to sell tobacco at international auction. Now the auction houses in Harare are silent—tobacco goes directly to China's 300 million smokers, as payment in kind for loans and investment from Chinese banks to Zimbabwe's bankrupt state-run companies. As Zimbabwe's agricultural sector collapses, the Chinese are taking over land the Zimbabwean government confiscated from white farmers, and cultivating the crops they need. On a recent visit to Beijing, President Mugabe—who was armed by the Chinese during the bush war against Ian Smith's Rhodesian forces—was given an honorary professorship at the Foreign Affairs University for his 'remarkable contribution in the work of diplomacy and international relations'. The same week, a UN report condemned his government for demolishing 700,000 homes and businesses 'with indifference to human suffering'.

In Freetown last June, rainstorms made the electricity cut out even more frequently than usual. The hi-tech console controlling the lights and TV in each room at the Bintumani bleeped in the night, as the power surged and faded. The new casino, a joint venture by a Chinese man called Henry and an Irishman called Derek with collar-length hair and a 1970s wide-lapel suit, was not busy. Chinese businessmen spun the roulette wheel, while a few glum Lebanese played slot machines, gambling with money they may soon lose anyway, as the Chinese break their traditional monopoly on trade in West Africa.

Sierra Leone's ambassador to Beijing, Sahr Johnny, was hosting a Chinese delegation planning investments in hydroelectric power and agriculture. 'The Chinese are doing more than the G8 to make poverty history,' he said. 'If a G8 country had wanted to rebuild the stadium, we'd still be holding meetings! The Chinese just come and do it. They don't hold meetings about environmental impact assessment, human rights, bad governance and good governance. I'm not saying it's right, just that Chinese investment is succeeding because they don't set high benchmarks.'

Like most African diplomats, Mr Johnny sent his children abroad to study. The two girls work in Britain, but his son is in Hong Kong, learning Mandarin and Cantonese.

Africa looks to China and sees success: according to the World Bank, the Chinese have lifted 400 million of their own people out of poverty in the past two decades. All the while, no one forced the

Lindsey Hilsum

Chinese government to have elections or allow its opponents to start newspapers. Many African leaders would love to do to their oppositions what the Chinese did to theirs in Tiananmen Square, but if they want Western aid money, they must abide by Western conditions.

Like most Western journalists and aid workers who have spent time in Africa, I frequently despair at the continent's problems, veering between blaming the aid donors, the African governments, and even at times the people. Western aid hasn't worked, so why was everyone demonstrating near Gleneagles so convinced that sending more would make things better? It cannot be good that African governments persist with human rights abuse, or perpetuate their rule against the desires of their peoples, but poverty remains Africa's greatest problem, and liberal concerns have not helped Africa's poor.

The Chinese come to Africa as equals, with no colonial hangover, no complex relationship of resentment. China wants to buy; Africa has something to sell. If African governments could respond in a way which spread the new wealth—a large if, of course—then China might provide an opportunity for Africa which Europe and America have failed to deliver. ☐

GRANTA

ANTEDILUVIAN
John Biguenet

New Orleans

To the inexperienced, hurricane stories always sound like exaggerations. My grandfather, for example, once told me of a hot afternoon in Waveland, Mississippi, when, drinking Dixie beers on his neighbour's porch, he noticed that the Gulf of Mexico had receded from the beach across the road. The retreating water had exposed nearly a mile of crabs and stranded fish; beachgoers ventured farther and farther out to pluck them from the wet sand for an easy dinner.

The neighbour, Alvin, decided to get his wife, who was repotting plants in a shed behind the house, to come and see the phenomenon. He started down the steps, accompanied by my grandfather.

As they reached the back of the little house, a wave hit the two men behind their knees. A few moments later, they were choking on warm, salty water.

They swam for a stand of pines a block farther inland and held fast to one of the tree trunks. By the time the water found its level, Alvin's house had disappeared, except for the brick piers upon which it had been built. As for Alvin's wife, they never found her body.

My grandfather swore their truth, but as far as I was concerned, the details didn't add up. If this was some hurricane, then where was the rain, the wind? The day I heard the story for the first time, he was already a one-legged old man, sitting across from me behind my father in the skiff the two of them had built and christened the *Squall*. My grandfather defended what he had said, explaining all this had happened back in the Thirties or Forties, before hurricanes had names.

'What's names got to do with it?' I persisted. 'Look to your cork,' my father interrupted, eyeing me into silence. I gave the speckled trout tugging the end of my line another few seconds, then set the hook, and reeled the fish in.

It has taken nearly fifty years, but I'm finally ready to believe my grandfather's story—and all the other impossible anecdotes I grew up hearing of what a hurricane can do to human beings.

In the two weeks after Hurricane Katrina sideswiped New Orleans and ravaged the coastal cities of Louisiana and Mississippi, I drove 2,200 miles, seeking first to escape the storm and then to find temporary refuge when its aftermath left my family homeless. Except in its particulars, our story is no different from that of the million other evacuees who fled the Gulf Coast in the hours before the hurricane, pushing a surge of water thirty feet high, came ashore near the border between Louisiana and Mississippi on Monday morning, August 29, 2005, killing hundreds and devastating everything in its path.

As we joined the mass migration, with all lanes on both sides of every highway away from the coast carrying traffic only north or west, we expected to be gone two days, perhaps three. My wife and son and I had a pair of small suitcases, hurriedly packed at dawn. Beside them in the trunk of my wife's VW Beetle, we slipped in portable computers, a book each (in my case, an unfortunately apt volume by W. G. Sebald I had begun the day before, *The Emigrants*), and the useless paraphernalia one thoughtlessly chooses when given an hour or two to abandon a home.

Thinking we would ride out the storm in the city, as I had every other hurricane from childhood on, we'd spent an hour Saturday afternoon stowing outdoor furniture and loose gardening gear in the garage. All we had left to do the next morning was carry in the shelves of orchids that thrived on our porch in the subtropical climate of New Orleans.

I knew the drill, and I thought I knew what to expect. As a boy in 1965, I had survived Hurricane Betsy at my grandmother's candlelit kitchen table, hunched over a transistor radio, listening as one of my heroes, Sandy Koufax, struck out fourteen Chicago batters in pitching a perfect game for Los Angeles.

My father had had to secure the construction site where he was overseeing the building of 400 houses, so I was left with my mother and younger brother and sister at my grandmother's. I remember wandering through the old shotgun house with a candle in my hand as the rain beat its heavy fists against the roof. The whole city was dark. The radio stations were on generators, fading in and out. My mother was furious with my father for leaving us during the storm. My grandfather had died the year before, making me the oldest male in the house that night. While my mother put my sister and brother to bed, I stood my candle in its tinfoil on the kitchen table and started playing with the transistor radio. All of a sudden, I was picking up a baseball game, the Dodgers against the Cubs. So I passed the evening with my head on my grandmother's table, listening by candlelight to a ball game half a continent away.

Just before dawn, my father shook me awake—I had fallen asleep on a sofa in the living room sometime during the night. Everyone else was sleeping in the back bedrooms. He was dripping wet and exhausted. I asked him what it was like outside. It was nearly over, but earlier it had been rough. After he had dropped us off, he was waiting at a red light with a policeman stopped next to him when the wind gusted and ripped the hood of the police car off, tossing it into a parking lot. Farther on, he was nearly hit by a huge metal mailbox torn loose from a street corner and tumbling down Gentilly Boulevard. I told him my mother was upset, so he decided to sit with me for a while as my grandmother's lace curtains paled with the morning light.

My most vivid memory of the hurricane itself, though, is something that had happened earlier that night. A few hours into the storm, the wind died. The rain pattered to a stop. My divorced aunt, also waiting out Betsy with my grandmother, gingerly stepped on to the porch. She called excitedly for us to join her. We ran out into the street and were amazed to see stars overhead. Down the block, a tree slumped against a crushed automobile. Not a single light was visible in any direction. But above us, the darkness yielded to more stars than I had ever before seen in the city. We stood with my grandmother's neighbours, astonished. Then, the oak trees trembled with a sudden twist of wind. As the curtain of darkness fell again after our brief respite, someone felt a raindrop. Children were hurried back into the houses. 'The eye,' my grandmother whispered to us, 'you've just stood in the eye of a hurricane.' And minutes later, the ferocious, snarling snout of the storm was again rooting at our doors, tamping at our windows, seeking something soft, something rotten, something that might give way.

Later that morning, my father drove us home. During the afternoon, a neighbour reported that water was rising in the eastern part of town. Just to be safe, we dragged our boat out from under the carport where it might get trapped if the water rose too quickly. Then we unbuckled the belts that secured it to the trailer and loosely tethered its bow to the telephone pole beside our house, so it might rise with the water. By evening, the flood lapped at our street. And to our great good fortune, that's where the water happened to stop. It stayed there, though, for over a week, stretching eastward for miles.

John Biguenet

In some places, the situation was desperate. A woman in St Bernard Parish had to stand on a kitchen chair with water up to her throat for two days before the police found her. Even for us, the situation deteriorated rapidly. The city's drinking water was contaminated. We had no power. Much of New Orleans was flooded. The perishables at neighbourhood groceries had spoiled, and the stores could not be replenished.

Finally, after a few days, my father sent me with a neighbour in his pickup truck to the French Quarter to see if we could find milk for the younger children in the neighbourhood. Rolling up to a stop sign halfway there, we saw a dead body in the gutter.

The only human corpses I had ever before seen were in coffins at the funerals I served as an altar boy. Habited in a little black cassock and a starched white surplice, I'd held for the officiating priest a silver bucket of holy water to asperse the dead or a smoking thurible of incense to perfume the remains. But those corpses had been rouged old women in pink chiffon nightgowns and waxen old men in blue suits. The black man in the gutter was starting to bloat. Flies clustered on his swollen lips. His hand swelled above the wrist shackled to the stop sign. A square of cardboard ripped from a carton and pinned to his chest spelled out a simple message: LOOTER. His white T-shirt was stained red at the belly. We pulled away and eventually found the milk we were looking for, though we paid three times what it was worth.

I thought I had seen the worst a hurricane could do to a city. And so, on Saturday, August 27 this year, we spent the morning on our usual weekend chores. At the grocery, we did buy more canned goods than usual, and we stopped off at a hardware store to stock up on fresh batteries for our flashlights. But we weren't overly worried. We'd been through this before, many times. We'd stay put.

Our plans changed late that evening when, working in my study, I heard a desperate voice on the television in the next room, pleading with one of the news anchors covering the approaching storm. The voice sounded exhausted. 'I'm lying in my bed, and I can't sleep. I've been doing this job for over thirty years, and I can't sleep tonight because I'm afraid thousands in your area could die on Monday when this hurricane hits. Tell your people they've got to get out of the way of this storm.'

By now I was standing in front of the television set. A caption on the screen identified the speaker as an official of the National Hurricane Center, phoning from Miami. Even the news anchor seemed shaken by the call.

I sat down and watched the weather forecast that followed. The satellite shot of Katrina's swirling cloud mass filled the eastern Gulf of Mexico. I had seen pictures like that every hurricane season. But the eye wall was gigantic, two or three times larger than usual. Then the meteorologist rotated the computer image of the storm from its cloud tops to what the hurricane looked like from the side: I saw a towering range of ragged purple mountains advancing on the coastline.

It was already after midnight. I got on the phone and called my son, who was out with friends. I told him we might be leaving town after all and to call us at seven o'clock the next morning from his apartment. Then I copied all my writing files on to a CD and slept for a few hours, waking in time to catch the five a.m. National Weather Service bulletin on the storm's progress. The hurricane had turned a bit more northward, on what would be its final course.

I started carrying books and files upstairs. At six, I woke my wife as gently as I could and told her we were leaving. She didn't ask why, simply got up and started gathering what we would need. Fifteen minutes later, she called our son, telling him to drive over as soon as possible with enough clothes for a few days away from home.

On TV, we learned there were no hotel rooms still available anywhere in Louisiana and Mississippi or even as far away as Memphis. We could see that the I-10 heading west out of New Orleans toward Baton Rouge and then Houston was already jammed with traffic. We'd have to find a different route to my brother's house in Dallas.

An hour later, having stacked chairs on tables and lifting what other furniture we could from the floor, we locked the door. Pulling my son's car into the garage, we unloaded his two cats into the backseat of my wife's Beetle, and I, extremely allergic to cats, slipped on a dust mask I would have to wear for the entire drive. We headed for the causeway north across Lake Pontchartrain.

Though the sky was blue, the lake—actually a bay of 600 square miles of salt water leading through another bay to the Gulf of Mexico—was already agitated. Overhead, high clouds scudded out of the east. The news on the radio was beginning to report that the mayor would call for a mandatory evacuation of the city by noon. Miraculously, the traffic leaving the south shore flowed smoothly. We crossed the first twenty miles of the bridge as quickly as we might have on an ordinary Sunday morning, but then, four miles from the north shore and still exposed to the open water of the lake, the traffic stopped. We began to inch forward. It took an hour to drive the final four miles across the bridge, and then another hour to drive the three miles to the entrance to the Interstate that would eventually take us north to Jackson, Mississippi, and from there on to Dallas.

Nearly blind with exhaustion, I pulled up in front of my brother's house just before midnight. A drive of usually eight or nine hours had taken us nearly twice as long.

In Dallas Monday morning, we watched on television as the storm's outer bands lashed New Orleans. The eye would pass to the east of the city. It might be bad, yes, but we knew from experience that the worst of a hurricane is in its north-east quadrant. New Orleans would be spared the brunt of the storm; only the trailing winds to the west of the eye would hit the city. But just after breakfast came news that a loose barge had breached a levee in the Industrial Canal; the Lower Ninth Ward was flooding. My sister-in-law sighed. 'Those poor people, they're going to lose everything.' I reminded everyone that our house, unlike most of New Orleans, was above sea level; in twenty-five years of storms, it had never once flooded.

That afternoon, we learned 200 feet of the 17th Street Canal levee had collapsed, allowing a torrent of water to flood the western half of the city. Then the television reported that a breach in a levee close to my childhood home was inundating another section of town. We had never before seen city levees simply crumble. Our conversation grew subdued as the day wore on, but on Monday night a message on the web site of our neighbourhood association sent us to bed with a great sense of relief. A man had heard from his father, who had refused to evacuate from the street next to ours. The entire neighbourhood was dry.

Only on Tuesday did we begin to understand that our lives were about to change. During the night, water had begun to rise in our neighbourhood. The city's pumps had failed, and a levee system that had received little funding over the past few years had given way to the swollen waters of Lake Pontchartrain. Houses that had survived a category-four hurricane the day before now stood steeping in up to eleven feet of water, our house among them. We watched with the rest of the world as New Orleans became a swamp of fetid water, where on every dry outcropping, stunned survivors begged for help.

As the water sat stagnant for weeks in the bowl-shaped city, the question became for us not when would we go back but would there be anything left to go back to. Mayor Ray Nagin announced, 'It's my take from talking to experts that most of the homes that were flooded, that stayed in the water for a number of weeks, most likely will have to be destroyed. My gut feeling right now is that we'll settle in at 250,000 people over the next three to six months, and then we'll start to ramp up over time to the half million we had before.' The mayor may have been overly optimistic; opinion polls of New Orleans' evacuees suggest that many intend to make their lives elsewhere. President Bush, castigated for his administration's indifference and incompetence in the storm's immediate aftermath, came to the city to declare that there was 'no way to imagine America without New Orleans'. But some people in his party did. Dennis Hastert, Speaker of the House of Representatives, said that it made no sense to spend billions of dollars rebuilding a city on such a naturally hazardous site: 'It looks like a lot of that place could be bulldozed.'

New Orleans has always been a city teetering on disaster, so often the victim of flood, fire, and fever. It was founded as a European settlement in 1718 by Jean Baptiste Le Moyne, *sieur* de Bienville, a minor aristocrat and a governor of French territories in the New World, and named after the regent of France, Philippe II, duc d'Orléans. The first French inhabitants lived on a strip of high ground used as an Indian portage between Lake Pontchartrain and the Mississippi River. Three years later, a Jesuit missionary judged it to be a 'wild and deserted place, at present almost entirely covered with canes and trees'.

My own family arrived soon after. A great aunt, the Mother Superior of an order of nuns, maintained that Biguenets had moved from Besançon in France to Philadelphia in 1752 and arrived in New Orleans in 1760, just before it was ceded to Spain. 'Probably looking for a decent meal,' my father would add, back in the days before Philadelphians began to take their restaurants seriously.

As the port at the mouth of North America's greatest river, the Mississippi, New Orleans flourished, superseding Biloxi as the capital of Louisiana in 1723, just five years after its founding. My ancestors arrived to a bustling town that depended upon the river trade in plantation crops such as indigo, rice, and tobacco, before the invention of the cotton gin in 1793 transformed the Southern economy. They would have survived the Good Friday fire of 1788 that in five hours destroyed more than 850 of the city's 1,000 buildings, leaving most of its 8,000 citizens homeless. (In a telling comparison to Bush's bungling after Katrina, Governor Miró was able to report to the Spanish king that shelter had been found for every single survivor within twenty-four hours of the fire.) By the end of its first century, the city had become the cultural capital of the continent. I would like to think that members of my family were in the audience in 1796 when a New Orleans theatre gave North America its first opera performance, and that they enjoyed some of the more than 400 opera premieres that followed in the next century, a higher number than in any other American city, even New York. Annexed to the United States by the Louisiana Purchase of 1803, the city expanded rapidly in the nineteenth century, reaching a population of nearly 170,000 by the outbreak of the Civil War in 1861.

From its earliest days, racial questions troubled Americans seeking to comprehend the city's diversity. Worrying about its integration into the United States, the American-born merchant Benjamin Morgan wrote from New Orleans in the same year as the Louisiana Purchase, '[U]pon what footing will the free quadroon, mulatto and black people stand; will they be entitled to the rights of citizens or not. They are a numerous class in this city...' (Morgan didn't quantify, but in his book *A Wilderness So Immense: the Louisiana Purchase and the Destiny of America*, Jon Kukla reports that the permanent residents of New Orleans in 1803 included '3,300 French-speaking Creoles, 2,800 slaves, and 1,300 free people of colour'.) Two hundred years have passed since Morgan posed his question, but as a lifelong New Orleanian, I do not think we have yet fully answered him.

The city has retained its ambivalence about race. At least until the hurricane hit, one could still dine there in a former slave exchange, where squatting slaves once waited to be auctioned.

Statues of Confederate heroes such as Robert E. Lee were prominent throughout the city; few whites paused to consider the affront to many of their fellow New Orleanians in honouring rebels who fought to defend slavery. Until a few years ago, an old laundromat I passed most evenings on the way home had on its front window a sign informing customers of a rule no longer enforced: NO COLOREDS ALLOWED (MAIDS IN UNIFORM EXCEPTED).

Yet in discussions about racism, white New Orleanians invariably insisted upon the close personal relationships they maintained with black friends. One of my teachers, for example, told me how his white Uptown family had moved their long-serving black maid into their master bedroom on the ground floor when she became too ill to climb the stairs, while they camped on a floor above for many months until the maid died.

I grew up to such heart-warming tales, smugly offered to refute the calumnies of Northern commentators on Southern racism. As in my teacher's anecdote, the object of a white family's affection was usually one of their household menials or an inferior at their place of business. And never once in my life in New Orleans did I hear an African-American acquaintance echo such a story.

People who wish to think of themselves as fundamentally decent have to find a way to shirk culpability for the sins of their society, either by asserting their own innocence or by isolating the evil outside the reach of their authority. So these stories also hinted at a kind of segregation that persisted in the imagination between two different and mutually exclusive cities that shared the same name. Whatever they might have believed about the feelings between individuals in the New Orleans they inhabited, few whites ever seemed embarrassed that the city's public school system, with ninety-three per cent of its students African-American, was bankrupt and in collapse. (The Louisiana Department of Education ranks forty-seven per cent of New Orleans public schools as 'academically unacceptable' and another 26.5 per cent on 'academic warning', the two lowest classifications.) Nor did they feel responsibility for the city's dilapidated public housing projects or its widespread poverty. (The city's poverty rate of twenty-eight per cent is more than twice the national average.)

Even if, as they would assert, racism was more often institutional than personal in New Orleans, the effects on the victims of that discrimination were certainly no less pernicious, and there can be no question that the division between races hobbled the city throughout much of its history. But racism alone did not set the city apart from other American cities. What made the city exceptional was something else.

I once heard a story in New Orleans about a pianist. Rehearsing for a performance one night at a club, the musician sat alone at the piano, gently but repeatedly striking the same key. Finally, the janitor, cleaning the floor in advance of the crowd, dropped his mop into its bucket and addressed the performer. 'Excuse me,' he said, 'but what exactly are you doing?' The musician raised his eyes, even as he continued to play that same note over and over again. 'Everybody else is just looking for it.' He struck the key again. 'I found it.'

That's the way New Orleanians described their city, indifferent to the reaction of others as they sounded the same note of self-satisfaction again and again. The returning native would always begin his account of 'abroad' (Washington, say) with 'You won't believe what those people up there put in their mouths' or 'You'd have to be deaf in both ears to listen to what they call music up there' or 'You ought to see the way those people up there treat one another'. It wasn't contempt, exactly, that New Orleanians felt for those condemned to live elsewhere; more a profound sense of pity for all those countrymen of theirs who obviously didn't know the first thing about eating and singing and living like a human being.

A national Gallup poll conducted this past summer among the residents of twenty-two urban areas found the highest level of satisfaction in New Orleans; fifty-three per cent of New Orleanians described themselves as extremely satisfied with their personal lives in the city, a figure that is even more surprising when one considers that under thirty per cent of the population is white. How could people beset by so many problems—endemic racism, wretched schools, vulnerability to hurricanes, corrupt government, a rising crime rate, and a stagnant economy—how could they possibly conclude that they were 'extremely satisfied' with their personal lives?

Perhaps they felt that way because in New Orleans, the personal has nearly always taken precedence over the institutional. What might be seen elsewhere as lax standards of official behavior, for example, was seen more indulgently in the city as the bending of unreasonably stringent institutional rules in the good cause of personal need. Every August when I was a child, my mother would dress my sister and brother and me in our worst clothes, and we would take the bus to City Hall to stand in line with other mothers and their children, all looking particularly grubby. Family by family, we would be admitted to the tax assessor's office to plead that our property was overvalued, that we had had a tough year economically, and that our taxes should be lowered. The assessor, a heavy man in a short-sleeved shirt and a garish tie, as I remember him, would then glance at an index card and ask about the health of one of our aunts or uncles by name. Before my mother could even answer, he'd already be examining the tax rolls and agreeing that, yes, something might be done for a working family like ours. Perhaps $25 would be cut from our tax bill, but as we were ushered out the assessor would always remind us children to tell all our aunts and uncles—and grandparents, too—what a friend he'd been to our family in a time of need.

Those interconnected family obligations tied the city together— often across racial lines and frequently extending for generations— and wove a community unusually impervious to outside opinion or change. Even 150 years after the Louisiana Purchase, my grandfather still called visiting tourists, 'The Americans'.

The eccentric charm, the distinctive cuisine and music, the reverence for the past, the inattentiveness to official corruption, the carelessness that characterized so much of its institutional life, the striptease clubs just a block away from the cathedral, the religious practices so devout they bordered on the superstitious (when we had trouble selling our first house, a local accountant advised us to bury a statue of St Joseph upside down in our backyard), and all the contradictions inexplicable to an outsider flowed from a culture that was utterly foreign to the Protestant ethic and the spirit of capitalism, that concerned itself not with the control of human appetites but with the desire to insure all those appetites might be well fed.

Is it any wonder that, despite all the faults of their city, New Orleanians were happier than their fellow Americans? Or that, at the moment of greatest crisis, all the institutions of government failed New Orleans and its people?

As I write, 1,300 miles from New Orleans in a town outside New

John Biguenet

York, I am thinking of our house on Bluebird Street. The water is probably still four feet deep inside. I imagine that in the ninety-degree heat a fine black filigree of mould is crawling up the walls, across the books on the upper shelves of the bookcases and over the paintings hung high enough to escape the water itself. The food in our refrigerator has rotted beyond recognition. The wooden legs of our chairs have swollen, crazing and shattering their finish. Every carefully copied recipe in our kitchen notebook has bled away. All the research for my new novel—the neatly trimmed newspaper articles, the photographs, the rare books on obscure topics acquired by chance, the maps, and the handwritten notes—is soggy pulp, adrift in my study. In our garden, the Japanese magnolias, as old as our children, are withered in the toxic water. Every plant we tended is dead.

But where we are now, the light seems wrong for the time of year. So as soon as the gates of New Orleans are opened again, we will choose homecoming over exile, even if the home needs building after we get there.

Union, New Jersey, September 2005

NOTES ON CONTRIBUTORS

Chimamanda Ngozi Adichie, who grew up in Nigeria, is the author of the novel *Purple Hibiscus* (Fourth Estate/Anchor Books). 'The Master' is taken from her forthcoming novel, *Half of a Yellow Sun* (Fourth Estate/Knopf).

Segun Afolabi was born in Kaduna, Nigeria and now lives in the UK. His short story collection, *A Life Elsewhere*, is published in April 2006 and a novel, *Goodbye Lucille*, will be published in 2007, both by Jonathan Cape.

Daniel Bergner won a 2004 Lettre-Ulysses Award for the Art of Reportage for his most recent book, *Soldiers of Light* (Penguin), published in the US as *In the Land of Magic Soldiers: A Story of White and Black in West Africa* (Picador).

John Biguenet is the author of a collection of stories, *The Torturer's Apprentice* (Orion/Perennial) and a novel, *Oyster* (Orion/Ecco).

Kwame Dawes's most recent collection of poetry is *Progeny of Air* (Peepal Tree Press). In 2004 he was awarded the Musgrave Silver Medal for outstanding services by a Jamaican in the Arts. 'Passport Control' is taken from his memoir, *A Far Cry from Plymouth Rock*, published by Peepal Tree Press in May 2006.

Nadine Gordimer was awarded the 1991 Nobel Prize for Literature. Her most recent novel is *Get a Life* (Bloomsbury/Farrar Straus & Giroux).

Helon Habila is the current Chinua Achebe Fellow at Bard College. 'The Witch's Dog' is taken from his forthcoming novel, *Measuring Time,* which will be published by Hamish Hamilton in the UK and by W. W. Norton in the US.

Lindsey Hilsum is the Channel 4 News International Editor.

Moses Isegawa was born in Uganda and now lives in the Netherlands. His previous novels include *Abyssinian Chronicles* and *Snakepit* (Picador/Vintage).

Geert van Kesteren is a Dutch photojournalist whose photographs of the Iraq war are published in *Why Mister, Why?* (Artimo). The essay on page 97 is part of his collaboration with the ecological organization Speaking4Earth.

Adewale Maja-Pearce lives in Lagos, Nigeria, where he runs Yemaja, an editorial services agency. His latest book is *Remembering Ken Saro-Wiwa and Other Essays*. 'Legacies' is taken from a soon-to-be-completed work of the same title.

Santu Mofokeng's photographs will be at the Mori Art Museum in Tokyo from February 2006. He lives in Johannesburg.

John Ryle is Chair of the Rift Valley Institute, a research and training organization serving the countries of Eastern Africa.

Ivan Vladislavic was born in Pretoria and is the author of five books of fiction. He has been awarded the Olive Schreiner Prize and the *Sunday Times* Fiction Prize. 'Johannesburg' is taken from his book-in-progress, *Portrait with Keys*.

Binyavanga Wainaina lives in Nairobi, Kenya. He is the founding editor of the literary magazine, *Kwani?* and won the Caine Prize for African writing in 2002. He is working on a memoir which will be published by Granta Books.